A GRADUAL RUIN

A GRADUAL

ROBERT HILLES

RUIN

a novel

DOUBLEDAY CANADA

COPYRIGHT © 2004 ROBERT HILLES

Doubleday Canada and colophon are trademarks.

NATIONAL LIBRARY OF CANADA CATALOGUING IN PUBLICATION

Hilles, Robert, 1951–
A gradual ruin / Robert Hilles.

ISBN 0-385-65961-X

I. Title.

PS8565.I48G73 2003   C813'.54   C2003-904405-X

JACKET IMAGE:
(girl and ruins) © *Bettmann/CORBIS/Magmaphoto.com*
(trees) *Philip Schermeister/National Geographic Collection/Getty Images*
JACKET & BOOK DESIGN: CS RICHARDSON

"The Wanderer," copyright 1930 by W. H. Auden, from COLLECTED POEMS
by W. H. Auden. Used by permission of Random House, Inc.

Printed and bound in the USA

Published in Canada by Doubleday Canada,
a division of Random House of Canada Limited

Visit Random House of Canada Limited's website: www.randomhouse.ca

BVG   10   9   8   7   6   5   4   3   2   1

In Memory of
Amanda Rae Richard (née Hilles)
(1981–2002)

Protect his house,
His anxious house where days are counted
From thunderbolt protect,
From gradual ruin spreading like a stain;
Converting number from vague to certain,
Bring joy, bring day of his returning,
Lucky with day approaching, with leaning dawn.

W. H. AUDEN

A GRADUAL RUIN

PROLOGUE

TOMMY WASHED HIS HANDS and lay two slices of dark rye bread on the cutting board. He wasn't sure that Judith would like such heavy bread, but the bakery—all the stores, in fact—were already closed and it was all he had. He was even less certain that she'd like whatever filling he chose, but it was too late now to ask her preference, and he'd only frighten her if he knocked with no better reason than a choice of sandwich.

At the commercial refrigerator he had installed the year before, he poked between several dozen bottles of cooling beer and wine to find the containers of sliced meat. He settled on hickory-roasted turkey, his own favourite and fresh only this past morning. From the bottom drawer he chose two crisp leaves of romaine lettuce. He fingered four or five tomatoes ripening on the kitchen sill and selected the perfect one for slicing.

He lifted the lid on his mother's porcelain butter dish, one of the few items he had kept from his parents' house, and spread a healthy portion on the bread, washed the romaine leaves, and trimmed them to fit. He smoothed the leaves flat and arranged turkey and tomato on top, careful to balance everything so that no large pieces of tomato poked out the edges. He added a dash of salt and pepper and carefully aligned the second slice of bread before he cut the sandwich in half diagonally, like his father had for his own lunches all through school. Not exactly the elegant sandwiches he often laboured over for his paying guests, but it would fill her stomach all the same. The way her eyes had lit up at the suggestion of a sandwich, she likely hadn't eaten all day, possibly longer. He was sure the turkey would suit her just fine. He'd once eaten raw chicken, he'd been that hungry. He and Freda had both devoured thin strips of it. He'd have to be more careful with Judith, make no mistakes this time, but if he didn't help her, who knew what would happen? He wouldn't have her on his conscience too. Besides, he could use the company. Even when his house was busy he often felt alone.

He placed the sandwich on one of the china plates from the living-room hutch and filled a tall glass with milk. At the last second, he remembered some cookies in the cupboard and arranged three of them on the side of the plate.

A gust of wind ripped the screen door out of his hand, but Tommy caught it with his foot in a practised movement that prevented it slamming against the house. He ducked a low branch on the Manitoba maple at the back door and followed the sidewalk to the carriage house. He noted that the flowerbeds needed serious weeding. Perhaps if she needed work she'd be willing to start there.

Judith's shadow behind the curtain stilled as his foot touched the wooden step. He lowered the plate to the stoop as he had promised and sensed Judith watching him. He knocked once and turned immediately back to the main house.

I

And the land shall mourn,
every family apart.
ZECHARIAH 12:12

ONE

THE ONLY DOCTOR IN TOWN was Tailgate Smith. He rode his horse four miles through deep snow to deliver Shirley, who was a blue baby despite his efforts. Had he not turned his head against a gust of wind, he would have missed the kerosene lamp her father had left flickering in the kitchen window and would have arrived too late to save Shirley from the breech position. With some work, Tailgate turned her around and delivered her. When he held her up to the light, her mother gasped at Shirley's colour—the other babies had been born without the least bit of trouble—but Tailgate put his mouth to Shirley's lips a few times, and slowly she turned pink. While he rocked her, everyone watched, as if he could suck the devil out of any one of them and breathe something good in its place. When he finished, he pulled on his heavy fur coat, shook her father's hand, and like a phantom finished with its earthly work, slipped back out to the snow and disappeared on his waiting horse.

From then on, whenever someone in the family needed a doctor, Wendell, their father, waited until it was absolutely necessary and then reluctantly yelled for one of his kids to get the Devil Doctor. To everyone else, he was still Tailgate Smith, the boy left by his unwed mother on the tailgate of his father's truck.

For years, Shirley's father called her the blue baby and said at first her colour nearly made his heart stop, no great feat since he'd had a heart attack at forty-two, only weeks after Alice's birth, two years earlier, on the cusp of the Great Depression. He claimed that his second daughter brought the depression with her, and so he called her the depression baby. His eldest daughter, Claris, had had a nickname at one time, but Alice couldn't remember it. As with Robbie, death protected Claris from their father's teasing.

Shirley was a cranky baby who kept everyone up with her crying, and even when she grew older, she seldom sat still for long, as though what Tailgate had blown into her left her jumpy and anxious. In the summer of 1947, when she was sixteen, she ran off with the first boy from Dryden who took a serious interest in her. Every day, he drove up to her school in his old Ford half-ton, shirt-sleeves nearly to his shoulder in a tight roll. Shirley watched for his dull red truck as she stood with friends smoking cigarettes, delaying the walk home, never in a hurry even when she knew she'd catch hell. She was accustomed to catching hell.

"Hey, Shirl," he'd say, leaning out the window to smile at her.

Shirley would smile back. "Don't he look *good?*" she'd say.

She liked it that Danny didn't swear or yell lewd comments like the other men from the mill who drove by.

He just revved his engine a few times to show off and drove away slowly as if he were in no great hurry to leave her behind.

The night before she left for good, Shirley didn't come home at all. Without a phone to bring them news, her parents worried that something, everything, had happened, and Wendell paced the floor alternately raging and mumbling. Alice covered her ears and turned to face the moon, full and steady out the window.

Shirley showed up with Danny about noon the next day, not long after her parents and Alice had finished a tense, wordless lunch of sliced ham and tomatoes, Shirley's favourite. Shirley slipped a cigarette from her mouth and said, more loudly than necessary, "This here is Danny, and we're getting married." Her father fixed a hard stare on her. Shirley took a drag on her cigarette, and for a moment it looked as if she would exhale in his face, but she held the smoke inside, daring him to say something, if not for her benefit, then for Danny's.

Her father walked slowly up to Shirley and hit her full in the face with his fist. Alice heard something crack, and everyone froze as Shirley dropped to the floor. When her head clunked down on the linoleum, the cigarette fell from her hand and she let out a sharp cry. She kicked at her father's legs, and before Wendell could move, Danny caught him full on the jaw and knocked him back against the kitchen counter. The lunch dishes crashed to the floor as her father thrashed to catch his balance.

Shirley rose to her feet. The left side of her face was red, the skin beneath her eye already swollen, and her makeup smeared. She wobbled a little and pushed away a handful of dishevelled red hair to see better as Danny helped steady her. They both watched her father and quickly backed toward the door. When they got inside the truck, they sat breathing heavily. Wendell soon followed them out of the house. He walked around to Shirley's side of the truck and stared inside.

Shirley spat at him, and saliva spread across the closed window, then slid in sad streaks down the glass. She glared at his cold, stiff face, and Danny stepped hard on the gas. The truck spun gravel past the old grey barn. Danny didn't ease off on the accelerator until the road curved east and ran alongside a row of wind-cut hazel bushes where Shirley and Alice had often hidden themselves in the fall, eating their fill of hazelnuts.

The dry summer day held the dust in the air until it drifted down and covered her father with a grey film. He didn't move for a long time, just dug in his pocket for his handkerchief and wiped the dust from his face. Alice sat still, not daring to look outside while Helen, her mother, straightened the kitchen, picking up dishes scattered across the floor. Some were shattered into pieces, and as she lifted each shard, careful not to get nicked, the glass caught reflections from the window and gave hard shapes to the afternoon light.

By 1947, Dryden had grown beyond the few gravel streets that began at the Wabigoon River and the town now extended east and south toward the muddy shores of Wabigoon Lake. While the streets remained unpaved, cafés and shops—including a Rexall drugstore and a movie theatre—lined several blocks along Queen, King, and Duke. Across the Duke Street Bridge, the paper mill, built in 1913, had expanded to include a hodgepodge of outbuildings, warehouses, and towers that had been added over the years with little attention to their perfunctory, drab appearance. For years the mill had dumped its milky-white foam into the Wabigoon River, but what the people of Dryden noticed more was the smell of rotten eggs that the rusted stack emitted almost daily in steamy clouds. Sometimes the smell was so heavy in the air that Alice and Shirley had covered their noses, trying not to breathe as they passed by on their way home from school.

Shirley never married Danny, just lived with him for a while in a small furnished suite they rented over the Fonda Café on King Street, where Shirley worked. Although she had moved only four miles, she felt as though she had gone a thousand. She missed her daily conspiratorial talks with Alice, but was compensated by freedom from her father's control. She stayed up as late as she wanted, even on work-days, and turned the volume on the radio as loud as she pleased during the day. In the evenings neighbours complained if she let the music play too loud, but accommodating others was always easier than obeying Wendell.

The one time Shirley saw her father in town, he stepped out of a building not more than fifty feet in front of her. She managed to duck into a storefront before he saw her, and she watched him cross the street to where her mother waited in the horse and buggy, transportation her father refused to give up for a car. He stepped up into the buckboard and, without saying a word to her mother or even acknowledging her, he set the horse in motion.

Neither her mother nor her father visited, only Alice, who came by after work one day that first autumn. The two giggled while Shirley served tea and shortbread cookies, as if they were still playing house, half expecting their father to poke his head inside the door and tell them to get back to their chores.

Shirley was never without a cigarette, and she removed one from her mouth as she leaned into the round grey Formica table.

"I don't miss *him*. Just Mom and you, Sis." She looked at her sister as if she wanted to save her, as if she should be able to but didn't know how. "What does he say about me?"

"He doesn't. Most of the time he pretends you don't exist, but I can tell he misses you."

Shirley smiled at that. "I'm glad he's hurting."

"The other day he was talking about the day you were born and about how much it snowed that day, like that was important. He said, 'She shouldn't have lived, all blue like that. She was born dead as sure as anything, if that Devil Doctor hadn't brought her back to life like that.'"

"Babies are born blue all the time, any doctor could tell him that." Shirley took a long drag on her cigarette. "Who does he think he is, needing to control everything and have the last word? It's as if he thinks between God and him no one else should get a word in."

Both sisters laughed uneasily, then sipped more tea, holding their warm cups as if all that was good in their lives was right there in their hands.

Danny came in from work and went straight to the fridge for a beer. His hands were covered with scars from freeing log jams on the conveyor belt. He sat at the kitchen table and in between two swallows of beer scowled at Shirley. "What's for supper?"

"Soup," she said, and laughed.

"We always have soup. Make something else."

"I already made it."

He took another swig, and then he stood. "I'm going to the café," he said, and he was out the door before either woman could say goodbye.

Alice stayed a while longer, until she noticed it was nearly seven and getting dark. "I'd better go before Dad wonders where I am."

"You should go your own way, Alice. Look at me. What's done is done and staying there won't bring Robbie back."

"I just don't want him ranting all night or taking it out on Mom."

"She leaves it alone but not him. Every time he looked at me, I felt I owed him something."

Alice stood and slid her chair against the table as tidily as she could.

"Leave it, I'll straighten up later. You can relax here." Shirley stepped closer to Alice, and they nudged their faces cheek to cheek briefly before parting, their eyes held tightly closed.

A few months after Danny and Shirley moved into the apartment, Danny changed. Not all at once, but bit by bit. He talked less about his dreams and about escaping

Dryden and more about work, often complaining about his foreman, who he claimed always gave him the dirtiest job. He had worked in the mill for nearly two years, and Shirley had been hoping that he'd tire of it, just as she had long since tired of the café. After all, how many Denver sandwiches can you serve before the work gets old? But Danny had little ambition beyond work and beer of late, and some nights she lay beside him in bed and wondered if in twenty years they'd be in this same bed, nothing changed except the date on the calendar and their weathered skin. She longed for the anonymity and flash of the city.

"I'm not leaving a good job in the mill to bust my ass unloading railway cars in Winnipeg," Danny said whenever Shirley broached the subject of moving.

Shirley left on her own one bright morning in April 1948, when she was seventeen. Danny had returned home from the night shift a few hours earlier, and she crept from the bed to the bathroom as she did each morning before going to work at the Fonda Café. She washed, collected all her things from the medicine cabinet, carried them to the bedroom, and got down the single suitcase she had recently bought.

Shirley watched Danny sleep as she packed. When she had nearly finished, he opened his eyes and said, "What the hell are you doing?"

"I'm moving to Winnipeg."

"Suit yourself," he said, and closed his eyes again.

In June, Shirley wrote to Alice, told her how she had no trouble getting a job as a sales clerk in a women's clothing store on Main Street, and how she loved walking the streets of Winnipeg, where no one knew her. She told Alice that she felt invisible for the first time in her life. *You'd love it here, too. They call Winnipeg the city of elms. Not poplar and spruce like at the farm, but American elms, and the street where I live is so thick with them that I can walk the whole length of it with my head leaned back and not once see the sky. Tell Dad that.*

Last week I rode buses all over the city just for the hell of it. Out on the edge of the city the land is so flat you can see forever in every direction. I was the only passenger on the bus and the driver got off and walked with me out into a field of tall wheat where I took a clump of it in my hand and carried it onto the bus, and all the way back into the city I smelled it.

You have to move here. My house has two bedrooms and one is waiting for you. There's a place nearby where they'll do your laundry cheap, so you won't have to scrub your clothes like at home, and there are dances and cafés up and down every street, so many of them that if you get tired of one you can just go on to another.

You can be whoever you want to be, and besides Dad will be too cheap to visit. I'm not kidding, this is the life for you and me.

Alice's father sat watching her read the letter at the kitchen table. She laughed when she got to the line about her father being too cheap. She covered her mouth with one hand and looked up guiltily.

"Don't laugh at the supper table. It's not polite," Wendell said. He slapped his hand down hard as he got up to leave the room.

Normally Alice would have sat chastened until her father came back for an apology, which she always provided, even if she believed she was in the right, but this time she left the table herself, despite the dismay on her mother's face, and ran until she was clear across the field in front of the house. At the edge of the bush, she stopped to catch her breath and sat on a rock and read Shirley's letter twice more. She tried to imagine the streets of Winnipeg lined with elms. She imagined visiting Shirley at work, could see Shirley picking out dresses or slacks for her, but what she couldn't imagine was how to get there. It was one thing to defy her father and leave the supper table early, it was quite another to pack her bags.

"Your mother and I are getting old, and it's a tremendous relief to have additional income," her father had said when Alice left school to work. He'd nursed his own mother until she died, that was why he'd married so late, and now it seemed he expected her to do the same.

She remembered two years ago, when Shirley was fifteen and Alice barely seventeen, when they had stopped across from the paper mill after school to watch the freshly peeled logs drop one at a time off the conveyor onto the large pile outside the shredding room.

"That's us if we don't leave here soon, just logs waiting to be used up. Promise me you'll come with me," Shirley had said, reaching out a hand for Alice to shake.

Alice enjoyed watching the logs drop in a nice rhythm onto the waiting pile, and on the days when the smokestack was dead, she loved the sweet, ripe smell of damp wood, but Shirley had always disdained the mill.

Shirley never shared her dreams with Alice, and that left Alice with the impression that Shirley was in a big hurry to go nowhere. Now Alice felt that she was the one going nowhere.

Alice stayed at the edge of the bush until well after dark. Several times her mother came to the door and looked out, but she never called to her, and when Alice finally went inside, the supper dishes were already put away. Her father had retired to his room, so Alice went straight to bed. She knew what really held her there, had felt it every day for years. Robbie had his big hands around her ankles and he wasn't about to let go.

Through the wall, Alice heard her father reading. His voice grew louder and louder until she imagined his lips tight against the wall aiming his words directly at her. She closed her eyes and covered her ears, and in her head, she walked the streets of Winnipeg.

Later Wendell came to Alice's bedside and stood above her. "How is she?"

"You don't have to worry about Shirley, she can handle herself." Alice could tell he wanted to ask more, but he held back until he sat on her bed.

"I've made mistakes, I know that. I was too old to have children and I wasn't as easy on you as I should have been. Getting old does that."

Alice saw her father's hands trembling but resisted the urge to hold them. She wrapped herself more tightly into the covers and closed her eyes to his pain. Anger had taken root in him a long time ago, and maybe now it had taken hold of her as well. She waited for him to speak, but he stayed silent, and after a minute or two more he pushed his hands deep into the mattress to balance himself as he stood up. When he was fully standing, she opened her eyes. She heard his shallow, quiet breaths and her eyes went to his grey hair catching the available light. She watched as he stood perfectly still for a few moments, his eyes marking off time with slow, heavy blinks.

Finally, he lifted his right hand and dabbed it beneath each eye. "Goodnight," he said. Alice listened as his feet padded along the flowered linoleum.

She had always associated the hush of his brown slippers with the war. At first, the war had barely touched Dryden or her family, but in 1941, the year Alice turned twelve, the Wartime Machine Shop Board encouraged the Dryden Paper Co. to begin producing parts for the war, and more families moved to Dryden seeking work. As the war effort grew, so did the town and the paper mill, each adding more buildings to accommodate the growth.

That year, her father brought the war home, lifted it from the wagon, and carried it into the house on his head. In the small living room, he lowered the dark walnut dome of tubes onto the worn mahogany table.

At first, all her father could coax from the radio was static. For a good half-hour, he worked the large tuning dial with rough fingers, and then suddenly a thick, heavy voice stuttered between static and went silent again. Her father tweaked the dial some more and the voice returned and steadied. Over the bleak winter months of low farm activity, her father sat for hours listening to any news of the war. Sometimes he sipped tea, other times he hardly moved at all except to lift a finger to his lips to quiet one of his children.

"You can't trust someone with a moustache that small," he said about Hitler one morning after Lorne Greene had delivered the grim news concerning some place in France called Dieppe. "My father had a broad moustache beneath his nose, and you wouldn't find a better man than him."

At first, Alice was afraid of the radio.

"Don't be such a sissy," Shirley said. "Everyone in town's got a radio." Even at eight, Shirley was afraid of nothing, except the wrath of her father.

Her mother knitted as she listened, and whenever Lorne Greene came on, her father hurried out of his room to join her. Greene's deep and trustworthy voice never cracked or slipped on a word, and over the next months and then years, the war was a small voice on the radio they had with an otherwise silent breakfast, lunch, and supper.

Once, when the death toll from the war was insufferably high, Helen snapped the radio off in mid-sentence. Alice's father, hunched over the shape of each word, sat straight up, his mouth agape. Helen didn't look up from her knitting, and Alice was certain her father would bellow at her mother, but he sat looking at her in silence, and then he nodded his head and drummed his fingers on the arms of the chair.

The war ended live on the radio, interrupting one of the songs played between war bulletins. Her father rose from his chair and applauded; he spun around on one foot, and turned off the radio, and then he sat in the quiet and grinned. Then he stood and walked back to his room. His feet, bound in wool slippers Alice's mother had knitted him, moved quietly along the floor.

Alice left home on the morning of August 9, 1948, without the fanfare of Shirley's departure. She rose early and dressed in her new full-length bluish-grey skirt and a ruffled white blouse with puffy sleeves. The previous day she had had a friend do her hair in a pageboy cut she'd chosen from *Vogue Magazine*. She did not tell either of her parents of her plans or that Shirley had sent her money for her ticket until her mother saw the suitcase, and brushed Alice's hair back from her face.

"Where will you stay?"

"With Shirley. She's got a place all fixed up." Alice did her best to sound as decided as possible even though her insides churned with doubts. She went to the front door, and as she put on her long navy coat and white gloves, Helen removed a handkerchief she had tucked into the sleeve of her sweater and dabbed her moist eyes. Tears formed in Alice's eyes too as she embraced her mother.

"Here, you'll need this." Her father thrust some crumpled bills into her free hand while Alice and her mother continued to embrace. His eyes were puffy and pink.

She squeezed her hand around the money and stepped back from her mother to stuff the bills into her purse. For a moment, Alice couldn't decide whether to run or come back inside, and she wanted to jam something in the door to keep it partway open forever.

At the train station, a young man sat down beside her, his hair neatly combed. He sent a few covert glances in

Alice's direction and then braved a bit of small talk. When Alice smiled and responded he told her that he was going to the University of Manitoba to study medicine.

Alice envied the young man's easy manner. She would never have spoken to him first.

"My father is Dr. Bailey. Do you know him?"

"No. The only doctor we ever used was Tailgate Smith, and I haven't seen him in years." Alice bunched the fingers of her white gloves unconsciously as she spoke.

The young man pushed into the stiff wooden back of the bench. "Tailgate retired a few years ago and moved to Florida. He had some health problems of his own, I think. My father took his place and I'll take his."

Alice hadn't seen Tailgate since 1938, the summer she turned nine. Alice and her sister Claris had both con- tracted a fever on Alice's birthday, and while hers soon went away, Claris's legs went limp and she began having trouble breathing. After sitting up with her several nights, Wendell reluctantly sent for Tailgate Smith. As soon as Tailgate saw her, he said, "You should have called me sooner. She has polio."

"It came and went with the other kids, even Robbie. I thought it was just a fever." Alice didn't like to see her father looking like a scolded boy.

"She needs to be treated—we need to get her to the hospital and in an iron lung as soon as possible."

"I can't afford that, I'm barely getting by."

"Worry about payment later, Wendell." Tailgate had looked so stern and serious, and now, waiting for the bus, Alice wondered if he had ever smiled. Do doctors smile?

Do they have good days too? She fumbled with a handkerchief just like her mother while the young man beside her was quiet, already practising to hold back.

Tailgate had brought the wagon around to the front door, and Alice's father carried Claris out and placed her gently in the back, on top of some blankets. Helen pushed Alice after Wendell at the last minute, to comfort Claris if she woke on the long ride into town. Alice climbed into the wagon with her sister, but her father shook his head.

"She's unconscious," he said. "She won't know you're there. Sit up front with me."

All during the wagon's slow progress, Alice and her father barely spoke. She'd made this trip so often along the winding gravel road to town that she knew every hairpin turn, meadow, and stand of balsam or poplar by heart. Normally she would have daydreamed most of the way, but that day she anxiously watched her father's weathered hands as they worked to keep the horse moving fast enough to make time, but slow enough for Claris's comfort. Alice turned back once to check on Claris and was surprised to see that Tailgate had come alongside the wagon and rode with his eyes fixed on Claris. Wendell forced Alice to face front again.

"She'll be all right," he said, but he spoke in such a quiet, uncertain voice that Alice knew something bad was about to happen.

About halfway to town, Tailgate hollered for her father to stop. Her father turned to look down at Claris. Immediately he thrust the reins at Alice and jumped into the back before the wagon had come to a complete halt.

By the time Tailgate dismounted, Alice's father sat cradling Claris with his face pressed into her shoulder. Alice had never seen her father cry before, and her strongest urge was to bolt from the wagon and run.

Tailgate joined her father, who relinquished his grip on Claris and climbed out to make more room for him. The doctor crouched next to Claris and felt for her pulse. He lowered her arm, dropped his head to her chest, and closed his eyes.

"I'm sorry," Tailgate said after a minute, and even though he must have uttered that phrase a thousand times before, Alice heard the words catch in his throat.

Her father climbed up into the wagon again and covered Claris. He rolled the blanket back enough to expose her face, and rested his head on her forehead.

Tailgate climbed up next to Alice. He touched her shoulder and let his hand warm into her. She looked into his old eyes and saw them filled with such sorrow that she dropped her gaze to the flecked and grooved wood of the wagon's buckboard. Tailgate sat so close Alice breathed in his musky tang, and she listened to his steady breathing. When he stepped back down to the road and remounted his horse, her father climbed down out of the wagon and stood resting his hand on the side of the wagon.

Death had run cold fingers over them and no one moved until something spooked her father's horse and it pulled the wagon away with such a snap of acceleration that Alice struggled to catch her balance and nearly dropped the reins. Finally, she managed to regain a full hold of them and pulled with all her might, but nothing slowed the horse. Tailgate flashed past in a crouched blur on her left. He leapt onto the back of her father's horse and gripped the reins with both hands, tugging until they slowed to a trot.

Alice clutched the edge of the wagon with white fingers, and without letting go, she looked back at her sister and saw her father running full out, and she bit her lip, fearing he'd have another heart attack. Even from a distance, she saw that his face was puffed with exertion, his cheeks bulbous as his hands and legs pumped. She'd never seen her father run before, and he looked awkward, his legs shooting out at odd angles, but he came straight at the wagon. Claris's eyes hadn't altered, and in that moment Alice understood death for the first time, how someone's body remained in the world after them, still bridled by the various forces of nature and yet no longer experiencing any of it. Claris's mouth hung open and her right hand pointed toward her father as if she too couldn't believe he would risk running.

When the wagon came to a standstill, Alice bolted from it and ran to the edge of the trees. Urine streamed down her legs, and she didn't want Tailgate or her father to see. When her father finally reached the wagon, he bent over and vomited into the tall grass at the shoulder of the road. Even from fifty feet away, Alice heard his laboured breathing. He coughed three times and then vomited again.

Tailgate put his hand on Wendell's shoulder. "I hope you won't do that often, not with your heart."

"I'm all right. Can't lose two daughters in one day." He spit again.

"We'll still need to take her to the hospital, Wendell," Tailgate said. "I can do it if you want."

Her father turned to face the beige blanket stretched over Claris. "No, I'll take her myself." He started when he saw Alice huddled beneath a sagging birch, and went to her, limping most of the way. Gingerly he lifted her and carried her back toward the wagon, but his strength gave out halfway. Alice fell to the gravel bed and he tumbled after her. The noise spooked the horse again, and the wagon creaked ahead a few feet, but Tailgate guided his horse in front of theirs, blocking the way until Alice and her father made it back to the wagon.

When they returned home, her father never said "Claris is dead" aloud. Instead, he stood at the edge of the bed holding his hat in his hands. Alice's mother knew without being told, and she wrapped her arms around herself and curled into the bed. Alice's father pulled the two girls and Robbie to him and squeezed them as Alice tried to wrestle free. No one spoke until, on the other side of her father, Shirley began to whimper.

"Quiet. Quiet," he said, and then he held her close, but Shirley wailed by then and Robbie joined in. Just when it seemed everything would come undone, their mother unfurled, sat up, and began to sing in a quavering, sob-torn voice. Wendell joined her, and finally Alice, and they sang until they drowned out Shirley and Robbie.

Most nights Alice fell asleep to the routine, muted sounds coming from her parents' room, the odd word, the drop of a shoe, the creak of floorboards, but not that night. *Claris is dead, Claris is dead.* She almost said it aloud to

Shirley, curled up in the bed next to hers. Shirley lay still, but Alice sensed she was wide awake.

Each time Alice closed her eyes she saw Claris's dead face. She remembered her father saying once, "When death comes, it surrounds you, drapes over you, and whisks you away." That wasn't her sister there; it was what death left behind. And she worried about her father. What if his heart gave out as he always said it could? She knew now what he might look like if it did, and she lay in bed, listening for any sound of him, wanting at least one sign that he was still alive, but all she heard was Shirley's occasional struggle to shift an arm or leg trapped within tight sheets.

Later, Shirley crawled in next to her, holding her, putting a damp cheek against hers, and for the remainder of the long, restless night they lay in each other's arms.

When the conductor called for passengers to board the train, Bailey waved goodbye to Alice and went to the club car, while she found a seat by herself in a half-empty car near the rear of the train. She didn't mind that her new acquaintance had gone off by himself, or perhaps in search of better company, and she kept her face turned to the window, watching rocky forests give way to the buttery blur of ripened wheat. The sun was setting when the train arrived in Winnipeg, so everything was lit with a glow that gave the city an aura of excitement. Alice disembarked and took in the warm evening air, and for the first time, she felt that she belonged to herself and to no one else. The whole future was a clean slate, no longer written over with guilt and disappointment and the expectations of others.

TWO

IN THE EARLY HOURS OF MARCH 29, 1945, after five and a half years of war and only five weeks before Germany would surrender, Tommy Armstrong woke from another dream of his dead mother. His mother wore a green dress as she rowed him across a lake in a small boat. The only thing she said to him was that green was her favourite colour. He woke realizing he couldn't remember her favourite colour and wondered if he had ever known it. In his memories, his mother wore every colour except black, a colour she loathed. Imagine being married to an undertaker and hating the colour black. In the dark of the barn, he lay in a greasy, stinking heap of rotting hay listening for the occasional thump of German 105 mm artillery. He knew that at first light, heavy Allied shelling would come again.

The severe winter across all of Europe had not completely abated, and in recent weeks with the lingering cold, dreams of his mother had become more frequent. He thought perhaps the cold caused him to think of Kenora in winter, of home, which he hadn't seen in nearly three years. Sometimes he woke in a sweat; other times, like that morning, he woke with the sensation that his mother was nearby, but that too brief moment of private reflection that follows waking couldn't last.

War has a way of stilling personal thoughts, and between the thunder of more planes carrying paratroopers even deeper into Germany, Tommy heard the lone, tentative footsteps of someone entering the barn. He inched deeper into the foul heap and slipped the knife from his belt. As someone started to rip the hay free, he held his breath and stiffened his legs from shaking. Before he was exposed, he pulled the intruder to him and pinned the knife against his throat. In the morning light, he saw a boy of ten or eleven, eyes wide in terror. Tommy removed the knife but not his grip on the boy.

"Mister, mister," the boy pleaded in a whisper.

Tommy felt his arms and legs relax as he released the boy, who stood slowly, brushing loose hay from his skinny frame and ragged pants.

"Yankee?"

"Canadian. How did you know I was here?" The boy pointed toward the door and Tommy understood—the door latched only from the outside and he had not been able to relatch once inside, though he hadn't considered that when he entered.

"Is good. Come, come. Okay?" The boy crooked his finger. Tommy hesitated at the door and watched the boy walk back toward the farmhouse. In the daylight, Tommy observed that a wall of trees hid the farm. All the same, he crossed the open space to the boy at a run. The boy eased the door of the farmhouse open, and with a nod of his head, he indicated that Tommy should enter.

Just inside the door, Tommy saw a man, a woman, and a girl of about five sitting at a large wooden table, waiting as if he were an expected guest. Like the boy, they all looked hungry. On the table were five bowls of a clear liquid, and in the centre of each bowl bobbed a small, withered potato. The man waved to an empty chair, so Tommy took chocolate out of his pack and passed pieces to everyone before he sat. The children ate theirs immediately, and after they all finished their soup, Tommy and the German farmer sat on the front steps and smoked Tommy's cigarettes.

"Farm *kaput. Deutschland ist alles kaput,*" the man said, lifting a handful of soil. He let the dry chunks slip through his fingers.

Tommy watched lumps of clay rain on the man's worn boot. His bare toes were visible and Tommy looked down at his own boots recently replaced in Belgium.

"*Die Soldaten,* there, there, there." The man pointed at three farmhouses a mile or so to the west.

Tommy ached all over, ached from lack of sleep and from muscles clenched with fear twenty-four hours a day. The man looked like his own father, the same deeply etched face and large hands. He judged by the way the man stroked the heads of his children at the table that he was a good father. Tommy lit another cigarette and then lit one for the man, who clearly savoured every puff. He wanted to be a father too, to have a family like this man, once the war was behind him.

The previous night Tommy had flown from Emmerich,

on the border of Germany and Holland, across the Rhine River into Germany, only four days after the start of a large Allied operation generally referred to as Operation Plunder.

Once across the Rhine, his mission was to form up with other paratroopers in the nearest wooded areas and drive the Germans east toward the Elbe River. Like most of the soldiers, and even the generals, Tommy hadn't known that the Allies were in a race with the Russians to capture Berlin; he just followed orders. B-17s carried British and Canadian paratroopers, while those less experienced, but willing to jump out of low-flying craft, flew across in gliders. Tommy rode in the British Horsa, made of light pine covered in canvas. Larger planes pulled these gliders two at a time, flying at 500 feet and only 120 knots. Set free, the gliders could not manoeuvre as deftly as powered craft and made easy targets for German ground fire.

Several times during the flight, the man beside Tommy leaned over and vomited, so that the glider smelled of puke and sweat, and each bank of the aircraft threw Tommy against the side panel. When they were over Germany, bullets ripped through the canvas and struck the young man beside Tommy who slumped against him, blood dripping from his mouth.

A moment later, German ground fire killed one of the pilots. As the surviving pilot struggled to keep the glider level, men began bailing out at thirty feet above ground. Finally only the pilot and Tommy remained. Tommy waited until they were nearly on the ground before he jumped. A few hundred yards farther, the glider crashed into a thicket of trees, the pilot failing to get out in time.

The night sky had continued to fill with a flotilla of pale bobbing mushrooms, some of them, Tommy knew from his training, attached to men already dead. From the position of the parachutes still in the sky, Tommy determined that his glider had crashed well south of the drop zone, leaving him alone in hostile territory. He had headed north, hoping to find the rest of his company, but after three hours without meeting anyone he lost hope and walked four hours more before he reached the barn. With the German soldiers precariously near, locating the Allied forces would be risky, but he couldn't remain put either.

Tommy waited until nightfall, then he said goodbye to the family and walked east down the gravel road away from the farms the German had warned him about. He hoped he could soon find someone from his company. For the first time in the war, he was lost, and truly alone.

Between bursts of artillery, dogs barked, and cows gathered in sad herds huddled against the dark. Others lay dead from the concussion of bombs, their feet sticking in the air, their bellies swollen. Tommy nearly fell into a crater the size of a tank, and saw more dead cows to his right and then the body of a paratrooper with his parachute still billowing up behind him. He could have been hit by German flak as he drifted in the night sky.

Tommy knelt down to retrieve the fallen man's identity disk and even in the limited light recognized the dark-headed Jamie Pakulak. Tommy convulsed involuntarily, and yet he couldn't look away from his friend's face. Only last week they'd got drunk together during furlough, sitting around a fire drinking whisky. His hands had glowed crimson in the firelight and made red arcs in the night.

Now those hands were hidden somewhere, caught in the chute that had bunched around him when he made impact. Tommy reached a hand around Jamie's icy neck and unfastened the clasp of his identity disk. He tucked it into his hip pocket and placed two cigarettes in Jamie's shirt pocket.

Drinking and smoking, spitting into the fire, it had been easy to believe that all one needed to survive the war was to proclaim survival loud enough for all to hear, as if saying so would make it true. When Jamie was so drunk that he could only mumble, he pointed an unsteady finger at Tommy. "Look in on my mother if anything ever happens to me, okay?"

Tommy cut the parachute free and dragged the sergeant into a field, where he covered him with his chute and weighted it with rocks. He gathered dry twigs and branches and piled them over the chute. When the mound of brush was thick and high enough, he stopped and bowed his head. He waited for words, but all he managed was a short, dry "Goodbye," uttered half aloud and half to himself. He thought of his own dead father, buried all those miles away from here.

Jamie had wanted nothing more than to go home to help his mother find a better life, and now here he lay wasted, on the ground like so many others across the countries of Europe, Africa, and Asia. Tommy had long given up the ghastly tally of friends he'd lost. He gave Jamie a single farewell tap before he struck the match.

Despite the danger, he stood next to the fire as the burning branches crackled and popped like a campfire from his childhood. When the flames reached the chute and the corpse, Tommy returned to the road. Almost immediately his toe connected with something solid, a helmet. He didn't care if it was Allied or German—he booted it as hard as he could, and then stumbled forward. Had it contained a head, he would have kicked just as hard. The fire glowed at his back until the road curved into a hedgerow.

The chilly March air forced him to bundle his jacket tightly around him as he followed the narrow gravel road cutting north away from Jamie and through more farmlands as flat as Manitoba and just as open. Tommy didn't have a clue where he was or in which direction he should move. For all he knew, he might be walking straight toward the enemy. The debris of retreating German soldiers littered the road: grey GM 30 gas masks, brown wool blankets, Mauser 98k and Kar 43 rifles, helmets, and even boots. He passed a long line of recently shelled Panzer tanks, supply trucks, and Kübelwagens, many of them charred black and spilling over with bodies.

A shell's impact separated a pile of helmets and masks, and several helmets rolled down into the ditch. He heard one bounce loudly against a boulder and in the next second a blast knocked his feet out from under him and tossed him toward the ditch. *This is it*, he thought. His head struck the ground first and he felt a sharp jab. When he finally came to rest, he lay dazed under a rain of clay and metal. The ground shook twice from artillery fire, and he trembled uncontrollably until he crawled down into the ditch and drew himself tightly into a fetal position. His heart raced as he took short tight breaths, and he expected the next shell or the one after to land right on top of him.

When the rifle fire quieted to sporadic intervals, Tommy felt safe enough to uncoil and roll onto his back. He ran his hands over his body and searched for wounds. He found none, but he was too shaken to stand, so he lay in the ditch for several minutes more. When he finally stood he could think no further than a safe place to have a smoke.

In the far distance he saw the lights of more farm-houses, and near him a herd of grazing cows bunched together so thickly they formed a single mound of steam-ing flesh. He decided they would have to do, and he left the road to wade into the midst of them. He ran a damp hand down the warm back of one of the sickly ones and felt numerous places where flesh sagged acutely next to bone. The cow lifted her head in Tommy's direction, but soon went back to feebly rooting dried tufts of grass. Tommy struck a match, cupped the tiny flame in his dirty hands, and drew the heat into his chest.

Even amongst the cows he thought he smelled fear. He could recognize that odour anywhere, had sniffed it too many times, as often from his own body as from others'. He leaned against the cow, dragged on his smoke, and watched more volleys light the night sky. Between drags, he clenched his jaw and drew on memories to calm him-self. He dreamed of sitting by the lake at Laclu after dark listening to frogs and loons mark off the night, as he'd done when he was twelve. He looked forward to waking as late as he wanted, and later, to dancing at the Kenricia Hotel on a Saturday night, or catching a movie with one of the young women who worked over at the Shop Easy. He ached for the war to be over, yet he also knew it would bring him closer to his father's death, and he wondered how he would manage the pain of standing over his father's grave. Fear, even panic, was useful, for he knew it kept him alive, and he felt plenty, right down into his legs, which burned and cramped at frequent intervals—but loss, how would he handle that, except to keep pushing it away? Now was no time to worry about it. He had to keep moving even if he was lost, because staying put meant capture or death.

As he edged back toward the road, he felt a faint grip on his right ankle. He quickly drew his knife. Below him, two faint eyes briefly caught the moon and he heard forced breathing.

Tommy held his knife in front of him and parted the grass for a better view. A young German soldier, sixteen or seventeen, lay with most of his bottom half mangled.

"*Helfen Sie mir*," the boy whispered. He pointed to his abdomen as if somehow he could still be helped.

Tommy lit a cigarette and put it between the boy's lips. The boy sucked, and Tommy watched the glow of the cigarette brighten and then fade in a carefully measured beat. Before the young soldier finished, Tommy moved to go— he couldn't risk lingering—but the youth caught his arm and held it. Tommy lit another cigarette and dragged on it. Unconsciously, he felt for his own leg, for his hip, and then, just like that, the boy's grip slackened.

Tommy waited until the lifeless hand slipped to the ground, then he broke for the road and walked east, the sky suddenly so empty that he saw stars for the first time that night.

He knew he shouldn't allow himself to feel anything for the boy's death, because he was the enemy and because there were too many dead and dying, and yet as he walked he couldn't help thinking how only weeks before, the boy had likely been loaded into a truck with other boys like him, too young to fight but conscripted all the same and dumped in some field not far from here and told to march or die. When the boy stared ahead, he would have seen the same things Tommy saw: smoke and fire. He would have breathed in the same air sour with rot. He'd managed to bring himself this far, and for what?

Tommy's father had been right to warn him. At any second he could end up like that boy, shot and left bleeding in an open field. Other soldiers maybe would give him a quick look as they passed. Maybe they wouldn't.

The last day of March brought a hard, punishing rain that stung Tommy's face and forced him to take cover under a bridge until late afternoon, when the heavy rain had reduced the road to a dark goo. His feet sunk ankle deep into a soupy mix of clay, gravel and topsoil that weighted each step, severely slowing his progress. Mud got into everything. He slept in mud, ate in it, and after hours walking in it his boots carried more than twice their original weight.

He had eaten little more than chocolate for the past day, so despite his fear of being turned in or captured, he stopped at a farmhouse separated from the road by only a hedgerow. Recent shelling had destroyed the second story of the house. The roof had completely disappeared and two walls had collapsed outward, scattering brick and timber along the ground. When Tommy knocked on the door leading to what remained of the house, the farmer and his wife yelled, "*Geh'weg. Wir haben nichts zu essen,*" Go away. We have nothing to eat.

He sat on their step, considering whether to force his way in and find out for himself what they had, but in the end he decided to try another farm, visible in the distance.

"*Holt.*" A German officer rounded the hedgerow, followed by a large company of young soldiers aiming their Mausers at him. Tommy dropped his rifle and raised his arms. A private approached him and searched Tommy's pack for grenades before poking him in the ribs with his rifle. The German company marched Tommy with his hands clasped on his head toward another farmhouse, where he joined seven other prisoners. He counted four American uniforms, two Canadian, and one British.

The Brit, a lieutenant though he looked barely twenty, greeted Tommy as casually as if they had just missed a trolley. "Bad luck, old chap, but the war will be over before these buggers can do much."

For a week, Tommy and the others were held in a makeshift compound and marched in monotonous circles until evening, when the guards allowed them to mingle. Then the prisoners played cards or exchanged stories. The next Sunday, German guards loaded them onto an eastbound train.

On Monday evening, not long after Tommy woke from his first real sleep in days, Soviet planes descended at full fire. Bullets tore through Tommy's car, ricocheting wildly off metal until they met with something softer like wood, upholstery, or flesh. He crouched beneath a seat and pulled his head into his chest, praying none of the bullets would strike him. He closed his eyes when the window above shattered and rained shards of glass. The screams and moans of the wounded filled his ears until they were drowned out by planes circling back for a bombing pass. Tommy's car was not hit directly, but still it shuddered and rolled off the track. He was tossed against the roof of the car and momentarily stunned, but he quickly regained his equilibrium and while it still teetered, he grabbed his pack and jumped through the buckled rear door along with a handful of other prisoners who scattered in various directions to divert any soldiers who pursued them in the dark.

Tommy ran alongside two Americans, until he dropped his pack containing his father's letters and stumbled in the mud to retrieve it. When he stood again he was alone, so he staggered, more than ran, for two hours through a steady, dense confusion of trees and undergrowth as branches scraped and slapped his face and hands until they stung with raw wounds.

When the wind shifted and brought rain, Tommy collapsed beneath a large spruce, shivering with exhaustion and cold. The dark blinded him to everything except the stabbing, frigid rain that pelted him even beneath the thick cover of the evergreens. He curled tighter into the trunk for protection, and found that if he moved around one side of the trunk he was sheltered from the wet, if not the biting wind. *I can do this*, Tommy told himself.

He felt inside his pack for the protected bundle of his father's letters. His father had been against the war. When Canada declared war on Germany, Tommy had been seventeen and still in high school, ready to quit immediately and join up like some of his friends, but his father had insisted that Tommy's education come first. As it was compulsory for all males sixteen or over to register for service, Tommy had done so, expecting to be called up against his father's wishes, but Mackenzie King's government was reluctant to legislate conscription because of the potential political fallout in Quebec.

Out of respect for his late mother, in 1941 Tommy enrolled in a bachelor of arts program at the University of Manitoba. And though his real ambition was to study medicine, he agreed with his father that an initial education in arts would be an advantage to a doctor.

Tommy had never heard his father complain about his own profession as an undertaker, and he certainly wasn't ashamed of it either. Still, he got the impression that perhaps undertaking hadn't been his father's own desire.

All Tommy knew for certain was that his father had always worked for Tommy's grandfather, who moved to Kenora in 1892, when the town was still called Rat Portage, not long before the railway arrived. Tommy's grandfather had opened the first funeral parlour during the Lake of the Woods gold rush, a timely decision, because all that prosperity brought its fair share of death. Tommy's father worked in the funeral parlour from the age of fifteen, obtaining most of his education at his father's side, and enrolled in an embalming school in Toronto for two months only when he was twenty, for testing. When Tommy's father turned twenty-one, the business was renamed Armstrong and Sons and remained that still. Tommy's grandfather died of a heart attack when he was only fifty, and left Tommy's father, a shy twenty-five-year-old, to take over the business.

Tommy grew up in a house in the Laclu area surrounded by the tallest poplar and birches he'd seen in the Kenora area, while farther back from the house pine and spruce forests encircled numerous small lakes. The Laclu district, six miles northwest of Kenora, contained mostly summer cottages and resorts. Tommy's grandfather had built the large house, only steps from the lake, in the early 1920s. Tommy had been born there, and his mother had died there. At the time his grandfather built the house, population was sparse and the road went no farther north, but later the area filled with Winnipeggers looking for a place to escape the city for the summer.

Every weekend in the autumn of 1941, Tommy had caught the train home from university. He was slow to make friends in the city, but by Christmas, some of his shyness had worn off, and his trips home became fewer.

By April, barely four months after Tommy's twentieth birthday, Parliament voted in favour of conscription. Mackenzie King delayed implementation, but Tommy expected that conscription was imminent and once again he longed to participate. Whenever he broached the subject with his father he got the same response.

"I know what bullets, let alone bombs, do to bodies. I don't want you facing that. You want to heal bodies someday, not destroy them. Besides, this is Britain's war, not ours. Just like the last one. Your mother wouldn't have wanted you to go to war unless you had no choice, and you still have a choice."

All of Tommy's friends from high school and even some from university had joined up. It infuriated Tommy that while he remained a boy they had become men serving a noble cause. Two of his good friends, Dennis and Herb, had been stationed together in a village in Sussex, where they awaited assignment to the Mediterranean. One morning, over cheese omelettes and cantaloupe slices, Tommy announced to his father that he planned to enlist.

"You think war is like the movies and the hero never dies. Well, I've got news for you. War is about killing, and the most heroic often die first."

"Give me more credit than that. Besides, I'll be conscripted anyway and I won't have a choice. It would be wrong not to go."

"How is it wrong to follow your conscience?"

"I am following it."

"Think it through. You have other choices."

"Like what? Running away?"

"I'm trying to keep you from making a mistake. In the last war I was just as eager as you to enlist. I tried to sign up three times but they rejected me because of my flat feet. They said I couldn't march. When I saw some of my friends come home without arms or legs, I was glad of my flat feet. Too many of them didn't come home at all."

"I know what I'm doing," Tommy said, no longer hiding his frustration.

"Do you?"

"You smother me," Tommy said, surprised he'd said that, as it wasn't true, but unable to articulate what he really felt.

His father looked hurt, and put his arms around his son, who remained rigid. "Let's sleep on it at least," he said.

By morning Tommy had cooled down enough to realize that perhaps his father was right. Maybe a lot of the older generation felt that way. And he knew that some of his friends had died already. Eddy had been engaged when he left last year and now Mallory wore his ring around her neck with his identity disk and hardly spoke to anyone when she left her parents' house.

Tommy shaved and put on cologne, and then he walked to the road and stuck his thumb out. He wore his baggy, zoot-inspired, low-crotched trousers with his navy cardigan and white shirt. He'd go into town and find some of his remaining friends. Bryce and Walter hadn't enlisted yet. Maybe he'd ask them why. The Reverend Lewis's banged-up Chevrolet rolled to a stop almost right away, and while he shifted papers on the front seat to make room for his passenger, Tommy checked his part in the side mirror and saw that curls had bunched over both his ears. Perhaps he'd stop at the barber's too.

The Reverend Lewis gripped the steering wheel as if he feared at any moment someone might force him off the road. He was a slight man with narrow shoulders and long arms, but what Tommy noticed most were the pronounced brown patches under his eyes.

"You're Tommy Armstrong, aren't you, the undertaker's son? I haven't seen you in church much since your mother passed on."

"Dad doesn't believe in church any more."

"What about you? You're old enough to think for yourself."

"I haven't decided."

"What's there to decide? I always enjoyed looking up and seeing your mother in the pew. She had such a lovely voice, always sang like an angel. Sometimes I'd slip in an extra hymn or two just to hear her voice above all the rest. Wonderful ballet dancer too."

"I don't remember much about her," Tommy said. He wished the Reverend Lewis would stick to his driving.

"Your mother was one in a million. Such a good Sunday-school teacher. She knew the meaning of the word *Christian* more than most, but she boasted about you all the time. I guess God'll forgive a mother that, but I remember you were real fidgety in church. Your mother used to calm you by tapping on your nose and smiling at you. Her and your father never missed a week." He looked over at Tommy and the car wandered into the path of oncoming traffic. "Sorry," he said, after he guided the car back onto the right side of the road. "I guess the Lord is looking out for both of us today."

Tommy slid down a little in his seat, not interested in being preached to.

The Reverend glanced at Tommy again. "Why hasn't a responsible boy like you signed up and gone overseas with the other young men? If I was half my age I'd be there too, alongside you, not with a gun but with this Bible." He tapped something hard in his breast pocket.

"I was thinking of it—"

"Well good for you. I'm glad to hear it. I don't like to hear some of these young boys who think freedom comes with no price."

They were nearing the turn into town. "My father doesn't want me to join. But some of my friends have signed up."

"It's a shame your mother's not here to guide you, but I guess I can't blame your father for being overprotective. You're all he's got. Your mother, though, she would have wanted you to go. Don't let your father tell you different."

"I don't think so."

"You were too young to see her passionate side. She fought for what she believed in."

"You can drop me off at Fife's Hardware," Tommy said. The last thing he needed right then was the Reverend's version of his mother. Tommy supposed he meant well, but how well had the Reverend really known his mother? How often would he have seen her—once, twice a week? But how well did Tommy know her? His father's memories of his mother had practically crowded out any of Tommy's own. He remembered the swoosh of her red skirt and the sound of her ballet shoes scraping on the floor, but nothing of what she smelled like or what her voice sounded like.

Instead of continuing down Main Street to Fife's, the Reverend signalled left just past the post office, drove to the train station, and parked. He turned to Tommy. "We all need a little guidance at times. Funny how the Lord works.

Any one of a dozen different people could have given you a ride today, but it turned out to be me. Maybe the Lord had a reason for that. Maybe he wanted me to remind you of your duty to your mother and your country. Enlisting is what she would have wanted. Women like a man in a uniform, she would have told you that." He smiled paternally at Tommy. "I could get you a ticket for Winnipeg if you like. You could be in a uniform tomorrow."

Within an hour, Tommy was aboard a train and he no longer doubted that his mother would have thought it was the right thing to do.

He wired his father from Winnipeg with the news. His father wired back a single sentence. *Take care of yourself, I love you, Dad.*

Tommy's father wrote him a letter every week without fail, even if only to comment on the weather or on who had died that week. No matter where the war took Tommy, his father's letters managed to find him. Tommy wrote back when he could, but his father never complained about Tommy's infrequent responses. Tommy was surprised, now, how much each of his father's letters meant to him.

Each letter began "Dear Tom," for his father continued to call him Tom, unlike his mother, who had preferred Tommy.

September 18, 1944

Dear Tom,
They cut our gasoline rations again this week although they continue to provide me with a little extra for the hearse.

Most people walk or stay home. I was happy to get your last letter. I don't know what I would do if anything happened to you. I know your mother would never forgive me.

The youngest Gow boy tried to cross the lake by himself in a canoe. The wind picked up and a swell must have tipped the canoe. They didn't find his body for a whole week. Even though I did the best I could with him, I know it wasn't enough. His mother would not go near his coffin and didn't stop crying through the whole service. The Reverend Lewis, the pompous old bastard, kept reading from the Bible, even though the Gows have never set a foot in his or anyone's church. Mr. Gow came up and shook his hand all the same. You'd think they'd been friends for years. He did something similar at your mother's funeral, kept us all singing hymn after hymn after hymn. It must be about time for him to retire.

I went fishing last week and wished you were with me. I caught one sucker, which I released. You remember how much your mother hated suckers. Too bony to eat, she said. When you get back, we'll drive out to Burnt Lake and fish for a whole week if you like. Some American got a huge pike out of there this summer. They had his picture in the paper.

I'll write again next week.

My thoughts and prayers are with you.

Love, Dad

His father ended every letter with "My thoughts and prayers are with you," even though Tommy hadn't seen his father pray since his mother died.

In December of 1944, near Holland, after ten success-
ful jumps Tommy landed hard, twisting his ankle. He
managed to get free of his chute, but before he could test
weight on the ankle, something burned the same leg. The
pain shot all the way up to his thigh, forcing him to the
ground. He pushed up his pant leg, surprised to see
blood. Only then did it register that he'd been shot. He
screamed and opened his eyes to see Jamie looking down
at him. Jamie carried him to the nearest jeep, and during
the trip to the Red Cross Hospital Tommy drifted in and
out of consciousness.

"Cracked your fibula," the doctor said. "That's the last of
your dancing days," he joked, and then, more seriously, "It'll
take a couple of months before you can walk on it. I'm
afraid we'll have to ship you to England."

While Tommy was in the British hospital, his father's
letters stopped coming. At first Tommy thought his father
might not have been informed of his injury or that the
Canadian mail corps hadn't been forwarding his mail to
the hospital in Kent. After Christmas, Tommy wrote a
short note to let his father know where he was, and while
he healed, he regularly read his father's last letter to keep
his spirits up.

December 11, 1944

Dear Tom,
Not much news this week. We had a heavy snowfall on
Tuesday and it closed down everything except the mill. My
work has been quiet for weeks, and I'm happy for the rest. I

have been feeling tired lately, so I've finally had a chance to putter around the house. It was your mother's birthday last week, and I didn't do much, just sang her Happy Birthday.

I gave the last of Jennie's pups to a nice family in town on Thursday. Their youngest boy reminded me of you, the way he kept hugging the pup.

I hope the war is over soon. They say on the radio Hitler can't hold on much longer. I don't listen to the radio that much though, I don't like all the war coverage.

If the war finishes up by late January, we can go ice fishing. I hope they're feeding you well and that you're keeping warm.

I miss you even more when it snows. It's so quiet here with you gone.

My thoughts and prayers are with you.

Love, Dad

Tommy received no reply to his note, so he wrote a longer letter, hopeful it would prompt a response. It also went unanswered.

In late January, a letter finally arrived. When the nurse handed him the envelope, his eyes lit up until he saw the handwriting and that the return address bore the name Reverend Lewis.

He took the letter outside to the terrace, even though it was chilly, and skimmed it the first time without taking a breath, and then he read it more slowly to let the details sink in.

December 20, 1944

Dear Thomas;
It saddens me to inform you of your father's passing. I do
not need to tell you that your father was well loved in the
community and will be sorely missed.

God works in strange ways, but I am certain that he
must have had a terrible need for your father to take him
so young. You must take comfort in that.

I saw your father in town a week before he died. We
had barely spoken in years but he looked so pale I later
drove out to see him. I volunteered to drive him to the hos-
pital, but he didn't want to go. He said in a day or two he
would be fine.

On December 14th, your father suffered a massive
heart attack. Not even the doctor knew your father had
been fighting cancer for some time, and it was the cancer
that weakened his heart.

Nearly half of Kenora turned out for your father's
service. We sang some of your mother's favourite hymns.
I know he would have liked that.

Tommy folded the letter and placed it in a pocket. The
hymns would mean nothing, he knew. What would have
pleased his father would have been to have Tommy there
with him. And of course nearly half the town turned
out—who wouldn't celebrate outliving the undertaker?

Likely, an undertaker from Winnipeg or Dryden had
been called for him. They would have first relieved the
rigor mortis by massaging and stretching his father's arms

and legs, and they would have washed him before making the tiny incisions in his neck and above his navel to drain his blood and replace it with embalming fluid. Only now did Tommy wonder how his father had felt preparing his mother in death. He had sensed how sad his father had been, but to think that he had to embalm her! Two or three small cuts were all that were needed, but it must have seemed like he was cutting her wide open, that his life drained away too as the blood flowed out of her.

Tommy had always taken his father's presence for granted, and when his mother died, his father had provided a shield for Tommy's grief, but there was no protection from his father's death, just the raw impact of it. He had no one to return home to—all that waited for him was an empty house and a few loose ends. Before the war, he'd taken those he loved for granted. He'd paid more attention to his mother after she died than when she was alive, and he neglected his father altogether. Perhaps if he hadn't, he would have recognized that his father was sick, and would have found a way to stay home as his father had wanted.

A young nurse found him and told him he could leave the next day. She smiled as she smoothed her dress at the hips and waited as if she expected him to be thankful for the news, but he felt only an urgent need to be alone. He closed his eyes to the nurse and remembered the story his father had told him of meeting Tommy's mother for the first time, in a hospital in Winnipeg. His father had come to pick up a body, and his mother was a volunteer at the hospital.

"I saw her standing over an older gentleman and I said to myself, that lucky codger, but I'm going to marry her."

All these years later, they were both dead and he was on the mend in a foreign hospital. He opened his eyes and retrieved the Reverend Lewis's letter, and the nurse stepped quietly back into the warm corridor.

Before he left the hospital, Tommy wrote a brief reply to the Reverend Lewis in which he did not mention his wound, but only thanked him for his letter and promised to stay in touch. As he handed the envelope to the mail clerk, it hit Tommy that there would be no more letters. *From anyone*, he thought, pain clutching at his heart like angry fingers.

These past two years, his father's letters had offered hope that any uneasiness between them could finally be mended. Tommy had even come to think of his father as a friend, and he had enjoyed his droll asides. The letters had provided insight into his father's personality, and Tommy felt he was beginning to know his father the way others had. He had imagined surprising his father in the kitchen, had seen clearly his father swinging around to grab Tommy in a tight embrace.

"Tom, thank God," he'd have said. "Let me look at you." And in that moment he would have known that this was not the same Tommy who came back, he would have been neither the boy nor even the man his father expected. Not once had Tommy ever imagined that his father would die before he returned home. He never told his father about the horrors he saw, or how he'd learned too late that his father was right about war, but he had promised himself that once the two of them were out fishing he would tell his father everything. What he regretted even more was not saying a proper goodbye. He understood now what a shock it must have been for his father to get the telegram.

Later, before shipping out again, he collected all his father's letters and placed them in a deep pocket of his pack for safekeeping. In the months ahead, he would command many to memory, and keep his father's voice alive a little longer, and more than ever, he wanted to return home, to keep his promise to his father that he would. Just as his mother never knew his father sang "Happy Birthday" to her every year, his father would never know whether Tommy survived or not, but that didn't change his need to do it for him.

The rain stopped, and for a few hours, Tommy slept. He woke, stretched, and rolled away from the tree. Both his hands felt raw and were caked in blood. He rose, still uncertain whether he stood north or south of Berlin, but he knew the train had crossed the Elbe early the previous morning, taking him many miles into enemy territory. The Americans lay to the west across the Elbe, the Russians to the east, and he and the Germans were caught between. On the ground, where random gunfire broke out without warning, east and west didn't matter because even friendly fire could kill him. His only chance of survival was to reach the Elbe before he was recaptured, so he travelled west at a brisk pace. Walking took his mind off the mounting fear that behind every tree enemy soldiers waited to ambush him.

Later that day, strobes of lightning and mortar fire came with the light rain as he walked west, where the horizon for a brief time glowed amber and then purple before dusk. He wasn't accustomed to rain this early in the year, for in Kenora they often had snow until the middle of April, but at the moment he appreciated neither. He longed for a few hours of direct sunlight, so he could properly dry out.

He kept in the trees on the edge of the road as much as possible. Nearly every building he passed had been reduced to ruins, and that night he cautiously approached a bombed-out classroom and crept around the building to make sure it was clear of enemies before he crawled inside. He hid himself behind loose bricks in one corner, and lay his head on his pack.

He woke to a stabbing pain in his ear. He swatted at the pain and struck a plump rat still nibbling. The rat squealed and tumbled noisily away into the dark. Tommy pressed his handkerchief to where the rat had nipped a small notch and stumbled in the dark away from the school, searching until he found a wooden hut, miraculously still intact. Because it was late at night, he felt safe making noise to scare off rats, and satisfied that none were about, he covered his head with his coat and slept. His ear still burned when he woke.

To the east, the first pale rays of the morning sun spiked around a remaining steeple and vanished into clouds of dust, and due west the full moon held its place against the day. He left the empty town, following the only road going west. For nearly a day, he hadn't seen any German soldiers and he hoped he was closer to the Elbe than he had first thought. The gravel road forked at a muddy field where dozens of horses, many dead or dying, formed a wall in front of him. The bodies of a handful of German soldiers lay amongst them.

He quickly retrieved a rifle, ammo, a knife, and supplies from one of the fallen soldiers. A few healthy but dazed animals wandered amongst the others, occasionally nudging the belly of a dead horse or soldier. Some of the wounded horses had managed to remain standing, and one amber stallion, much larger than most of them, bobbed its head in pained protest. Tommy stroked the horse until it calmed.

Tommy felt the stallion shiver under his fingertips, and as he leaned down to survey its underbelly, he saw that its right hind leg had been ripped through by shrapnel and the animal had lost so much blood that the hoof of its mangled leg touched down in a dark puddle. Tommy whispered into the horse's ear. He then stepped back and fired one shot between its eyes. The horse dropped slowly, its shredded hind leg buckling first, then the other before the front ones sagged together. The animal sighed once, tossed its head, and went silent.

A motor rumbled somewhere to the south, and Tommy ran toward a stand of trees. Fresh horse blood splattered his pant legs and added to all the other detritus as if he were a living artifact of the whole bloody mess.

He reached the trees and slowly crawled on all fours between them, stopping often to listen. Anyone could be hiding in bush this thick, even a Red Army company, who were as likely to shoot him now as any Germans were, unless they saw his uniform first. He slid along the ground to remain as hidden as possible, pushing aside thistles and shrubs in his way. Several times he nicked his hands and legs on thorns, and most of the time he crossed in mud, except for the odd patch of snow hidden from the sun. Twice he pulled himself up next to a tall pine long enough to get a reading of what lay ahead.

He crawled a good distance into the forest before he heard the whimpering. At first, he thought he imagined it, fatigue playing tricks on him. But as he moved forward, the sound grew stronger. Worried that he was stumbling into a trap, he thought for a moment about heading back, but his heart drew him to the sound against his better judgment. He inched closer, and the sound became more clearly that of a crying child. Near the source, the bush opened up, and he saw someone lying in the dirt, so covered in filth and blood that at first he couldn't make out whether it was a girl or boy. He pulled himself to within a few feet and the sobbing stopped. The girl had seen him, but she made no attempt to flee or defend herself. Tommy reached out a shaking hand to brush aside the dirt and mud, and she screamed so loudly he clasped his hand around her mouth, but she bit him and he had to let her go. Her hair clung to her head in matted, muddied clumps. She was only thirteen or fourteen.

"I won't hurt you," he said, keeping his voice as calm and low as possible. She spit at him and screamed again, then scrambled to her feet as if to make a run for it, but suddenly a gunshot cut through the brush and Tommy grabbed her and pulled her next to him as he rolled to one side to free his rifle. More bullets whizzed by. As soon as

Tommy spotted the rifle's spark, he shot five times in that direction. After the fifth pop, he heard a single groan and the shooting stopped.

The girl shivered next to him, and as he held her tighter to shield her, she shook even more. Tommy remained perfectly still and considered his options. He didn't want to die this close to the end of the war, so he couldn't afford the added liability of the girl, yet what chance did she stand on her own? His parents would never have forgiven him if he'd walked away from a child. His father had instilled in him the idea that the strong should protect the weak. "That's what ethical humans do," he said. Even in war that had to be true, especially for the children. Children were not the enemy. No matter how much his father prayed for Tommy's return, he would have told him he needed to do what was right. Tommy also knew he'd never be able to live with himself if he left her behind, prey to the next German or Red Army soldier who came along. He'd saved her life, and he couldn't leave her here to die. She was his responsibility at least as far as the next village.

He rolled away from her and lifted his head to survey the vicinity. "*Alles klar,*" he whispered, and waited for the girl to respond, but she simply stared at him, trembling. Her dress was badly soiled but bore the contemporary cut and style of someone from Berlin or Hamburg. Her left eye had swollen nearly closed, and dried blood smeared her face. Scratches covered her right cheek, her torn blouse exposed her navel, and her dress was ripped in several places. She held her left leg stiffly at her side. Broken, Tommy thought, by the look of it.

"Tommy," he said, pointing to himself.

"Freda," she said.

The wind picked up and the tall pines swayed and Tommy knew their rustling would prevent him from hearing any enemy movements. He and Freda were both in jeopardy as long as they stayed there, for a forest this dense was certain to attract more retreating Germans.

Tommy pointed ahead to indicate that they had to move, and at first Freda appeared reluctant to go with him, but after a moment, she nodded and pointed at her leg. He dropped his pack, secured his rifle over his shoulder, bent to his knees and offered her his back. She carefully worked herself into place next to him and eased her bad leg through the loop of his arm. He grabbed his pack in one hand and slowly lifted her. Freda weighed more than he had guessed, and she groaned whenever he touched her bad leg, but she maintained a steady grip around his neck. With less than five hours of daylight remaining, Tommy continued walking west.

Branches slapped against them as Tommy pressed through the thick undergrowth. He did his best to keep the larger ones from hitting Freda, but his back ached from her weight, and he had to stop often, so that it took almost an hour to reach the other side of the forest. There, he gently lowered her to a sitting position against a large pine tree and sat some distance away so as not to frighten her.

Two hundred feet in front of them was a paved road, its surface riddled with craters from weeks of bombings. On the other side of the highway, an even larger stand of trees blocked all views to the north. The highway cut through a narrow valley that extended as far as the horizon, but in the east, the valley widened, and Tommy saw a village several miles away.

He waved in that direction, but Freda vehemently shook her head. Tommy pointed in the opposite direction down the road, which led to a steep hill. She shook her head again, so he pointed at the forest across the road, and she nodded.

For the next few hours Tommy stopped at each cross-road and pointed in various directions until Freda signalled her approval. In this manner, they grew to trust each other and moved through a land made more chaotic each hour.

THREE

UPON ALICE'S ARRIVAL IN AUGUST 1948, she moved in with Shirley and her new boyfriend, Rudy. They shared a small house on Alfred Street, not far off Main. This was one of the oldest parts of the city, with a large working-class population and many recent arrivals to the city. Alice liked the various exotic smells and sights she encountered on her daily walks to work.

The asphalt shingles on their roof curled up, the blue paint on the trim peeled, but to Shirley and Alice the house glowed with unlimited promise. They had running water, electricity, and even a telephone, and best of all, their childhood home was two hundred miles away, as distant as death.

Not long after Alice moved in, Shirley discovered she was pregnant, and she and Rudy, a red-headed farm boy from Beausejour, began to argue more. Rudy flirted with Alice at every opportunity and often put his arm around her shoulder or squeezed her in an embrace to get a rise out of Shirley. Alice would blush and try to wriggle free, and then Rudy would turn his smile on her.

"I'm just playing," he'd claim, even as Shirley would shoot him a dirty look.

Rudy frequented the many booze cans that operated in this part of Winnipeg and sometimes didn't make it home until dawn. One night Shirley woke Alice at three with a loud rap on her door. "Alice, get up. We've got to find the bastard."

The two of them walked to Flora. Despite the hour, the street was alive with lights and people, and at several buildings people spilled out into the streets. Shirley walked straight into each establishment with Alice in tow. "Come on, he's got to be here somewhere. I'm not letting him get away with it again." When they reached the last house on Flora, they went south to Stella, and there they found Rudy in a white-brick house lit up like it was still the supper hour. Rudy sat smiling in an easy chair while a young woman balanced on the arm of the chair and whispered into his ear.

When Rudy saw them his eyes darted between Alice and Shirley, and then his smile disappeared and he sprang to his feet. "What the hell are you doing here?" he yelled above the din.

"Just get your ass outside," Shirley said, and dragged him by the arm. At the front steps, she pushed him toward the street.

"You better watch yourself," he said, but he staggered like an obedient child to his car angled awkwardly at the curb.

"So drunk you can't even park right," Shirley said as she got behind the wheel. Rudy slumped in the passenger seat and didn't answer.

Shirley pulled out onto the road. "I don't normally give second chances, but I'm knocked up so I'm breaking that rule. You've got one more chance, get it?"

Alice, in the back seat, thought Rudy nodded his head, but it could just as easily have bobbed in response to the motion of the vehicle. At the house, they left Rudy in the car and went inside.

Alice kissed her sister on the cheek and then went to her room. As she lay in her small bed under the moon's bleary light, she thought about Rudy left hunched in the car to sober up. She wondered if she could be as strong as Shirley, and as firm with her ultimatums.

Once, when Shirley was nearly three months pregnant, Alice woke in the middle of the night to find Rudy standing naked with an erection by her bed, and without thinking she reached out and touched him. He didn't move, just allowed her hand to grip him as if he were some prize she wanted to claim. Several nights later, he appeared again, and when she did nothing to stop him, he slipped into bed with her. She pushed his hands away when he tried to touch her, and lay stiff and silent beside him, rebuffing his few advances, until he finally left on his own.

The following morning, Alice woke feeling as though she were hung over. She dallied in bed a long time, unsure why she had not told Rudy to leave, or why she didn't get up now and confess everything to Shirley. She owed her sister that at least, but she felt she had something new, a power over Shirley that even as the older sister she had never felt before.

She remembered the time Shirley was eight and had

climbed a tree and sat on a branch nearly twelve feet off the ground. Shirley had always been the daredevil, the one to test their father's limits, and that day, although Wendell pleaded with her to get down, Shirley had laughed and said, "Catch me." Before their father could say anything, she jumped, and he caught her in the nick of time. Shirley had received a mild scolding about how she could have broken an arm or even cracked her head, but it wasn't enough to prevent Alice from wishing she had been the one to jump into their father's arms. She didn't even have the nerve to climb the tree.

The next week, Alice woke to Rudy's warm hands sliding over her. This time she allowed him to continue. He breathed her name into her ear, and she felt a warm sensation start in her stomach and spread outward. Up close, Rudy smelled different than anyone she'd ever been near—a little spicy, like Tailgate that day Claris died. His hands explored her, and he moistened her lips with soft, light kisses and then heavier ones until he gently parted her lips with his tongue. She bit down, held him in her mouth, and drew him closer.

Afterward, they fell asleep nested in warm covers.

Shirley's scream woke them. "Get out, bastard! Bastard! *Bastard!*" She pounded on Rudy's head with her fists. "Get out, you son of a bitch. If I see you in hell, it'll be too soon. You goddamn asshole. I'm pregnant, and you do this?"

Rudy leaped naked from the bed and ran into the living room, both hands raised to shield himself from Shirley's blows. Alice closed her bedroom door and lay trembling, her skin cold even beneath the covers.

"Asshole! Never come back!" Alice heard Shirley yell, and then silence. She didn't dare leave her room. Several times she heard the screen door strike against the side of the house, and tears formed but stopped at the corner of her eyes. She wished the wind would break through the bedroom window, sweep her up, whisk her away.

Eventually, when Shirley's crying had abated, Alice ventured timidly from her bedroom. The brisk September wind gusted unhindered through the open doors, and Alice hugged her arms around herself.

Shirley sat with her head pressed back against the doorframe, her eyes closed, and Alice slipped past her and tried to close the screen door, but her sister's leg prevented her. Alice waited with the door slightly pressed against Shirley's leg. Shirley opened her eyes, and with her other leg, kicked tamely at Alice, who stepped aside, leaving the screen door to flap open. Alice went to the kitchen and took a glass from the cupboard. The water gurgled in the bottom of the sink as it ran cold on her hand, her fingers disrupting the flow. She took several gulps of water, then refilled the glass and took it to Shirley, who had closed both doors and was sitting in a patch of moonlight in the middle of the living-room floor. Her toes fished in the carpet as she hugged her bare knees.

She looked up at Alice with a cold stare even as she took the glass and put it to her lips. After she had taken a sip, she said, "What's this? To make more tears, is that it?" When Alice didn't answer, she said, "Him I could understand, but not you. Why?"

"Some things just happen."

"Nothing just happens. There's a reason for everything. You can blame me for Robbie if you want, Dad does. But this makes no sense. We're *family*, Alice. Family doesn't do this."

"I'm sorry, Shirley, I really am. Don't hate me."

"Rudy I can hate, but not you. Right now I can't even think about forgiving you, but I'll have to, won't I?"

"I hope so, and you're wrong about Dad. He doesn't blame you, he blames me."

"Let's not start that again. I'm so damn tired of our family. I just wanted to get away from all that. I thought it could be different for you and me."

"It *is* different."

"No, it isn't. If you want to get back at someone, get back at Dad. How do you expect me to feel? Rudy, he's nothing but a shit. There'll be other men. He's not worth fighting over, but we're for life." She tried to stand, but her legs buckled a little, and Alice reached out to help her.

Shirley brushed her hand away. "I can do it on my own just fine."

When she stood she teetered, and Alice embraced her to steady her. At first, Shirley stood with her hands stiff at her side as Alice squeezed hard, but slowly she gave in and lifted her arms.

Alice was three and a half months pregnant when she met Peter. He came into the café one day and sat in a corner booth, drinking black coffee and watching her work. He was in his late twenties, shy and awkward, as if he was taking his own sweet time to grow up. He didn't have Rudy's looks, but something in the way his eyes followed her made Alice take notice. After his fourth coffee, Alice asked if he wanted anything to eat, but he shook his head and went on sipping his coffee, elbows on the table, holding the cup a few inches from his face all the time.

"You're pregnant, aren't you?" he asked when she brought him another cup.

"You can tell? I'm hardly showing."

"Lucky guess. You run your hand over your stomach as if you're protecting something. I like that." He took a quick, nervous look down the narrow length of the café. "Your husband must be happy."

"No husband. Just some bastard long gone. Excuse my French."

"Must be a bastard to leave you high and dry. I'd marry you in a minute."

To Alice, he looked young and naive, but his large, rough hands around his coffee cup made him seem older as they opened and closed several times and fanned the stale, smoky air. She caught his eyes on her bare fingers still nervously clutching the coffee pot, and she realized that neither of them had spoken for more than a minute.

"Are you always this nice?" she asked.

"I try." He flashed a smile and then ducked his head to hide his crooked yellow teeth, but when she moved away, she saw that his eyes had returned to her.

After her shift, Peter drove Alice home and they sat in the heated front porch for several hours talking. Both Peter's parents had died when he was a boy, and his aunt and uncle had raised him on a farm west of Winnipeg. He had come to the city after the war and worked in the rail yards loading and unloading boxcars.

"Can I feel your stomach? I've never touched someone pregnant before."

"Here," she said, and gently placed his hand on her belly, leaving her hand on top of his. "I felt the baby move for the first time a couple of days ago. I was lying in bed falling asleep and I felt something vibrate for just a second. My sister insists it's too soon for me to feel any movement unless it's a boy because her doctor said boys are more active at night, but I think it's a girl."

"My aunt said a mother knows these things best. She and my uncle never had kids, never wanted them either, she told me. They weren't too happy to have me, either, until I was old enough to work on the farm. I'm glad you're already pregnant. It means we can begin our family sooner."

Alice started when he said that, but he smiled as if he could have been teasing and leaned over and kissed her softly on the cheek. Then he stood up and walked away whistling. Halfway to his truck, he turned and waved, and she waved back, her thin fingers held high in the street light.

Every night for the next month and a half Peter arrived at the café an hour before Alice's shift ended and drank coffee until she finished. Each evening they sat in the porch, and often he asked to touch her stomach. At first, it struck Alice as strange to be joined to this man through her unborn child, but slowly she began to count on it.

One night Alice got off work early, and they drove to Assiniboine Park and sat in the idling truck beneath a grove of American elms with branches so broad and dense that even without leaves they managed to block the stars.

Peter held Alice's hand, and later he placed his head on her stomach and listened for signs of life. He talked more than usual, and as he caught sounds of movement or felt a kick, he made up stories for Alice about the baby.

"She's going to be a mechanic," he said. "No. A movie star. And she's got red hair and freckles just like me."

Alice laughed. Peter wasn't like the other men who saw her belly and turned away, and when the moonlight caught his red hair and filled it with pale highlights, Alice could see her new baby with red hair and freckles just as he said. She decided then that she would marry him if he asked.

Peter and Alice didn't make love until her sixth month of pregnancy. Until then, Peter had seemed content with hand-holding and goodnight kisses, never pressing her to do more, but Alice wanted more herself, and she realized she would have to make the first move.

She still lived with Shirley, and she felt uncomfortable bringing Peter to her room, given the incident with Rudy, but Peter lived in a boarding house with even less privacy. To complicate things, Shirley was nine months' pregnant and moodier than ever. She and Alice argued whenever they spent more than half an hour together, but fortunately, Shirley now went to bed early most nights.

Alice and Peter sat in the porch as they did every night, and when Alice saw Shirley's light go out she knew this would be the night, though her belly was so large she wondered if Peter would want her.

When there was a long break in the conversation, a more regular occurrence now, she stood up to stretch. Peter took this as a hint he should leave and stood too, but Alice grabbed his hand and led him into the house.

"We don't want to wake Shirley," she whispered as they sat on her bed, the only place in her room they could sit.

Alice placed Peter's hand on her covered breast, although she longed to feel his hand on her bare skin. She moved it slowly in a circle over her blouse, and Peter followed her lead and moved with an attentiveness that caused her cheeks to flush hotly.

When they lay naked on the bed and Alice wanted him to enter her, Peter hesitated.

"Won't it hurt the baby?"

"Don't be silly," she said. She realized she sounded like Shirley and stroked his face to soften her words.

He entered her from behind and moved slowly inside her, careful not to pull too hard on her abdomen. This was so different from Rudy's raw quickness, and neither of them spoke as their bodies moved to a slow, building rhythm, but they communicated all the same, with soft sounds, and movements, and ever-deepening desire.

The strangest part for Alice was how they made room for the baby, both of them acutely aware of the presence of another, so that it seemed to Alice as though the first time they made love, they also cradled her unborn child.

A week later, they drove the streets in search of For Rent signs.

"This one's pretty," Peter said, stopping in front of a modest wartime bungalow on Walker Avenue.

"I love the porch. It'd be a great place to rock the baby," Alice said, snuggling closer to Peter and looking down at the shaded roundness protecting her child. She had just begun to include "the baby" in everything she said and thought.

Within a week, they had moved in, wanting to be settled before the baby arrived. A narrow carpeted hallway connected the living room at the front of the house to the small kitchen at the rear. They bought a new refrigerator with Peter's savings, and Alice soon took to holding its door open in search of something to satisfy her cravings. The linoleum floor in the kitchen and bathroom needed replacing, and there was a curled-up corner of brown just in front of the electric stove that made her long for the day when she could afford to rip it up, but all in all, she was thrilled with the house they had found so easily.

Peter now worked closer to home, at the Red Roses Flour Mill, where every day his red hair turned white by the end of his shift. Each night he left a trail of small white prints through the living room and into the kitchen, where he would retrieve a beer, open the back door, and drink slowly as he surveyed the back yard.

Peter seldom talked about work, so when Alice nudged up behind him, drawing as close as the baby allowed, they spoke mostly about the people they knew, or the coming baby. Peter's truck broke down frequently, and on Saturday mornings, he rose early to work on it. In the afternoon he'd come inside covered in grease, and Alice, who paced the house wanting all the waiting to be over, would stop at the sight of his glistening hands.

"Don't bring that inside," she'd say, and he ignored her until one day she took him by the hands and marched him to the back door. "Clean up outside first. All week you *have* to get dirty but on the weekends you choose to, so don't bring it in the house."

From then on, Peter cleaned up before he left work, and on the weekends, he washed his hands in the old metal washbasin Alice left for him in the garage. Sometimes when she noticed, Alice kissed his red, swollen hands, pulled them behind her and drew them into the small of her back.

Two weeks after Shirley gave birth to Cathleen, Peter and Alice had a courthouse marriage with only Shirley and one of Peter's co-workers as witnesses. Alice didn't even consider telling her parents she was getting married. They would get their news all at once—one marriage, two grandchildren—and later, when she was strong enough to face their disappointment and disapproval.

On June 16, 1949, Alice rose earlier than usual with mild lower back pain and stood before the bathroom mirror running her hands over her swollen belly. The baby had dropped three weeks before, and Shirley had told her then, "With Cathleen I only had to wait two weeks to the day after she dropped."

Damp traces of Peter's morning bath covered the edges of the mirror, and a few rivulets bordered Alice's reflected face. He must have left for work just minutes ago, although she hadn't heard a thing before her bladder woke her. She streaked one finger along the moist glass in a quick swirl as she looked in the mirror, trying to find her old face in its new roundness, and she said aloud, "Today's the day the baby's coming." She smiled at that thought and moved slowly to the kitchen, where she found a note from Peter that said, "Telephone if there's any news." She considered calling him to say she had a feeling about today, but she wanted to wait until she was certain—Peter's boss was not the type who liked false alarms.

The night before, Alice and Peter had walked along Portage Avenue at midnight trying to induce labour. They held hands and Peter said, "We'll walk all the way to the west end of Portage if that's what it takes."

They both tired after about three miles, and Peter had hailed a cab, but the walk had helped her sleep well. Now clear morning light fell across the kitchen table as she sipped coffee and listened to the first few birds and stared out the back window at Peter's oily car parts already littering the scruffy yard, as if they'd lived here for years rather than weeks. A half-gutted truck sat at the back fence, its hood yawning toward her. It was an ugly yard, but at least the house *had* a yard, and it was fenced as well.

Alice considered her baby's coming journey. How would she know it had started for sure? She had heard of false labour, and she worried she'd call Peter for nothing. Not only that, but what about the pain? She knew it would hurt, but how much? A lot, or only a little? She leaned back in the chair and looked at the row of hubcaps Peter had propped along the east fence. Her lower back continued to ache, so she drank her coffee, and then, instead of doing her morning chores, prepared for the baby, just in case.

She collected some older, rose-coloured towels from the back of the closet and set them next to the tub as she'd seen her father do before Robbie was born. Shirley had delivered Cathleen at home, all by herself, and had called Alice only when it was all over, saying, "She's as healthy as an ox and I did it all by myself, just like Mom. I thought it would be harder than it was. Mind you, it hurt like a son of a bitch, but she's all mine."

Peter, on the other hand, was cautious. "Call me if there's any sign and I'll get you to the hospital. You need a doctor."

Alice ran the water, not too hot but not too cold either. No baby wants to emerge into the cold. She dropped her robe and tested the water with her toe and right then she felt the first light tug she could have missed if her attention had been elsewhere. She stood waiting for another one, and when it came minutes later, it held longer and was no tug but a real pain. Alice settled into the water and lay her head against the back of the tub, waiting.

By the time the contractions were five minutes apart, the water had cooled and Alice had begun to shiver. The contractions had strengthened into sharp pains that made her moan and grip the side of the bathtub. When her head cleared, she knew she had to get out of the tub, that Peter was right and this was a bad idea. Her legs trembled and nearly gave as she climbed out, but she made it to the bed and pulled the covers over her head, and then she vomited a big brown coffee mess off to the side. *This is not good*, she thought. *Call Peter. Breathe. Call Peter!*

The contractions took her away from the room, and

when they let go, she lay dripping in sweat under the grey cotton bedspread and white flannel sheets that she and Peter had splurged on at Eaton's before moving into the house. When she did manage to focus, her eyes kept falling on the limed-oak vanity with rounded metal handles she had brought with her from Shirley's. Across from it, Peter's dresser contrasted with the lighter coloured, mismatched vanity, end tables, and headboard.

She closed her eyes again to contain another stab of pain, and this time screamed so loud she hoped the neighbours would hear, but no one came. She felt herself begin to push the baby as though she had a heavy, dead stone in her and not a baby at all.

Between the contractions she had no strength, could not even turn from side to side, and she knew her child would be born, dead or alive, here in the soiled bedding. Alice probed inside for the baby, and when she brought her hand back, it shone with bright red blood. In a moment of reason, she thought, *What if the baby is breeched like Shirley?* for there was no Tailgate to turn the baby around. She screamed again, and her whole insides clamped in a further spasm as she reached down again for the head. At first she found nothing, but she pushed her fingers farther up and touched the head, which felt softer than she expected. The pain pulled her further under and still the hard shape needed pushing out. She coughed and pushed harder, and for the first time she felt the baby slide along inside her.

The baby's head emerged from her without a sound, and her hands between her legs felt her child still half inside her, so she tugged with both hands and the baby dropped onto the sheets.

Alice couldn't tell whether her baby, all smeared in blood, was a boy or girl until she drew the infant to her. The umbilical cord reminded Alice that she'd forgotten a knife, but she was too weak to get one now, which was just as well because she couldn't remember what Shirley had told her about cutting the cord. Was she supposed to do it immediately or wait for the afterbirth? She breathed through the receding pain as her daughter squirmed on her stomach, and as Alice started to drift off, she thought she heard the front door open and Peter come in with a dog, but she realized the sound was the first whimper from her daughter.

When Alice opened her eyes again, she saw by the clock that nearly half an hour had passed. She tried to lift herself up, but her arms couldn't hold her, and when she reached between her legs, she drew back damp, blood-stained fingers. The pain had subsided but not stopped completely as Shirley had promised, and now Alice worried that the bleeding wouldn't stop either and that Peter would find her dead, because she didn't expect him home for several more hours. The baby cried, and Alice forced her eyes open and saw that her daughter had tangled herself in the cord. Alice managed to free her and slid her as close to her face as the umbilical cord allowed. "Judith," she whispered.

A hand eased onto her forehead and Alice opened her eyes. Peter looked grave and appeared to be moving in slow motion.

"She's beautiful," he said. "Are you okay? I called, and when you didn't answer, I came straight home." He leaned in a little closer to Alice and stroked her face. "I've called for an ambulance," he said, and added, "I'll get you some water."

"Thank you." She hadn't realized she was parched. "What about the cord? Can't you cut it?"

"They will. I don't want to lose either of you."

"I've made a mess of the bed. I threw up, and the blood—"

"Who cares about the bed," Peter said. "Look what you made!" He left her then, and brought back a large glass of water, and later in the ambulance, Peter smiled at her and said, "Judith has red hair just like I said."

Alice wrote to her parents a month after Judith was born and told them everything, even sent them photographs of Judith and Cathleen taken together at a Simpson Sears studio. The babies wore matching pink cotton dresses and bonnets and resembled their father rather than their mothers.

"Why'd you do that?" Shirley asked. "I don't want him getting to know Cathleen. He'll just say we're bad for getting pregnant, and for not being good Christians, or something equally stupid. At least you're married. They'll forgive you, but not me."

Helen wrote a cheery letter back, saying both babies looked beautiful, but there was no word from their father, not even a little note attached at the end. *I hope you'll bring the babies down*, her mother had written, but made no mention of her or their father coming to Winnipeg.

"I told you not to write," Shirley said after she read her mother's letter.

Alice continued to write, though, and the frequent letters she received in return provided Shirley with the only news she got of her parents.

When Judith was eight months old, Peter said, "We should make a trip down sometime and visit. I think it's time you and your parents patched things up."

"It's not that simple," Alice said.

"Maybe not, but I'd give anything to have my parents back."

And so they drove to Dryden early that winter, in Peter's truck with the broken heater. But to Alice's surprise, and pleasure, her parents, particularly her father, doted on Judith, and Alice saw for the first time how he may have doted on her when she was a baby.

"She's nearly as beautiful as you were," Wendell said as he rocked Judith, and then later, when they were leaving, he took Alice aside and said, "Tell Shirley to bring Cathleen for a visit—we'd love to see her too. We're getting too old to make the trip to Winnipeg, but that doesn't mean we want to ignore our grandchildren. Both you girls turned out fine, all on your own."

One afternoon in September 1950, Alice heard a single firm knock, and when she opened the door, Rudy stood smiling at her.

"Aren't you going to invite me in?"

"No, I'm not. I'm married now."

Rudy reached out to place a hand on Alice's shoulder,

but she pulled back and held her ground in the doorway.

"I want to see my baby. You owe me that."

"I don't owe you anything."

Rudy stepped closer. His breath smelled of whisky, and a yellow taint surrounded his irises. Alice blocked his way, and as she watched him stagger, she wondered how she had ever allowed him to touch her.

"It was you I wanted, not Shirley. That's why she kicked me out."

He moved forward to kiss her and she pushed him firmly back from the door. He stumbled down a step and looked up at her.

"I want you back. And my baby."

"I'm happy now, so take the hint and don't come back." Alice slammed the door and locked it with a quick flick of her wrist. She leaned into the door for support until it cracked from the impact of Rudy's shoulder.

She jumped back and watched the door anxiously. "I'm calling the police!" she yelled, and through the thin wood she could hear him swear.

She pressed a hand to the door but felt nothing. Then she felt Rudy push on the other side, testing, and she pressed back. She felt the door give a little but hold, and then she heard, "Shit," followed by irregular footsteps to the curb.

Judith began to cry, and Alice went to her. She found her daughter sitting up in bed, her red hair messed to a curly ball. She had her father's same grey eyes, except that where Rudy's eyes darted back and forth, seldom fixing on one thing for long, Judith's held steady. Alice breathed in Judith's baby scent, sensing that Rudy would be back.

"Horny, most likely," Shirley said later when Alice called her. "He'd pretend to be the pope if he thought it would get him into your pants. It's his notion of charm, and if he didn't think with his cock he wouldn't think at all. He'd like the extra challenge of a husband and child."

Alice planned to tell Peter about Rudy, but that day Peter's truck broke down and he didn't arrive home until well after dark, so tired and irritable that he cleaned up and went straight to bed. As Alice lay beside him that night, she convinced herself that she had been wrong. Rudy wouldn't be back because there was nothing to come back for. She'd made that clear.

The next week brought cooler fall days. The beginning of the month had been exceptionally hot, and Alice was grateful for the colder temperatures because with less heat, Judith napped for an entire two hours without waking. Alice used the time to read and listen to the radio—usually CKY or sometimes CBC—or to do the crossword puzzle in that day's *Winnipeg Tribune*. Most of her day was filled with tasks related to Judith—cleaning up after her, washing diapers, washing clothes, preparing her food and bottles—so occasionally when Judith napped, Alice napped herself. Otherwise, she went to bed every night exhausted and couldn't really say what she'd done to tire herself out except look after Judith.

Rudy began showing up every afternoon while Judith napped. It didn't matter what time Alice put Judith down, within ten minutes Rudy would be at the door. His timing gave her chills. She thought he must be watching the house. All he ever did was knock twice and wait, while Alice sat quietly on the couch waiting for him to give up, which he inevitably did.

Each day she told herself she would tell Peter that night. Each day she hoped Rudy would finally get the message and go away once and for all.

One morning she woke to a familiar feeling in her stomach. She vomited several times, while Judith ate breakfast in her high chair, and even without visiting the doctor, she knew she was pregnant.

That afternoon, when she walked into the kitchen to prepare Judith's lunch, Rudy was sitting at the table.

"How'd you get in?" Alice asked, her voice trembling with a rush of adrenalin.

"You got any coffee?" Rudy had a pleased look on his face, his head cocked to one side.

"Please *leave*." Alice spoke as calmly as she could manage.

"Worried your husband might find us?"

"Leave before I call the police."

"What will you tell your husband?"

"Fuck off," she said, and bolted for Judith's room. She worked her nursing chair under the doorknob.

"Alice, let me in. I'm staying here until your husband comes home."

She heard him slide down the door and imagined his back propped against it, his heels dug into carpet.

She quickly dressed Judith and eased the bedroom window open. She returned to the door and pressed her ear against it. She thought she heard Rudy stand up and pace the living room. After another minute, she felt him slowly push against the door, testing. The chair cracked under the pressure. Alice tiptoed to the crib, bundled Judith in her arms, and hurried to the window. As she straddled the sill, the door rattled and the chair gave a warning snap. Without hesitation, she dropped her feet to the ground. She wrapped Judith tighter to protect her against the cool air and ran into the street, ran to a confectionery several blocks away and slipped inside.

She huddled behind a shelf full of Campbell's soup cans stacked three high, her eyes darting to the door each time it opened. Finally, she saw a bus approach. She replaced the can she'd been holding and ran outside to board it, surveying the street as she eased her way to the back of the crowd.

She watched for Rudy at every stop for the first ten blocks until she was certain he hadn't followed her, and at Portage and Main she transferred to Shirley's bus.

That night, Peter came for them. When Alice opened the door, he stood on the steps with his worn blue cap in his hand. "Are you okay?"

She threw herself at him. "I was so scared," she said as he held her.

"I hoped you'd be here. When I got home, Rudy was sitting out front smirking, as if he was waiting for me. 'You lost your wife?' he said. 'She's my daughter and don't forget it.' He told me he'd been trying for days to see Judith. Is that true?"

Alice nodded, watching his face.

"Why didn't you tell me?"

"I don't know. I was afraid you wouldn't believe me. That you'd think I'd encouraged him." She wanted him to argue that, to say, "Of course I'd believe you," but he didn't, he only shook his head and held her against him again.

"I called the police from the neighbour's and waited outside in the truck. It took two officers to carry him off." He stopped and took a breath. "The police said we can't keep him away from Judith unless we get a court order. He's one crazy son of a bitch. I wish you'd told me."

"Me too." Alice recognized the concern on Peter's face, but she thought she saw something else as well, not disapproval so much as doubt, or even jealousy.

Peter moved them inside. "I don't want us to have secrets. I knew he was a bastard, but I never thought he was a lunatic. What if he hurt you?"

"But I avoided him, didn't I?" Alice wanted him to see that she was stronger than Rudy and that if she couldn't always tell Peter everything, he should trust her anyway.

Peter drew back from her and his eyes measured her. "You still could have been hurt."

"Maybe I should stay here awhile," she said, not sure she meant it.

"I'm not leaving you here!" Peter said. "What's to stop him from coming here?" He put his cap back on his head. "We'll get through this. I just don't want anything to happen to Judith. She's mine now too."

"Ours," Alice said. Everything he said was right, but that look was still there in his eyes. He thought she had something to hide and he was jealous.

"I can look after us," Alice said. "And I haven't done anything wrong!" She walked away, hoping Peter would follow her, but he didn't. She heard the door latch as he left.

"Peter's outside sulking in his truck. You two have a fight?" Shirley asked when she returned from shopping a little later.

Alice told her what had happened.

"You're both acting like babies," Shirley said. "If you don't watch it you'll let Rudy fuck up a good thing, and he isn't worth that. You don't need to be afraid of him—he's all wind."

"I'm not afraid of Rudy."

"Why'd you come running here, then?"

"He tried to break down the door!"

"That's just for show. He's a little man inside, which is why I was glad to get rid of him. You stand up to him and he'll turn into a worm." Shirley puffed on her cigarette and then grinned at Alice. "Take my word for it. He loves it if you run, but if you stand up to him, he'll slink away."

Judith, who had begun to walk in the past month, teetered toward her mother. Alice drew Judith to her with one arm while she opened the curtains with her other and saw Peter's truck still there. Did he think he had to stand guard? She saw Peter in the cab, a cigarette secure in his mouth. When did he start smoking again? He had pushed his cap back to reveal his high forehead, and Alice watched him exhale a large cloud of smoke before she let the curtain drop and pulled Judith up onto her lap.

She fingered her daughter's hair, a pretty tangle in the living-room light, and she felt again the strong love she had for Peter. Peter had never been judgmental, or jealous, before. She knew she had complicated the situation, but Peter had allowed suspicion to form a rift between them, and he was the only one who could mend that.

Two hours later when dark began to fall, Peter's truck was still there. Earlier, he had killed the engine, but as the night air cooled, he kept the truck idling.

Shirley said, "You should either go with him or tell him to bugger off." She sat down facing the back of her chair, her chin resting on her arms folded over the curved back.

Alice had already put Judith to sleep on the couch, and had spent much of the rest of the evening by the window.

"I'm going to sleep on it. I've had enough for one day."

She lay down next to Judith, and as she curled around one child, she sensed the new baby inside her, nothing more than an urge for life her body could still refuse, that seed busy making its own body out of bits of hers. Judith had been no different once, but now she belonged in Alice's life as no one else had. Not Peter, nor her parents. Her children needed her, both the born and the unborn, but they needed a stable family as well. They needed Peter, all three of them.

Several times that night, Judith's whimpering woke Alice, and each time, Alice held her daughter's damp face against her own to calm her. At four o'clock, Judith kicked wildly at her covers. When Alice couldn't soothe her, and went to the refrigerator for milk, Peter's truck was still there, and he remained hidden in the dark of the cab. Alice pressed her forehead against the window and squinted into the night before she returned to the couch and waited for Judith's breathing to become regular again. In the morning, Shirley and Cathleen were already gone when Alice woke. So was Peter.

A few hours later, when Alice had just gathered her and Judith's things in preparation for leaving, Rudy came into Shirley's kitchen from the living room and took Judith up in his arms. "You look just like your dad, don't you? Except you're beautiful like your mother." Judith squirmed out of his grip and toddled across the linoleum to her mother.

Alice lifted Judith and went to the telephone. "Why don't you leave us alone?"

Rudy stubbed his cigarette into the tabletop and placed the butt in his jacket pocket. "Cathleen could be anybody's kid. You know Shirley. She's frisky. But Judith is mine and I want to see her."

Alice started to dial.

"You think I'm afraid of the police?" Rudy smiled but didn't get up from the chair. "I could take her with me right now if I wanted to."

"Over my dead body! You might have fathered her, but you'll never *be* her father. If you really cared about her and wanted to be a part of her life you wouldn't be acting like a criminal." Alice put the phone down and carried Judith into the bedroom. She put her in Cathleen's playpen and returned to the kitchen.

She looked hard at Rudy, who still sat at the kitchen table with a new cigarette in his mouth. "I've had enough of you. Get out of here." Alice opened the back door and motioned to him to leave, but he didn't move. "This isn't about Judith at all. I've learned a lot from Shirley and one of the things I've learned is that you're not worth shit. You tried to break down my daughter's door. Do you think I'll ever forget that? Judith is my child and Peter's, and we'll never let you have her. Now get out!"

When he still didn't move, Alice shrugged. "Suit yourself, but I don't want to see you ever again." She left him in the kitchen, put on her coat and fetched Judith. She left by the front door.

All through her second pregnancy Alice sang. Most of the songs she made up herself, playing them on an old piano Peter bought several weeks after she told him she was pregnant. Whatever she had seen in his face that time had disappeared, mended by their night apart, and he sometimes sat at the piano with her, holding his hand to her belly as she played.

He was more attentive and considerate than ever, and during the long, cold winter months of her pregnancy, Alice would lie in bed nights with Peter spooned behind her. On the days the extra weight caused her feet to swell, he massaged them, sometimes for hours. He seemed to take nothing for granted.

"Will you love them both the same?" Alice asked him.

"Of course," he said, as if there could be no doubt, and he was true to his word.

Adam was born thin and frail, with red hair and a thick forehead—the spitting image of Peter. Alice contracted influenza and was sick for two weeks after his birth, so she couldn't leave the hospital. When she did, she remained so pale and sickly that Peter had to stay home with the children. He lost his job at the flour mill, but for some time he and Alice had been planning to leave the city for a quieter place, so they moved east to Kenora, where the post-war boom allowed him to find work quickly in the paper mill.

The next summer, Peter built a house at Burnt Lake, ten miles straight south of Kenora on the Trans-Canada Highway. He set the foundation on the southern tip of the lot and created floor joists out of the straightest spruce he found on the lot. He peeled them by hand and supported them on concrete blocks. The rest of the house he constructed from whatever scraps of lumber he could salvage. At auction, he bought an oak ceiling from a recently demolished school and used it to floor most of the house. The long, narrow kitchen was brightly lit by five full windows, and across from the sink, Alice arranged the turquoise Formica table with chrome legs and matching chrome and plastic chairs. If she stood on her tiptoes in front of the kitchen sink, Alice could glimpse peekaboo views of the lake through the trees.

Burnt Lake was seven miles long and a mile across at its widest point, where it flowed into Lake of the Woods.

"Not many boats come to this end of the lake," Peter had said when he first showed the land to Alice. "This is Edna Bay, and we'll have it to ourselves most of the time. The children can swim in the summer when they're older, and it has a natural sand beach." He reached a hand in the water and withdrew a dripping clump of sand.

Alice dipped her hand after his in the warm water, and kept it there, not believing. Warm as her skin. The sun skimmed along the surface and disappeared between the branches of a row of trees that formed a second ridge just at eye level across the bay. A thumb line of thick spruce, as straight and even as a carpenter's plumb, spanned the western shore of the lake, adding to the privacy.

Down a narrow path between tall, weathered white and red pine, Peter rolled a boulder to the shore for Alice. She often perched on it with Judith curled up next to her while she held Adam in her lap. They were willing passengers in their mother's arms as her feet made circles in the water.

Peter cleared a little field behind the house and slowly filled it with junk. His projects gave him a reason to get up each morning, and he cared little that they were always abandoned partway through. Over the next eight years the backyard at Burnt Lake became cluttered with machines and equipment that didn't work and no one else wanted: washers, cars, tractors, plows, wood stoves, miles of rusted pipe, barn doors, power saws, winches, skidders, even a small Jeep snowplow that had been used during the war. Peter hoped he could repair and eventually sell these goods to someone, although he never did. Small buildings appeared here and there, too, huddled communities of abandoned chicken coops and old sheds where a plethora of carburetors, fly wheels, rear ends, and tie rods accumulated at an ever-increasing rate.

Like all his other projects, Peter never completely finished building the house. Just off the kitchen he enclosed a small, partly insulated room where in winter a slop pail collected their daily wastes. The kitchen cabinets were unfinished wooden skeletons where dishes collected in no particular order. Only the cups were arranged together, hung on large, ugly nails. The kitchen floor heaved the first winter and from then on it had a large hump in the middle as if something had tried to push its way out of the ground beneath them, but Alice cared less about the interior of their home than she had in the past and spent more time outside with her children.

Judith changed after Adam was born. Although she was already two, she stopped sleeping through the night. Nightmares woke her almost nightly and she would crawl into bed with Peter and Alice until one of her parents coaxed her back to bed. Sometimes Peter with his deep-throated voice hummed to help her settle down.

Shortly after Judith's third birthday, the nightmares magically stopped, and for two glorious years Alice's life was tranquil and content. Her one regret was how little she saw Shirley and Cathleen, for they rarely visited, and never stayed the night.

On her first visit, Shirley had made it clear how she felt about Alice's move. "I couldn't live here, I would have packed my bags by now and moved back to Winnipeg. I'd have thought you'd have more ambition than this, and Peter too. He seems nice enough, but is this all he wants?"

"We're happy here," Alice said, which wasn't entirely true, but Alice hated how Shirley put her on the defensive, when she seemed neither settled nor happy herself. She lived in a rented apartment in the city, with nowhere for Cathleen to play outside, and she changed jobs and boyfriends several times a year.

"Mom and Dad came for a visit," Alice said to change the subject.

"I don't get so much as a letter from them. Not that I'd want to."

"Dad's not well, and most of the time he hardly left the kitchen, but he was awfully good to Adam and Judith, had one or the other on his knee the whole time."

"He could turn on the charm when he wanted to, but I don't miss him, except for Cathleen's sake. She might like to know Mom."

Cathleen and Judith no longer played well together, and they fought on every visit, with Cathleen usually pinning Judith until she screamed for help. Alice had to separate them, because Shirley hardly cared.

"Leave them," she'd say. "You and I were worse."

That may have been true, but Alice wanted more for her children, and she thought Shirley should want more for Cathleen as well.

When Judith was particularly difficult, Alice reminded herself that her daughter was also Rudy's daughter, and to prevent her from being like him, Alice grew more determined to parent her well. As Adam got older that became increasingly difficult because Judith and Adam fought constantly. On a trip back from Dryden, Adam slapped Judith's hand away as she teased him, and Judith wailed for the last hour of the trip. Alice almost reached back and slapped her, she grew so tired of her carrying on, but Peter bit his lip and kept silent, so she did the same. Once she turned up the radio in an attempt to drown out Judith, but that only added to the racket. Whatever had happened to her sweet child?

One Saturday, when Judith was seven, Alice took the two children down to the lake with her as usual. She held both of them as she perched on the rock and dangled her feet in the water.

The sun stretched in thin strips along the tops of the trees on the facing camelback hills, as Peter called them, two large lumps like a Bactrian camel. That was a word he must have learned long before Alice met him because she never saw him read anything except the Kenora newspaper, and even then he only perused the front page before passing it to her. Judith had studied camels in school that year, and she brought home a picture to show Alice, who smiled when Judith said "Bactrian," for suddenly the two halves of her life fitted together.

Alice heard the plop in the water before she realized that Adam had plunged, fully dressed, into the lake. He dropped straight to the bottom and looked toward the surface, his eyes bulged in terror. His cheeks swelled and then his mouth opened to shape a scream but only a single bubble emerged. Alice pushed Judith aside and dove into the water. Her green checked dress darkened, ballooned, and then her weight drew it under.

She heard nothing but the odd flap of her own feet until she grabbed Adam and broke the surface with a gasp. Adam's startled face followed. He choked and then coughed as his body shivered in his mother's arms. She carried him ashore and laid him on the sandy ground. His red eyes stared at her in confusion as he spit wet, unfinished words, and Alice rolled him on his side and patted his back a couple of times. Already the lake and all the disturbed water had calmed, as if nothing more than a small stone had broken the surface.

Alice hurried Judith ahead of her and rushed Adam back to the house, where she wrapped him in a blanket and rocked him, holding him tight. Peter came in from the yard and stood over her.

"What's wrong?"

Alice didn't answer, so Judith blurted it out. "Adam almost drowned."

"Jesus, Alice, what happened?" Peter sat next to her on the couch. He didn't seem to know at first whether he wanted to comfort her or take Adam. Finally, he pulled Alice to him and with his other hand stroked Adam's cheek. After a moment, he put his arm around Judith too. "It's okay," he said, "We're all safe now."

FOUR

AS NIGHT APPROACHED, Tommy and Freda stopped to rest on the edge of a recently tilled field. On the far side, he saw a single farmhouse backed against a stand of maples dotted with the occasional silver fir, and next to it, a wire fence formed a rectangular pen. Tommy gestured a route around the farmhouse, but Freda pointed directly at it. He shifted her carefully on his back and walked toward the house. As they neared the pen, he saw several dozen milling chickens and rabbits. He felt their animal attention as a large rooster moved determinedly in his direction for a moment and then stopped. Partly devoured carcasses were strewn across the floor of the pen, indicating that the animals had been eating each other.

The contents of the dark farmhouse lay smashed out front. Fragments of porcelain bowls and vases littered the ground, and torn linen and shattered pictures were heaped over splintered wooden furniture. A small library of books had been torn and strewn around.

Tommy left Freda on the front porch while he searched the house. He found the remains of a man and woman in the kitchen, both of them shot at close range and laid side by side next to the table. The clogged air reeked with death, and along the dark edges of the kitchen, he heard the restless shuffling of rats. They had worked slowly through the corpses, and as his muddied boots scraped on the wooden floor, they scurried to new hiding places.

Satisfied that there was no human danger, he returned for Freda. He shielded her eyes as he passed the couple on his way to the bedroom, and when he had lowered her onto the bed, he dragged the farmer and his wife out to the barn, planning only to lay them inside, as he could not risk the time to dig graves. When he swung the barn door open, Tommy froze. Against one wall two girls hung— likely the couple's daughters. Neither appeared to be more than sixteen, and they'd been crucified, even their heads nailed in place. The horror of what he saw forced him to close his eyes. He felt himself wavering on his feet but could only open his lids reluctantly. He had heard rumours of crucifixions like these, and while the war had shown him much to hate about humanity, nothing he had encountered had prepared him yet for the pure evil of this. He shook, and their dead eyes held him, so he could not immediately look away.

The barn door creaked, and cool air chilled his neck. His stomach knotted, and his fists curled while his arms remained stiff at his sides. He had to resist giving up, slipping into the warm hay and closing his eyes for good. Each new horror caused him to wonder why he kept going. At this moment there was Freda to consider, but even if he managed to save her, what would it matter? What was the point? His only comfort was the tenuous belief that beyond war the world still existed more or less as he had known it, and he clung to the idea that if only he could get home, his life would begin to make sense once again.

Tommy squatted, rocking on his haunches, knowing that during the years before the war, this father might have returned tired each day from the fields and embraced his daughters. Before bed, he may have read to them, and that last night, when he heard the soldiers coming, he had certainly hoped they were friendly. In all likelihood, their mother had awakened the daughters and all three had rushed to the cellar. He couldn't bear to imagine what had happened next, but the gruesome ending was foretold.

A rat crossed in front of Tommy, pausing to sniff first the mother and then the father, and Tommy stood and stomped his foot to drive it back into the shadows, where he heard it tunnelling through the dry hay. The wind lifted one corner of the mother's dress and Tommy could see that her leg had been gnawed.

He wanted to free the crucified corpses, and with his hands he tried with the younger one, but after he struggled for a few minutes, the smell forced him to retreat from the barn.

Knowing that darkness was only a few minutes away, Tommy took some air and returned to the barn. He searched it for tools, and at first he believed everything useful had already been stolen, but eventually he found a shovel. With it, he pried the corpses from the wall and placed the daughters between their parents. His eyes burned and his breath came in shallow gasps, but he felt a need to hold this grim gathering in his head. He closed up the barn and lay several nearby planks under the door to keep out animals and turned his back on it.

A bright moon spread a thin glow over the surface of the pen where the chickens restlessly pecked. He selected one of the healthier ones—a Lakenvelder—killed it, and plucked the hen's white and black feathers. In limited moonlight, he gutted the bird, carried its pink flesh inside, and laid it on the table. Tommy pounded the chicken meat flat and cut it into strips and quickly swallowed one strip raw. He offered a strip to Freda, but she looked at him in fear and shook her head.

A while later, she called from the bedroom and pointed at her mouth. He placed a few thin strips of mashed flesh on her tongue and she swallowed reluctantly. Freda ate more until the taste caused her to gag, and when he motioned her to lie down and rest, she did, offering him a cautious smile before closing her eyes.

Tommy returned to the kitchen and lay on the floor near the front door to keep guard. A cold spring wind howled during the night and he slept in spurts, getting up now and then to check on Freda. He woke again at dawn to a shaking farmhouse and Freda's screams. He ran to her and found her on the floor trembling. He lifted her to the bed and went to the window. In the first light, he made out the hunched shapes of at least half a dozen Panzer tanks heading straight up the road toward the farmhouse.

Freda quieted as Tommy scooped her up and made for the cellar stairs as the house shook violently. The cellar smelled of decay, and he felt his way along the damp, crumbling wall. Freda whimpered and buried her face in his tightened chest. He kicked at the rats that gathered at his feet.

Freda clung tightly to him as the floor above them creaked and groaned in response to the thunder of the tanks. Tommy huddled in a corner as far from the stairs as he could, and held Freda close. Rats nipped at his clothes and bare arms. He swatted at them, but they were undeterred. The tanks had shaken them past the point of fear.

In all the noise, Tommy heard firm footsteps overhead. Light broke at the top of the stairs, and a fresh wave of rats flowed down into the dark fleeing the light. Dozens of rats chirped and the light went out. "*Kaput,*" a voice said, and the sound of wood sagging and yielding followed. Boards snapped and groaned and dust rained down on Tommy and Freda as both stifled coughs.

Something heavy dropped with a crash, a tank motor revved, and the demolition above stopped. For a few minutes more, the ground vibrated until the sounds faded to a few sporadic tremors. Most of the rats drifted away, except for a persistent handful, which eagerly continued to prowl until Tommy grabbed several and tossed them squealing into the dark. Freda screamed and Tommy covered her mouth until she quieted. When he removed his hand, she gulped air with rapid, irregular breaths.

Tommy waited almost two hours before venturing upstairs. Morning light shone down the stairs as Tommy pushed the trap door open and carried Freda out of the cellar. The stairs ended at open air—the whole front of the house was reduced to rubble, a Nazi preventative tactic meant to leave the Red Army with no place to take shelter. Thick, rank dust filled the air and made breathing difficult.

The bed where Freda had slept remained strangely untouched, and Tommy saw that the tossed blanket looked as if it had been that way for weeks. He motioned her to sit on the bed, and Freda obeyed, her eyes dark and still suspicious. As Tommy examined her bad leg, he moved gently, not wanting to frighten her. The skin around her calf was rubbed raw, indicating that she had been tied up for some time, and bruises covered the length of her leg. Tommy tapped her swollen knee gently, and when she cried out in pain, he gestured that he wouldn't do that again. He carefully lifted her from the bed and lay her on the floor. He tossed the straw mattress aside and stripped two thin boards from underneath. He tore strips from the wool blanket and wrapped them around the boards to form a splint.

Her leg buckled a little when she tried to stand, but she did manage to straighten up and support herself. She smiled and attempted a step forward but winced in pain. Tommy knew walking would be difficult for her, but they would make better time if she walked, even slowly. She swept a few strands of matted sandy hair from her freckled face. When she smiled, Tommy saw straight, well-cared-for teeth, but her thin, sunken face reflected months of meagre rations. They both smiled and walked into the front yard, where the sun already shone higher than Tommy expected. The razed earth outside steamed with columns of mist, and a few flattened chickens and rabbits were scattered about the yard.

Without warning, one after another, airplanes dropped out of the clouds and banked from the east. As they approached, they filled the air with a deafening howl, and within minutes, a whole squadron crowded the sky. At first, Tommy couldn't tell whose they were, but as they flew closer, he made out the star insignia of the Soviet air force. He motioned Freda to crawl beneath what remained of the front porch, and despite her injured leg, she quickly slid into the dark gap. He crawled after her just in time as the lead plane strafed the clearing. Chickens appeared out of nowhere, running wildly in all directions. Several bullets passed through the thick timber porch and stirred dust around Tommy, and then a long hiss preceded an awful thump so close he thought his eardrums would burst. A second bomb hit farther away, and a third rapidly followed. Tommy dug his hands into the ground as if he were hanging on to a steep cliff.

When the sky quieted again, he turned to find Freda in the dusty haze. She lay no more than three feet from him, with her head down, motionless. Tommy feared that she had been hit, but as the dust settled he saw that her eyes glowed with terror.

He crawled to her on his elbows and held her. She felt cold, and her breathing was shallow. They huddled together for a half-hour before smoke from the barn forced them to back out from under the shelter. Flames engulfed the barn and Tommy smelled burning flesh. He and Freda coughed and spit mouthfuls of dark dust, and then Tommy brushed the dirt and dust away from Freda's face, and she did the same for him. Her scarred hands brushing his bearded cheek provided the first gesture of tenderness he had received in months.

Freda moved first, heading south and west away from the tanks. She walked faster than he expected, and they quickly left the farm behind, veering off the only path, which was too well travelled to be safe. The rolling land was sparsely treed, and to their north, they saw tanks burning in the morning sun, victims of the Soviet planes.

Freda pointed to a narrow road that wound through some open country, and eventually they encountered a German family walking with a single donkey carrying their belongings. Freda left Tommy and approached them. They spoke in friendly tones for a few minutes and occasionally pointed at him. He nodded his head slowly and they nodded back. When Freda returned, Tommy motioned toward the family to indicate that she should join them if she wished, but she shook her head and handed him a small sack of grain.

They sat and ate several handfuls of the sweet raw grain. Tommy watched Freda chew and noticed that her eyes were lit a little more brightly than they had been, and her swollen eye had begun to heal. A part of him had hoped she would join the others, freeing him from any responsibility for her, but another part was grateful for her company, however limited their communication, and he wondered if his own eyes showed signs of new light as well. Now and then, groups of villagers or farmers passed, but for the most part they travelled alone, even the sky quiet and unthreatening, the sun warming their shoulders.

Late that afternoon, they came upon a crowd swarming

the wreckage of a freight train. The opaque smoke issuing from the mangled locomotive made breathing difficult, but cautiously, Tommy and Freda approached and slipped in unnoticed to join the fray. Tattered and emaciated refugees, many of them women and children, rushed toward the centre, where men broke into one of the over-turned boxcars and heaved chocolate bars into the waiting crowd. People fought to scoop up some of the bars, and Freda and Tommy joined in until their pockets were full, and then they retreated and turned west again to follow the afternoon sun.

They stopped to eat chocolate well clear of the crowd, gesturing now and then in celebration of their good for-tune. Tommy savoured several mouthfuls of the dark, slightly bitter confection. Suddenly Freda took his hand in her cold one and kissed it lightly. He whistled "Danny Boy," and she whistled too but couldn't follow the tune, so they laughed together.

At intervals as they walked, Freda spoke to him in German. He knew only a few words here and there. *Großeltern*, grandparents, *Bauernhof*, farm. Occasionally she sang in German, in a rough voice, not at all like his mother's.

Tommy wanted to tell her everything about his life, and to ask her the same, but he didn't know where to begin, so he took out his wallet and showed Freda pictures of his parents. "*Mutter, Vater*," he said.

Freda looked at them and smiled, and as she sat beside him he could almost imagine she was the sister his mother had promised him for years. Then, he hadn't wanted a sister, or even a younger brother, but with both parents gone, he now wished for one, so at least someone would be waiting for him to come home.

"My parents are both *tot*," he said. That was one German word he had heard often enough. *Dead.*

Freda squeezed his hand.

"My parents were madly in love. I want to love someone the way my father loved my mother. He never loved anyone else," he said, although he knew she didn't understand a word. He pointed at Freda. "*Mutter?*" he asked.

"Berlin," Freda said.

"*Vater?*"

"*Soldat. Tot.*" Her face remained composed, and Tommy could see that war had already hardened her.

"Berlin?" Tommy said and pointed at Freda.

She looked confused. He pointed at the two of them, made a walking motion with two fingers, and again said, "Berlin?"

"*Nein. Berlin kaput. Mutter ...*" Freda made a shoving-away gesture with her hands. Her mother must have sent her away from Berlin. She pointed west toward the Elbe and said, "*Amerikaner.*"

So, filled with chocolate, they continued in the direction of the Elbe.

"My mother loved the ballet and she and my father took the train once a month to Winnipeg to see a production. My father always said that my mother swept him off his feet, although I think it was mutual. My father couldn't dance at all, and he always complained about his two left feet, but my mother said he wasn't so bad."

Freda nodded, although he knew she had no idea what he was saying. In faltering German, he asked her if she had brothers or sisters, and she told him two brothers, both soldiers, both dead.

Tommy told Freda of how his father's death troubled him and how he had not dreamed once of his father since he'd learned of his death. He found that odd, and worse was that for weeks now he could hardly recall his father's face. His mother's, yes, but not his father's, as if somehow he'd erased everything except the sound of his voice, saved by the letters he still managed to keep safely in his mangled pack.

For a little while, as they talked, the war faded to distant artillery fire north of a hump of hills ruggedly treed with spruce and pine, like those around Kenora, although Tommy couldn't have felt farther from home.

"When this whole mess is over, I'm heading straight for Winnipeg. I'm leaving all that bush behind me. I've lost nearly three years of my life and I plan to make up for lost time. I could never live in my parents' house again with them gone, so I'll sell it, and then I plan to find someone who'll love me despite all this war business. We'll start a family in the city, boys or girls, it doesn't matter to me, and live a normal life."

Tommy wondered what Freda's dreams were, beyond surviving the war. He imagined her dancing like his mother, although her wounded leg would hinder that. He wished he knew the German word for dreams, but then it occurred to him that she might be too young yet to have those kinds of dreams, and that only caused him to wonder what she did think about. He hoped her thoughts went back before the war, to some happier time when she was younger and her family was all together.

The next evening, to Tommy's surprise—he had been certain that the train had taken him much closer to Berlin—they reached the Elbe River. The road they'd recently joined stopped abruptly at the muddy springtime river. Three concrete columns stood intact above the half-sunken ruin of the bridge.

"There is a rail bridge at Tangermunde, one day's walk north," a woman assured Tommy in broken English. She carried a brown suitcase, and a green handkerchief covered her hair. "*Der Heimgang,*" she said, and moved off. Going home. She looked back at them but continued walking south, the opposite direction of everyone else.

Late the next day, they reached the bridge. Bombings had left it leaning at a forty-five-degree angle, and a slow line of refugees trailed from the bridge, each patiently waiting a turn at the precarious crossing. Tommy put off an attempt until nightfall, when he hoped the line would thin out.

Dirt and mud caked his clothes and his skin itched where red sores had formed beneath his soiled uniform. His ear had begun to heal where the rat bit it, but it still felt hot and swollen, so when he spotted a clear pool where a wide creek eddied before being sullied by the heavy brown flow of the Elbe, he took the opportunity to wash. He left Freda at the road and clambered down the embankment, pushing aside prickly dried shrubs. At the water's edge, he stripped to his waist and waded in. The grime and stink eased off him in water so frigid he would have normally scrambled out as quickly as he had gone in. Instead, he washed until his arms and fingers numbed in the cold and his sores were temporarily soothed.

Freda watched from the bank for a while and then half hobbled, half slid down to lower her feet into the river too. Tommy slipped out and approached her. He could see that blisters covered both her feet, the red traces of blood streaking the water briefly before being drawn away. When she had finished, Tommy adjusted her splint and dried her feet in his one dry shirt before putting it on.

That evening, Tommy and Freda progressed slowly in the dark because the lean of the bridge was more pronounced than it appeared from land. They planted each step into the ledge made by the rail and used the higher rail for support against falling into the icy water. The river's gentle lap against the bottom of the bridge belied the strong current beneath, and although Tommy led Freda by the hand, halfway across, she froze, sobbing.

"*Nicht weit*," Tommy said—not far—and waited. Several boys and an older man approached.

"*Schnell*," the man said and pressed firmly into Tommy's shoulder.

"*Das Fräulein ist verletzt*," Tommy said. The girl is injured.

"*Schnell! Russische Soldaten.*"

Tommy lifted Freda higher onto the bridge while the man and boys passed. From the top rail, the water sounded more dangerous, and in the moonlight, he saw more refugees approaching. He lowered Freda to the bottom rail and quickly followed her. The lip of the rail dug painfully into his arch but he managed to keep his balance. He stepped past Freda and crouched enough for her to put her arms around his neck. He carried her this way the remaining two hundred yards, stopping only long enough to get his breath.

Across the bridge, they approached a group of refugees gathered around a fire.

"You are safe," a man said, "*Amerikaner* are nearby."

Tommy and Freda warmed up and shared a bar of chocolate with the others, and moved off into a cold but calm night with renewed energy.

They continued in the dark for several hours along a main road. In the distance Tommy could see the silhouette of a medieval castle on a rounded, deciduous hill and caught the fruity scent of a nearby orchard in blossom. They passed cows with steam pouring off their backs, and Tommy knew if he approached one he'd find its udder hot as he slipped his hands below for warm milk, but he stifled the impulse, afraid that stray German soldiers may have taken refuge in the nearby farm.

Instead, he and Freda stopped at a small lake, its dark water misty and cold, its perimeter surrounded by bare maples and birches, while on the far side a castle's lone tower remained intact. Tommy couldn't see any way around the lake except to follow the road they were on, so he found a haystack not far from the water and dug a hole big enough for both of them to crawl inside later. Then they sat by the lake eating the remaining grain, careful to keep enough for morning. Tommy pointed to himself and held up his fingers twice to indicate twenty-two. Freda answered fourteen and then flashed a shy smile. When Tommy pointed at her cheek and knee, she said, "*Russische Soldaten.*"

"*Ist sicher,*" he said. We are safe. "Americans *hier. Nein Russische soldaten hier.*"

"*Yanks gut?*" she asked.

"*Ja, gut.*"

Freda nodded. Dark, layered strands of cloud had knitted out the moon until Tommy could barely discern shapes around him, so he motioned Freda to lie down and covered her with clumps of hay before covering himself. He left their faces free and piled more hay so that only an air hole joined their cavity to the world outside. "*Gute nacht,*" Freda whispered. "*Danke.*"

When Tommy woke the next morning Freda was gone. He pulled himself from the haystack into the gloom of fog and the odour of smoke, while German airplanes searched for targets above the thick cover Freda must have disappeared into. Between the planes and his heartbeat, he couldn't hear anything else, but after the planes had gone, he called her name. He got no response.

His whole body ached, especially his legs, from the strain of crossing the bridge, but he made his way to the edge of the lake and took a drink. It was possible she had decided to strike out on her own, but gauging from the short time he'd been with her, he thought that unlikely. He worried that she had wandered off looking for food and fallen and injured her leg more.

He washed his face in the cold water and by then the fog had lifted a little off the lake, but he still could not see across. All the same, it had been light for only a couple of hours, so she couldn't have gone far. Could she? He had just moved away from the lake to seek a better vantage point when he heard a scream that sent him scrambling up the steep incline. As he broke the crest, he saw Freda surrounded by six American soldiers in a makeshift camp.

The soldiers laughed as they taunted Freda, and he saw that she clutched two pieces of meat she must have grabbed from their fire as they slept.

"Leave her alone," Tommy yelled, running up to them.

The sergeant looked him up and down and said, "Fuck you, pal. She's a Nazi thief and we're going to deal with her."

"She's with me. Besides, we're all on the same side, right?" Tommy pushed his way into the middle where Freda stood trembling.

The sergeant leered. "What do you want with her?"

"Can't you see she's hurt and hungry?"

"Fuck you." He pushed Tommy back while the other men levelled their M1s at Tommy.

Tommy shoved past the men and took Freda by the hand. She dropped the pieces of meat as he pulled her toward the lake. Tommy heard the rifles cock but kept walking. Freda trembled by his side, her eyes once again red and devoid of any emotion except fear.

The sergeant ran in front of Tommy and pointed a revolver into Freda's bruised cheek. She slumped to the ground and the sergeant made to kick her, but Tommy pushed him to the ground.

One of the other Americans slammed a rifle butt against Tommy's head, and he dropped to the ground and covered his skull. His whole head throbbed, and the ringing was so loud he thought he'd gone deaf. He spun toward the Americans, brandishing his knife.

The sergeant had already come to his feet and he kicked Tommy's chin, knocking him back on the seat of his pants, and when his head hit the ground he blacked out for a second or two. When he came to, he managed to stand and lunge at the sergeant, sweeping the air with his knife.

Several sets of hands grabbed Tommy and tossed him to the ground. He hit hard and heard a snapping sound, but continued to lunge blindly with his knife. He felt the blade enter something spongy and stop at hard bone.

"Shit!" the sergeant yelled, and then another kick square in the face sent Tommy sprawling on his back. Two Americans pinned him to the ground, but he continued to kick and thrash his arms as best he could despite the pain radiating from his jaw. His lips felt swollen and he tasted blood.

The sergeant kneeled over and spit into Tommy's face. "Stupid fuck," the sergeant said, barely opening his mouth to speak, his face cold and determined.

Tommy struggled to free himself but three men now held him flat on his back. Above him he could see Freda's pale face lean over him before the sergeant pushed her out of the way.

"Be reasonable and let us go," Tommy pleaded through his painful jaw. "She's just a child."

"Get rid of this piece-of-shit Kraut lover," the sergeant said. Freda screamed and bit the sergeant's arm until he hit her on the swollen side of her face. She slid to the ground and moaned.

Tommy kicked out again and managed to knock over one of the soldiers pinning him down, but another quickly took his place.

"Fucking tough bastard, aren't we?" the sergeant said, and swung a rifle butt against the side of Tommy's head.

They kicked Tommy until he lost consciousness, and then they dragged him by the arms back to the lake. When he regained consciousness one of the soldiers kicked him squarely in the stomach and knocked the wind out of him again.

They left him then, and he lay alone in the mud, his uniform soiled by muck and piss. He heard Freda scream and attempted to get up, but he couldn't raise his head without it spinning. German bombers criss-crossed the sky dropping bombs, and the earth shook.

II

For a small moment I have forsaken thee;
but with great mercies will I gather thee.

ISAIAH 54:7

FIVE

ALICE WAS SEVEN AND SHIRLEY five when their
mother gave birth to Robbie in 1936. All through her
mother's pregnancy, Alice hated the thought of having
another younger brother or sister. Shirley already tor-
mented her, and if a sister was so stubborn and annoying,
how much worse would her lot be if she also had the misfortune of a brother? Robbie was nearly a month overdue
and Helen had swelled bigger with him than with any of
the other children. Then, a few days before her mother
went into labour, the baby stopped moving altogether, and
Alice hid in her bedroom. She had wished the baby dead.
What if wishing had made it true?

When her mother's water finally broke, their father boiled
water and sent Alice and Shirley out to the well for more.
Robbie arrived while Shirley and Alice were on their second
trip. When Alice got to the house, her father was beaming.

Fresh from her mother, a small tuft of dark hair crown-
ing the top of his head, the new baby was hideous. He had
big hands and feet, but his eyes were small and set deep
into his large head. *He's deformed*, Alice thought.

That night in bed she buried her face in her pillow and held her eyes tightly closed, trying to muffle the sound of her father and mother talking excitedly in their bedroom. Neither of them said what Alice knew—that Robbie was the ugliest baby ever born.

Robbie didn't sleep through the night until he was three, but Alice's father dragged his favourite chair from the living room without complaint, and left it near the kitchen stove so he could get up and rock Robbie back to sleep whenever he needed to.

In the years after Robbie's birth, the depression gave way to the prosperity of the war years. Their farm flourished and for the first time Alice had store-bought clothes. In the summer of 1940, their father took them to the beach in Dryden every Saturday while their mother stayed at home to rest. The beach formed naturally where the dammed Wabigoon River swelled to a wide, shallow bay. Here the water warmed enough to permit swimming, and every day in summer the beach filled with families seeking relief from the heat. Alice watched her father play with Robbie with an affection he had never publicly shown his daughters.

He told all of them, "If you can swim fifteen feet in one direction and fifteen feet in the other without touching down, you've learned how to swim," but he helped only Robbie and left Alice and Shirley to learn on their own. Each time they went to the beach, their father carried Robbie through the crowd of midday swimmers and dropped him where the water reached to just below Robbie's armpits. He placed one hand on Robbie's stomach and lifted him until Robbie balanced on the flat of his father's strong hand and paddled in the water.

"Kick," he told Robbie.

Later, their father left Robbie in the water and stood on the shore to watch, his white legs visible to his knees. Alice had never noticed her father's bare legs before this summer, and she was surprised at how thin they were. Stick legs with thin blue veins all down the front and back, meeting at his slightly yellowed and turned-under toes.

Robbie never swam very far by himself before he gave up, and all summer their father encouraged him, unable to entirely conceal his disappointment.

On the way home, Robbie sat next to his father on the buckboard and Alice watched Wendell pat his head. "You'll learn soon enough," he said. Alice sat next to Shirley in the back of the wagon, cupping a handful of stones she had collected, wanting to throw them at her brother.

"He's timid in the water," Alice heard her father tell her mother. "He only wants to play and he never goes out over his head. He bawled like a baby the first time I took him to the water and he wouldn't even put his foot in. When I dropped him, just to his ankles, he screamed. But now he loves the water and doesn't want to leave it. Now he cries when I take him out, so he's bound to learn once he can get those big feet of his to work."

By the end of that summer, neither Robbie nor Shirley could swim. Only Alice swam the vital fifteen feet in one direction and fifteen feet back without touching down, and yet, no matter how many times she demonstrated this skill, her father never praised her. In fact he seemed not even to notice as he watched from the safety of the beach, his eyes fixed on Robbie's futile splashes.

The next spring their father discovered that Finn Lake curled toward their property and he spent several weeks cutting a narrow path through the half mile of bush to a natural sand beach. Finn Lake at this point was no wider than a river and surrounded by white pine and birch. Ten feet off shore, the sandy bottom washed to a soft, waiting mud and soon dropped to unknown depths in the middle.

The beach was no more than a hundred feet from where Allison Creek spilled spring runoff into the lake, and the path Wendell cut began behind the house, crossed the hay field, and carried through dense, unforgiving brush. Along the way, the path crossed Allison Creek twice and passed through two natural meadows thickly scattered with wildflowers.

Alice turned twelve that summer, and as soon as school ended she taught Shirley to swim. She tried teaching Robbie and succeeded in showing him how to dog-paddle enough to keep his head above water, but not even that elicited her father's attention. During the first weeks of July, the days were so hot Alice woke sweating by eight each morning and baked in her room even with the window wide open. Playing outside was impossible, and the heat proved too soporific for reading, so each morning dragged until early afternoon, when she and her sister were permitted to go to the lake.

Alice and Shirley walked barefoot to the beach, and on the way Shirley liked to run through the tall, aimless stalks of wildflowers and trample whole clumps of them, leaving a cloud of petals behind her. By the time she reached the lake, her feet were stained with rainbows. Alice preferred to pluck a single flower and take in its scent as she cupped it in her hands.

That summer Alice's body began changing, and sometimes she got headaches so intense she put a pillow over her head to keep the light and noise out, so she loved how the lake engulfed her and cooled her skin.

In late July, heavy rain replaced the heat, and Alice stood indoors watching rain batter the tall grass behind the house until the whole field flattened, stalks glistening as they arched into each other just inches from the ground. She watched and wished for a break in the weather, but for a solid week, the rain never let up. Finally, on Sunday, she woke to an early heat worse than any so far. Years later, Alice would still be struck by how quickly a day could become one that would forever haunt her.

The heat was so great that their mother allowed them to go to the lake early, and it was barely past noon when they crossed through a willow grove at the far end of the field. Robbie came running after them, shouting, "Dad says take me, take me. I want to swim too."

Shirley broke off a branch and waved it at Robbie. "We're not taking you. You can't even swim properly."

"It's okay, I'll watch him," Alice said.

"Get walking, then," Shirley said, swatting his legs with the branch.

Robbie ran ahead, and Shirley caught up to him and poked him in the back with her willow branch.

"*Alice!* Shirley's poking me."

"Leave him alone! Why do you have to tease him so much?" Alice glared at her sister and let the two of them go ahead. She pretended she was an only child and that they were strangers she could choose to ignore. The damp grass felt cool on her bare feet as she waded through twisted stalks flattened by the rain. She kept her head down and fell farther behind.

Near a puddle, she found a frog with its hind legs squashed. Blood and other strangely coloured liquids oozed from its flattened legs, and Alice gingerly lifted the frog from the soggy ground. She felt the body twitch in her hand and saw its mouth open several times before going still. She lowered the corpse into the creamed-coffee water and it floated belly up, its mangled legs dangling toward bottom. She pushed the white underside with her finger and watched the frog float lifeless across the same puddle it had been safe in all morning.

Alice noticed blood on the inside of her leg and she touched it, thinking it was frog's blood, but when she followed the trail of colour upward, she saw that it was her own. She tore fronds of grass and wiped the blood from her leg and then took the small face towel she always brought with her and stuffed it between her legs.

Between the trees by the shore, Alice could see Robbie already splashing in the water. He waved and Alice waved back. She turned to face Shirley, who had already lifted her dress over her head and tossed it onto a branch. She stood thin and naked in front of Alice, smiling as if she didn't have a care in the world.

Alice caught sight of Miner's Rock, which looked

cold and deserted even on this hot day. Her father said a boatload of miners drowned off that rock the summer of 1921, the year the road from Dryden was built. All that summer the miners had searched for gold on the north shore, but found only the cold bottom of Finn Lake. Finn was the man who spotted the boat going down and swam out to try to save them, but only he made it back to shore alive.

Robbie dog-paddled out toward where the bottom turned to mud and then slipped below the surface, but Alice was so worried about how she could undress without Shirley seeing the blood between her legs that she didn't notice until Shirley screamed and ran naked toward the water, her bare feet slapping the surface of the lake with quick barks.

"What?" Alice's eyes followed Shirley and scanned farther out expecting to see Robbie chest high in the water. Instead, the bay lay calm and empty, only a few expanding ripples marking his point of entry.

Not until after Shirley dove beneath the mud-brown surface did Alice understand what had happened. She immediately chased after her sister and once in the water she kicked hard with both feet, afraid both her brother and sister would both be swallowed by the lake. Frantically, she felt through the stirred-up water, which had turned even murkier, and held herself under even as her lungs burned. When her fingers struck the mud bottom, she kicked with all her might and shot to the surface and greedily gulped air. Shirley screamed behind her, but Alice's eyes had blurred from grit and she couldn't see a thing. She kicked her feet to move in the direction of Shirley's scream, and when Alice's vision finally cleared, she saw that Shirley had already reached shore and stood stooped over Robbie.

"Alice, help! Help me!"

Alice pushed through the muddy water until she reached sand and could run. She tripped at the water's edge and put out her hands to break her fall. She landed near her brother. His hazel eyes were open, and his lips— blue, nearly purple—bubbled with yellowish froth. *He's okay, he's okay*, she promised herself. He couldn't have been under the water more than a couple of minutes. He couldn't be dead. *Could he?* His eyes stared straight into the bright afternoon sun.

"Do something!" Shirley shouted.

Alice dropped to her knees and pressed her ear to Robbie's chest. When she heard nothing, she pounded on the space between his ribs. "Breathe!" she shouted.

"Get out of the way." Shirley pushed her sister aside, lifted Robbie to her bare shoulder, and raced down the path toward the house. Partway her legs buckled, but she managed to steady herself and kept going. Robbie's large head bobbed against her shoulder.

Alice overtook her just as Shirley collapsed on her knees. Robbie's head struck the mud and Alice lifted her brother and carried him as fast as she could. Shirley ran alongside, and within no time Alice felt her chest constrict, but she dared not slow her pace. Despite her effort, valuable minutes passed before she reached the halfway point of Allison Creek. By then, her lungs burned and she was forced to take short, quick breaths. Her arms and legs felt rubbery and she worried that she would collapse any second, but she pushed on. Just when she was about to drop in total exhaustion, the sight of the house provided her with a burst of strength. She struggled to speak, "Get Mom," she managed.

Shirley spurted ahead, screaming as loud as she could.

Both parents came out of the house before Shirley reached it, and as soon as Helen saw Alice carrying Robbie, she sprinted toward Alice. Shirley, still naked, gave her father a wide berth and kept running.

Helen lay Robbie gently on a patch of dry grass. She pushed her fists into his small chest and moved his arms back and forth, then she turned him on his side and put her fingers down his throat to clear his airway of vomit and water.

Wendell leaned over them, breathing heavily.

Alice dropped to her hands and knees, wheezing in the background while her mother worked on Robbie. Without warning, Wendell stepped close to Alice and stooped to slap her so solidly on the side of the cheek she was knocked onto her back.

When Alice opened her eyes, Shirley's face was just inches from hers. Shirley hugged a scratchy olive-green blanket around herself, and tears formed at the corners of her eyes. Alice held her so close she could smell the lake on Shirley's neck. They clung to each other for several minutes, rocking together without making a sound. When they broke apart, Alice's mother was carrying Robbie to the house. Her father, next to her, supported Robbie's head. They moved slowly and cautiously, as if Robbie were asleep and they didn't want to wake him. Alice lay back in the tall grass next to Shirley.

For the longest time she couldn't move, and her limbs felt so heavy she didn't know if she could lift them, but finally, the damp towel between her legs felt cold, and she forced herself to adjust it, which left dark blood on her fingers. She had the irrational thought that maybe the blood leaving her body was Robbie's.

Shirley huddled again beside Alice, and Alice had never seen her sister so still. Alice listened to the wind cut swaths across the freshly dried grass and tried to hear Shirley's breathing over the wind. With her eyes closed, she could trace everything in the field, even the placement of the house and where she lay under the shelter of a caragana bush, one of several that lined the halfway point across the field. In the evenings, their father had often brought Robbie out this far to throw balls. Alice used to watch Robbie run from bush to bush chasing the worn baseballs her father kept in a special dish on top of the radio.

She marvelled at how her father could always pinpoint a ball's location in the tall grass, so that once Robbie reached a ball, he could drop his large hand into the grass and lift it triumphantly while her father hollered praise. Alice's gut cramped again and she lowered her hand to the spot. Shirley didn't move.

After dark, the wind quieted, and Alice sat up and watched light spill from every window in the house. She knew what her parents were busily doing inside, because she'd been through it all before with Claris. She couldn't face any of it, not yet, least of all Robbie's body, rigid like Claris's, trapped for good in his final gulp of air.

They spent the whole night lying in the grass. Alice woke several times from the cold and nestled closer to Shirley for warmth. Once she looked into the dark sky above, and for the first time, it looked round and not flat. She saw that there were stars behind stars, and later the moon edged its way across the sky, so she could make out her own arms and legs and even the crushed-rock path that started at the road and ended at the house. She imagined Robbie lying on his bed, his eyes open but unable to take in the toys that likely lay where he'd left them.

Shirley woke once and asked, "He'll be all right, won't he?" and Alice said yes. They held hands and squeezed so tightly their fingers hurt.

As she lay quietly beside Shirley, Alice remembered how the afternoon after Claris's death, her father returned with Claris from the hospital and lowered her gently to her bed. Her mother undressed Claris and called Alice into the room. She raised the warm cloth from the basin and wrung it dry. Her mother worked slowly from Claris's stiff face, down her body, over her burgeoning breasts, and on to her feet, catching all the tricky places—behind her ears and between her toes. When she had finished, she wrapped Claris in a blanket and looked straight at Alice.

"Doesn't she look beautiful?"

Alice agreed but didn't look at her sister, instead looked just above her frozen body, at a small dot on the wall—a fly, or a smudge. Maybe the same mark Claris had stared at night after night before falling asleep. Alice thought

Claris was likely just that size now, a small cinder inside her hollow body. That's what her father had told her. "Without our souls, we're hollow inside, like an old rotted-out log." She had stepped back from her sister, leaned into her mother, who sang softly.

It made Alice shiver to think of her mother washing down Robbie's body. Just one look at his face would be enough to send Alice running. She should have been paying attention every second he was in the water. She would not soon forget the sour smell on her brother's lips, or how all night the blood had not stopped but continued to stain the towel, or how she stood on the shore unable to act while Shirley ran for the water, or most of all, how swiftly he had died. She had thought she hated him, but now he was gone, she only wished he was back.

When the sun broke over the top of the far spruces, Alice raised her head and slid a hand down to the place where blood still flowed out of her. She got up, careful not to wake Shirley. She removed the damp towel from between her legs and looked at it. She had expected more than one dark patch not even half the size of her palm.

In the kitchen, she found a tea towel and positioned it where the towel had been. She washed her hands, opened the garbage, and worked the stained towel beneath a layer of coffee and eggshells.

She stood outside her brother's room and wondered if her parents had covered him in blankets or left him on top of the covers, his hands folded on his lap like her sister's had been.

For weeks after, Alice could not go into Robbie's room. She would stand outside his door and imagine him in there playing or asleep, but never as he must have been that morning.

Alice expected her parents to collect all of Robbie's things and put them in a box, air out the room, even fix it up as a spare room, but they left the room untouched at first. Then her father started to sneak in things like a new baseball, glove, or cap. He tried to hide them, but her mother usually found them.

Later, as a mother herself, Alice understood her father's sorrow, but never the blame. The day Robbie died had changed her as much as it had changed him, or all of them for that matter. For years no one talked about the drowning, although her father spoke of Robbie often, saying, "Robbie was so good at catching a ball. Robbie had a natural ear for music. Robbie was so bright, I'm sure he would have been a doctor."

Robbie's death had elevated him even more in her father's mind, and praise for Robbie was parcelled out nearly as generously as blame for Alice and Shirley. Sometimes their father was direct. "I would have thought you girls would have learned from what happened with Robbie not to ..." Other times his blame was nothing more than a look he gave them at supper or when one of the girls came inside from playing. A look that said, *Robbie doesn't get to eat or play, does he?*

SIX

THE PAIN IN HIS GUT and the swollen eye made it difficult to move, but Tommy managed to stagger back toward
the embankment. As he scrambled up the hill, he saw the
smoke from the Americans' fire. He hadn't checked his
watch, so he wasn't certain how long he'd been out, but he
knew from the position of the sun that it must have been
nearly an hour.

He edged along on hands and knees, working past the
pain, his rifle hung over his shoulder. Below him a
makeshift tent flapped wildly but he saw no sign of the
men. He crouched as low to the ground as possible and
shimmied down the slope. His stomach felt better for
moving but breathing was still difficult as his heart beat
loudly against his chest.

As he neared the camp, he saw that they had fled, leaving behind the tent and a dying fire. Around the fire, the
tracks of the men flattened the ground. In the mud he saw
the direction from which they had come and the direction
they had gone. Near the fire, they had stood in pairs, some
footsteps deeper than others, marking each man's weight.

When he didn't find Freda's footprints, he slipped the rifle from his shoulder and stuck the barrel between the tent flaps. She lay on her stomach, and for a moment, hope allowed him to think she slept, but when he knelt down to her, her skin felt cooler than it should have. He shook her arm several times, and then he saw the scarf around her neck. He lay down beside her, his body too heavy to hold upright, his breathing coming so hard he closed his eyes and tried to measure and slow the rasping gasps in and out.

He struggled to his feet and lifted Freda onto his shoulder, the feel of her limbs having become, in such a short time, so familiar. Though they had removed her splint, she felt much heavier than before. He balanced her on his shoulder and curled one arm around her waist, and as he carried her he was struck by the bitter, terrible irony. Her trust in him had been misplaced and his efforts to save her useless. If he had left Freda where he had found her, she might still be alive, saved by a passing German farmer or his family. She may have lived a long life, raised many children and grandchildren, but his own hubris and his belief that he need only cross the Elbe to save her had got her killed.

All night he carried her as he followed the Americans' tracks, unsure what he would do when he found them but knowing he had to do something. The pain of his wounds slowed him, so he wasn't sure if he'd ever catch up to them, but they were in no hurry, and just before daybreak he overtook them without being noticed. The orange glow of their fire guided him the last quarter mile, and about a hundred yards from their camp, he lowered Freda between two trees and watched the men warming their hands.

Several times, he lifted his rifle and aimed at the sergeant, who staggered from side to side in front of the camp. Tommy's finger trembled on the trigger and each time he squeezed a little harder, but in the end he couldn't. It was one thing to shoot someone in a German uniform, certain he'd be killed if he didn't, and quite another to shoot an American in revenge. He lay for a long time with the rocky ground pressed into his stomach, and at dawn, a jeep arrived from the west. The men climbed into it, and they sped off.

Tommy fed their fire and removed the bracelet Freda had on her wrist. Perhaps he could return it to her mother. When he looked at it more closely, he saw it was engraved: *Freda Wenders 1931*. He slipped the bracelet into his pocket and then used the butt of his rifle to dig a hole two feet deeper than the usual wartime grave so that no scrounging animal would uncover her, and he buried her, and when he finished, he sat by the fire until it died out. All that day and through the night, he lay by Freda's fresh grave. Never before had anyone's trust in him gone so disastrously wrong.

He thought of the day his mother died. Tommy was waiting outside her room when his father came out, and grey and tired as he was, he managed a faint smile when he saw his eight-year-old son standing expectantly in the hall. For weeks now, his mother had been too ill to leave the bed, so Tommy would visit in the afternoon for a short while, and on the days his mother felt stronger, she would read to him, but most of the time she lay with her eyes closed and he held her hand, waiting for her to squeeze it and acknowledge that she knew he was there. He had believed his mother would get better. He thought only old people died, that everyone else who fell sick eventually got better, just as he had in the past.

"Your mother can't see you right now." His father's words came out flat, and although he usually maintained eye contact whenever he spoke to Tommy, that day he looked off to one side until, as if he were suddenly aware of that fact, he placed a firm hand on Tommy's shoulder and fastened reddened eyes on his son. "Your mother has passed away."

Tommy bolted from his father and made for the door, but his father stopped him and guided Tommy to his own bedroom.

"Wait in here," he said. "She wouldn't want you to see her the way she is."

Tommy watched his father move with a lethargy so unlike his normal self, and later, when his father went out to the garage to ready the hearse, Tommy disobeyed him and crept into his mother's room. The sight of her stopped him. She lay on her back with her head turned a little to one side as if she were trying to look out the window. Her mouth gaped open in a way she would never have permitted in life.

"Mommy?" Tommy called. He stared at his mother's face and blond hair, both paled by the afternoon light covering the bed. His legs trembled and he said, "Mommy, wake up."

He heard his father call him, but Tommy ignored him until his father slowly but forcefully led him out.

Before his mother died, Tommy had perceived her as the permanent one in his life because his father was so often in town "attending to people's sad times," as his mother put it. She had seemed to him the stronger of his parents, an impression that may have had everything to do with the bear she shot when Tommy was six and his father was at work. All through the summer of 1928, bears bothered the town, picking through garbage and entering houses. One day Tommy heard one scratching on the outside wall.

Tommy's mother came into his room and whispered to him, "Stay under your bed no matter what happens. And cover your ears," she added before leaving him.

A few moments later, he heard two loud pops.

"You got it clean through the eye," his father said that evening, walking around the animal, surveying the corpse as if he planned to embalm it.

"Lucky shot, I guess."

"More than luck."

His mother had been a ballerina in Winnipeg before Tommy was born, but she had quit because of arthritic knees. She told him that someday he would be a famous dancer, performing on all the great stages of Europe and North America, and she poured all her energy into her son's dancing. She had started ballet lessons at the age of five, so not long after Tommy's fifth birthday he began his. Every day for two hours his mother called out a random combination of turns, jumps, and steps for him to perform.

She taught him numerous ballet moves—*cambre, détourné, relevé*. Tommy especially liked it when she rolled her r's, but he loved even more her excited praise whenever he successfully completed a new move.

By the time he turned seven, he was graceful and coordinated enough to imagine he could be the great dancer his mother hoped, and after she died he continued his lessons three times a week before school. His father drove him to town and waited while Tommy danced, and for eight more years he persevered, despite a gangly teenage body and a new discomfort with himself. Almost overnight he lost whatever finesse and edge he had, and gradually he became more fascinated with the natural world than with dance. Whenever he had a chance he explored the ponds behind the house, where frogs and snakes gathered at the edges of the water, and his father often found him there when it was time for his ballet class, until they agreed finally that his heart was no longer in the dance.

By morning, the cold brought him to his feet. The war had already swallowed the Americans. They had stepped away from war to murder and then stepped back in, and no one but Tommy knew the difference.

He went east, toward Berlin. He knew he risked being charged with desertion, but he needed to find Freda's mother; at least he could keep her from a futile search. If he joined up with the Allies he might never get to Berlin, but this way he was still a POW at large, free to go where he wanted. Tommy had no allegiance now, only his and Freda's, the allegiance of those wanting a normal life.

He passed people of all nationalities fleeing west. The crowds were thicker than before, and many sat along the roadside, too weak to walk, while others had already come so far they moved ever slower through the mud. One small boy of about eight pushed a bicycle with flat tires. Two girls, barely younger than Freda, sang softly as they passed. Together they formed an unpredictable parade marching away from the Russians, a ragged sea of countless children, many barely old enough to speak. A few rode on the backs of older children, and some carried a bag or two, but most walked empty-handed, owning only the torn clothes on their backs. Now and then, he saw German soldiers on foot. Almost everyone travelled west, but Tommy moved east toward the coming Russians, away from the Americans.

This time the crowds on the bridge were so thick he had to wait until three in the morning to cross against the flow. Even then, he continuously moved aside to make room for people going west. After he again crossed the Elbe, he waded up to his neck into the same frigid eddy and twisted back and forth to rinse his soiled clothes with none of the enthusiasm he had felt when Freda accompanied him.

When he passed the point where he'd met Freda, he continued east even after fleeing Germans warned him that he was less than twenty miles from Berlin. "*Berlin ist kaput*, only Russians there. Are you crazy? They will kill you." At first, he ignored the warnings as he had others, but that night he woke from a dream of his father for the first time since he'd died. "Get out, get out of there, before it's too late," his father implored, and he woke recognizing the foolishness of his plan.

Freda's mother could already be dead, and if not she most certainly had already joined the thousands of Germans fleeing Berlin by the hour. Berlin was the last place he was likely to find her, and as well-meaning as his plan might have seemed at the time, it would do no good to enter the city now.

Once again, he turned west, joining the ever-thickening flood of refugees. Along the way, he heard rumours that Germany had surrendered, but he would learn too late that the rumours were true.

The following day marked a week since Freda died. Exhausted from days of little rest or food, he lay down close to the edge of the trees and slept. He woke to four sets of Soviet eyes peering down at him. One of the soldiers motioned for Tommy to stand, and once on his feet, he pointed to his Canadian uniform. The Soviet soldiers only laughed.

"Friends?" Tommy said, and extended a hand to shake.

The man in charge ignored Tommy's proffered hand and pointed at his own Soviet uniform, laughing again. "*Komm.* War finished." He pulled Tommy in the direction of a waiting Soviet jeep. None of the Soviets raised their weapons, but neither did they welcome him as an ally. He hoped they were taking him to a Canadian company. The Soviet sergeant hustled Tommy into the back of the jeep, and two other soldiers sat on each side of him. Only then did Tommy realize that they had taken him prisoner. As the jeep sped off, he closed his eyes and fingered Freda's bracelet in his pants pocket.

His captors were taking him in the direction of Berlin,

and he worried that once there he would face a quick execution for desertion, if they waited that long and didn't leave him in the ditch somewhere along the way. He saw Soviet soldiers on the side of the road busily replacing German signs with Russian ones, and as they entered the city the road clogged with fleeing Germans. Many lay dead beside their meagre belongings, and some were separated from their limbs. Wild horses, freed of their burdens, roamed the city. Horses hit by fleeing vehicles or bomb concussions rotted on sidewalks, their bellies torn open by packs of rats or dogs.

Through this confused bustle, the jeep made slow progress, and when they turned into a deserted side street and stopped he was so certain they planned to shoot him right there that his legs began to shake. The surrounding buildings, many of them brick warehouses and foundries, were intact, while in the distance Tommy saw the gaping holes of Berlin's collapsed core. The sergeant ordered Tommy out of the jeep and pointed down the alley, saying, "*Davay*," and Tommy took his order to mean the opposite. For one jubilant moment, he believed they had released him, until he heard the Soviets fall in behind him.

As they neared the end of the long side street, the sergeant pointed Tommy toward two large warehouse doors. In the badly lit interior, Tommy could barely make out a group of people standing around a small fire in the far corner. The sergeant motioned Tommy to join the others, and then he saluted the Soviet junior lieutenant in charge, who saluted back.

The lieutenant pointed at Tommy's pack, then at a table. Tommy pushed the pack at him with a roughness he couldn't contain, and another soldier searched him twice while the lieutenant watched. Satisfied, the lieutenant carried Tommy's pack to an office at the back of the warehouse, leaving five Red Army soldiers to guard twenty prisoners. Most of the captive men were German, but Tommy recognized a few American and French amongst them. As far as he could see, he was the lone Canadian.

Each prisoner was permitted a small space on the dirt floor around the perimeter of the fire in which to sleep. Tommy stayed as close to the fire as he was allowed, but still his body shook, whether from fright or cold he couldn't have said. Guards permitted prisoners to move freely but they couldn't speak and they had to maintain an arm's length between themselves and any other prisoner. No one told them that, but if they got too close, a guard would hit them with his rifle and push them apart.

The next morning, a young German boy crawled in through a window, likely seeking refuge. Tommy could see that the boy had one leg and was only about seven years old. When he looked up and saw all the men in uniform, he gasped and frantically hopped back toward the window. The Soviet officer in charge called, "*Holt!*" but the young intruder kept going. One of the Red Army soldiers grabbed the boy and hauled him away from the window. When the boy bit his hand, the soldier punched him violently in the face a number of times, until the boy collapsed to the ground. The soldiers left him there for nearly half an hour, and Tommy kept looking over at his still form, thinking of Freda. The Soviet soldiers laughed amongst themselves and then the youngest, not much more than a boy himself, walked over to the body and put two bullets into his head. The child's leg twitched a little, and Tommy turned away, unable to watch as the young Soviet guard dragged the body out to the street.

From the moment of his capture, Tommy was certain that in time the Soviets would discover their mistake and release him. He stood when they told him to stand, ate the bread they brought him, slept when they indicated he should sleep, but on the third day of his captivity, two Red Army soldiers escorted him to the small office at the back of the warehouse. A single bulb dangled from the ceiling and its stingy yellow glow lit the room's only furniture—a small plain pine table and several wooden chairs. The soldiers directed him to one of the chairs and stood guard just behind him. They kept him waiting all morning. If he let his head drop or his shoulders slouch, one of the guards slapped him on the side of the head. Finally, a small man with wire-rimmed glasses entered and sat in front of him.

"Name and place of birth?"

"Thomas Edward Armstrong. Canada. Kenora, Canada."

"Cigarette?" The man lit one himself and offered another to Tommy.

Tommy shook his head because he thought that if he said yes, the man would slap him.

The man's face remained impassive as he returned the cigarette pack to his coat pocket and blew thin strips of smoke toward the high ceiling. Tommy watched him act like he had all the time in the world.

"Tommy, tell me, what is your crime?" He spoke in nearly perfect English.

"I haven't committed a crime. Why are you detaining me? The war is over."

"Who said the war is over?" The man slapped Tommy's face so hard he spit blood. "Spy," he said, and spit in Tommy's face. "We have places for spies. You'll be sorry that you ever came into our hands. I can shoot you right now, or I can shoot you tomorrow or the next day. German spies are everywhere. Many with uniforms just like yours."

With that, he left the room, and as soon as he left, the guards grabbed Tommy by the collar and dragged him back to the other prisoners.

All that day and the next, soldiers dragged prisoners to the office to be interrogated, until finally each of them signed a paper written entirely in Russian. When Tommy's turn came, the same bespectacled man looked up briefly at him and then slid the papers toward him. "Sign these, please."

Tommy knew there was no point in arguing. He scrawled his name on the papers and pushed them back across the table. The man picked them up without looking up at Tommy and placed them on a large pile. He retrieved the next papers and read the name on the top as a signal for Tommy to move on.

After two weeks, Soviet soldiers loaded the prisoners onto trucks and locked them inside; a heavy tarp hung over the back so that no one could see out. For one whole day and night, the trucks drove, stopping only to refuel, until they came to a stop in the dead of night. Guards tossed back the tarp and pointed rifles and flashlights inside.

"*Komm*," one of them said, and the Soviet soldiers took turns holding the prisoners at attention for the rest of the night, until the sun broke over the horizon in a pale orange spill, and the guards finally loaded Tommy and the others into railway cars. For two days the train didn't move, and then, early in the morning of the third day, the train crawled toward the rising sun, eventually picking up a lethargic rhythm. After little more than an hour, it stopped, and it occurred to Tommy that the Russians had no plan at all. The whole next day they stayed put, until near midnight, their car suddenly lurched forward, accelerating until the train travelled at a good clip.

Most of the time Tommy kept his face covered from the stench, but once a day, he took his turn at the air holes. He would never have guessed that fresh air could feel so good. Each man was allowed a half-hour before he was expected to move back and let others take his place, the sombre rotation all any of them had to look forward to aside from a short meal stop, which never changed—one small cup of potato soup with a few bits of grain in the bottom.

Each night, bug bites, the stagnant odours of too many unwashed others, and constant nudging made sleep difficult, but in the end, because of fatigue and the motion of the train, everyone succumbed for at least a few hours crammed tight against others and folded into awkward postures that made real rest impossible. Sometimes Tommy woke knowing that he had dreamed of Freda, but every detail escaped him, and he was left only with the sensation of her being next to him. She had become trapped in the recesses of his head somewhere, and his dreams acted as a flashlight, scanning the dark for her face.

At times he was gripped by a great fear that only death lay ahead. As each day passed he perfected the fantasy that the Soviets would realize their mistake, that people would act in a way that made sense, and he would be set free. But the longer he was on the train the more that seemed unlikely. Many of the prisoners appeared numb, even resigned to whatever lay ahead, and if he also looked numb on the outside, inside his self-berating had been replaced by boiling anger. Three nerve-jangling years of combat had taught him that anger was a great motivator.

Tommy seldom talked to anyone. When the British or especially the American prisoners attempted conversation with him, he muttered few words in reply and waited for the other man to give up. Some of the men must have thought the war had turned him mute. When he could, he moved through the car, squeezing between men already too close together in order that he never stayed long in one place. Some men made room for him but others didn't, and sometimes the restless swaying of the group moved him smoothly along the length of the car like a marble between fingers.

At one end of the car, three German boys huddled together talking. They never left their end of the car to take a turn at the air hole and slept on the floor in each other's arms, talking long past any others even when they were asked to pipe down.

On the fourth night, when they still talked and laughed

after everyone else had fallen silent, a bulky man near them squeezed closer and yelled at the boys in a language Tommy didn't recognize. It was too dark to see much, but Tommy heard nervous laughter, followed by a struggle and then a chilling scream.

The next day until meal time, the boy's body remained where he died. The other two boys shrank away from him. When the train finally stopped, two Red Army soldiers took the body away. Those who could see out reported that the train had stopped in a stubbled field. It stayed there for another night and day.

One English-speaking German prisoner drew Tommy's attention because he bore a remarkable resemblance to his own father, right down to a similar rumpled linen suit and glasses. Tommy struck up a conversation with him so he could look at his face for a while, and the man told Tommy about the night the Soviets marched into Berlin. "I hid in a basement while Red Army soldiers dragged women from houses and raped them. What could I do? The soldiers broke down doors and took away the women, shooting men or dragging them off to be shot later. They raped in pairs, one standing guard while the other pushed the woman to the floor. I watched from the basement window as women were dragged into the street, and I did nothing. I thought only of saving my life.

"Before the war, I was a doctor. That night I became just another animal huddling to stay alive. I thought all night of my wife and daughter deep on the other side of Berlin. I thought of them being dragged out into the street too and I wept that night as never before. I planned at daylight to go for them, but I never got a chance. Those Soviet bastards dug me out from the basement, and now I can't escape the screams."

Only weeks ago he and Tommy might have killed each other, and now they spoke with words weighed down by all they'd seen. *We're all fleeing such guilt,* Tommy thought, and he shook the man's hand. The ebb and flow of bodies parted them as mysteriously as it had brought them together.

SEVEN

SPRING ARRIVED LATE IN 1963, and the ice on Edna Bay remained dark and thick even into the last week of April, when Peter keeled over without a sound as he sharpened the large blade of his sawmill.

When he didn't come in for lunch, Alice went to see what kept him and found him lying flat on his back. She got down on her knees next to him and felt for a pulse. When she found none, she pressed her ear to his chest as she'd seen Tailgate do and lay that way for a long time, her head resting on Peter's hard ribs, until she saw that Adam and Judith had come from the house and stood quietly above her.

Judith, who was thirteen and already taller than her mother, touched her mother's neck until Alice stood up. Against hope, mother and daughter scanned Peter's body for the slightest sign of life, and then Alice buried her face in Judith's shoulder.

"Go phone for an ambulance," she said after a minute.

Adam ran to call, but Judith remained behind. She wanted to believe her father was only playing one of his tricks. She took Peter's arm and shook it like a rag doll.

"No," Alice said. "Judith, don't, he's gone."

Judith kicked Peter in the ribs with all her might. When his heavy body shuddered and a soft moan escaped him, she ran screaming to the house.

After the ambulance attendant had loaded Peter onto the stretcher and covered him with a sheet, Alice stood at the front door, and she saw once again all the rough joins Peter had attempted when making the steps. Everywhere she looked she saw his mistakes, and with that realization came the understanding he'd never correct them.

"Are you sad?" Cathleen asked Judith after the funeral.

Judith acted as if she had not heard. Of course she was sad, but she knew from experience that Cathleen wasn't likely to offer comfort. When they were six, she had made Judith stick a nail in an electrical outlet, and had convulsed in giggles when Judith nearly electrocuted herself. At nine, she twirled Judith's kitten by the tail and would have released it in mid-air if Judith hadn't tackled her first. Every time Cathleen visited, she invented some fresh way to torment her cousin.

Shirley was no help. When Judith ran protesting to her aunt and her mother on one of Cathleen's visits, Shirley only shook her head and laughed. "Shit runs downhill," she said. "I get mad at her, she gets mad at you. She's an angry kid, there's no doubt about it, but you've got to be tough right back."

So Judith said nothing, just turned away and picked at a scab on her finger.

"Do you miss him?" Cathleen asked.

"Of course."

"You shouldn't, you know. He's not your real dad." Cathleen said this with smug, restrained glee, well aware this would be news to Judith.

"You take that back," Judith said. She lunged at Cathleen but only succeeded in slapping the air in front of her.

"We have the same father."

"My dad is your dad?"

"No, stupid. Rudy's our father."

"That's not true! My dad's dead, and if you don't take that back I'll smash your face in."

"It should make you feel better to know your dad's still alive. I heard Mom tell one of her *men*. She said, 'That son of a bitch knocked us both up and now look at us with nothing to show for it but two red-headed kids.'" Cathleen flashed an unfriendly smile.

Judith felt her stomach go cold. She said, "Dad had red hair and he's my real father."

"Your mother married him because he had red hair, that's what my mom said."

Judith lunged again but only caught a piece of her blouse as her cousin slipped out the door, leaving Judith to sit on her bed and bang her heels against the floor. Cathleen could be right—she didn't look like Peter, but she wanted him to be her father, not Rudy, a man she had only heard Shirley refer to alongside *bastard*, *prick*, and *shithead*. Her mother never mentioned him at all, but still her stomach tightened with the logic of the revelation until she could hardly breathe. She picked at the ribs of her pink chenille bedspread and tried to hear the voices in the other room, but all that passed through the door was a dull murmur and the clinking of dishes.

Before Peter died, Alice had taken pleasure in visiting each of the children's rooms as they slept. Judith slept restlessly on her stomach with her neck twisted at odd angles, and sometimes the only part of her covered was her head, the rest of her kept warm by flannel pyjamas.

Even at eleven, Adam often took a toy to bed—his favourite was a small wooden locomotive that had been Peter's—but unlike his sister, he didn't move much in his sleep. His little mouth fluttered with each breath, his lips pursed as if he were on the verge of saying something. He still wore faded Roy Rogers and Trigger pyjamas with the legs cut into shorts. They matched his Roy Rogers bedspread and a Roy Rogers banner that he had pestered Peter to buy.

After Peter died Alice didn't go to their rooms as often. She couldn't stand how much Adam looked like his father when he slept, and Judith had started to close her door, first only at night before she went to sleep, but more all the time, whether she was in there or not.

"I want some privacy," she said, her voice still small despite the loaded words. "You can still come in, just knock first."

Alice rarely knocked except at meal time because each day meant a new struggle. She remembered how Shirley had been as a teenager, staying out late, running away from home. Alice had thought she and Judith would always be close, but sometimes Judith acted as if she hated her, just as Shirley had hated their father.

Behind her door, Judith usually lay in bed with her legs tangled in the matted blankets and listened to her mother make noises in the kitchen. She resented how neatly her mother kept house since Peter died, as if she cared more now that he was gone, so she left her room as messy as her mother let her get away with. Peter had been messy, and Judith missed how he had resisted her mother.

Leave me alone, she wanted to scream at anyone who came near. With her door closed, she listened to the murmur of her mother's voice filling that outer space. Judith knew that some people talked to the dead and told them what happened each day, and she wished she could talk to Peter that way, but each time she tried to, she felt silly and stopped. She wanted Peter to remain her father. She didn't want some stranger for a father. How could her mother not have told her about Rudy, if what Cathleen said was true?

Sometimes she went out and sat with her mother, trying to take up her father's part of the conversation, but more and more she wanted to stay in her room. Her mother and Adam annoyed her in ways she'd never noticed before—the way they crunched their food when they ate, or said "What?" every time she looked at them.

Lately, when her mother knocked on the door and said, "Judith, time to help with the dishes," Judith would yell back, "Why?" If she got no response, she'd stay where she was.

Every night she listened to WLS from Chicago, which she tuned in through some trick of the atmosphere, but nothing she heard on the radio could change the sameness of each day. She was trapped in a grey life, as if any previous momentum had been paused permanently by Peter's death, while her mother continued to knit a long burgundy scarf in preparation for winter or read another book, as though nothing important had changed.

During the week, Alice got off work in time to meet the school bus at the highway, and as soon as they were inside the door, she made Judith and Adam do their homework before supper. For Judith, who was now in grade nine, homework took hours, and after homework there was supper and then chores—Adam's outside, Judith's in the house. She couldn't count how many loads of laundry she'd had to do since Peter died. Before that her mother had done most of the chores. And then there was school: Judith didn't have a single good thing to say about school. She hated nearly everyone, including the teachers who kept saying she wasn't working to potential. What potential?

On Sunday nights, they watched *Ed Sullivan* and *Bonanza*, Peter's two favourite shows. Judith sat on the far end of the couch from her mother, and Adam curled up in the chair that Peter had always occupied, the one with the wide red cushions and maple arms, as if he had inherited it.

The TV shows were drab in black and white, but that didn't prevent Judith from envying the people who each week waited behind Ed Sullivan's curtain for their lives to change, just like that, through the eye of the camera, so that they were suddenly famous to a world that hadn't previously given them a thought.

Judith soon began to forget what Peter looked like, and she kept checking photographs of him to remind herself.

Sometimes she'd be certain that she had his face right in her mind and then she'd look at the wedding picture on the TV and see that she had his nose wrong, or the way his eyebrows met, or even the shape of his mouth. She wondered if in ten years his face would be completely altered in her memory so that one day she'd look at a photo and not recognize him at all.

Sometimes she took a photo to the bathroom and compared his face to hers. The eyes were the same grey, and her hair just as red as always, but other features had changed, and if they had ever resembled his, they didn't now. Her neck was longer and thinner, her face had filled out, and her jawline was less defined. She wondered if she had put on weight and checked her stomach, but it was still flat. Worst of all, her nose kept getting longer. She pushed on the end of it as if she could stop it from growing and wondered how others saw her. If she couldn't recall Peter's face from one day to the next, maybe no one ever remembered anyone exactly as they were.

On school days, Alice made breakfast, and Judith waited until her mother had called her three or four times before she got out of bed. Then she and Adam walked a quarter mile to the bus stop, and once a car full of high-school boys slowed down beside them. A boy in the back seat stuck his head out. "You want a ride?"

"No."

"Fuck you," he said.

"Fuck *off*," Judith yelled back, and the boys all laughed and waved and one of them yelled something she couldn't hear. Judith saw her brother's shocked look, a look that said, *I'm gonna tell.* "Boys are creeps. Don't smile, don't laugh. And don't say anything to Mom either. They think they're smart, but they don't know shit. A car doesn't mean shit to me and if you're ever like that, I won't talk to you. I'll pretend I don't even know you."

The bus that day overflowed with noisy elementary kids from Adam's school, and Judith sat in the middle, keeping a whole seat to herself and staying away from the few high-school boys who crowded the back and hollered insults at everyone. She was in high school herself now, but she was only in her first year at Lakewood, which made her a baby in the eyes of the boys at the back, as if she cared.

She piled her books and coat on the seat beside her and watched out the window as the bus snaked through granite and slate rock cuts as high as five-story buildings. She'd seen the explosion that made the cuts only once, when the construction company blasted near their place at Burnt Lake. The blast was going to be close to their home, so they had got into a Department of Highways truck and been taken to the safety of a nearby hill, where she had watched the earth rise up in a grey cloud before she heard the explosion. When the cloud settled, a heap of misshapen boulders formed a massive mound like that over an enormous grave. Peter grinned when he saw the explosion as if he'd never seen anything like it in his whole life.

"Look at that," he said to Judith. "Isn't that something?"

After school, when Judith should have been working on her homework, she listened to the radio and wrote out a list of promises to herself. *I will not stay here. I will be somebody. I will not be boring like my mother.*

A few days later, Judith skipped her last class and went to the Woolworths store. She put a pair of red panties in her front pocket and just walked out. Half a block from the store, she still shook with fear and excitement as she ducked down the alley behind Main Street. The trembling stopped, but when she took the panties out to look at them she couldn't like them the way she had in the store. There they had seemed daring and beautiful. Now that she had them, they were cheap and ugly. She felt sick just looking at them, and when she was sure no one could see her, she dropped them in a garbage can as she walked by and ran as quickly as possible to the bus stop. But right away she wished she had them again, and she felt a small crack of happiness enter her life for the first time since Peter had died.

EIGHT

ON THE EIGHTH NIGHT, the train pulled onto a side rail, sounded one hollow whistle, and creaked to a stop. When someone asked a soldier where they were, he barked, "Wait. You will see."

In the morning, the soldiers opened the doors of all the cars and shepherded the prisoners out. Tommy shielded his eyes against the bright angle of the early sun, but when his eyes adjusted, he saw slightly rolling fields with little sign of life, except to the northwest, where several thick stands of oak marked the presence of farms. Next to the track the dry grass had withered to a powdery brown, but ran to emerald along the west bank of the broad river he later learned was the Dnieper, which flowed into the Black Sea.

The empty train pulled away, leaving behind a dozen shabbily dressed soldiers, most with gaping holes in their pants or coats, and their charges—some terrified, some sick, some nearly numb from the journey. Tommy stifled thoughts of impending death and forced one foot to follow the other as the prisoners were marched north for an hour.

At last they halted before the gates of a large enclosure, and they were made to stand in the sweltering heat of late June, and by afternoon Tommy fought to keep from passing out. The guards allowed each prisoner only two quick mouthfuls of stale water to ease their parched throats, and next to Tommy a French prisoner shook constantly and spit on the ground whenever the guard turned away. One American prisoner stood completely at attention, and Tommy wondered how the man found strength to hold the pose for so many hours. When one of the older prisoners collapsed in the bright sun, he was forced at gunpoint back to his feet.

No one spoke—they intuited that to do so could mean death for everyone. Some tired from the strain and leaned against others until a surreptitious finger in the ribs straightened them. In the late afternoon, more prosperous looking guards replaced the shabby ones and herded the prisoners through the gates and into the centre of the enclosure. The prisoners lined up twenty abreast in rows flanking a squat, windowless building that every so often emitted foul bursts of steam. These soldiers, too, left the prisoners to stand the rest of the day in the heat without offering any food, and by nightfall, when a senior sergeant finally gave the order to sleep, Tommy dropped into a space near the building and fell immediately asleep.

In the days ahead, Tommy discovered that he was being held outside Dnepropetrovsk, in Ukraine, and that from here all prisoners were sent to Siberia or points in between, their destination depending on the designs of someone higher up. At first he still hoped that officials would notice their mistake and send him home, but he soon realized that none of them would be going home and now hoped he would at least be sent to a camp near Moscow. He'd heard that no one survived Siberia.

Guards shouting "*Khleb!*" passed between the sleeping prisoners at daybreak. Those who did not immediately wake were kicked in the ribs. Tommy rose quickly and stood favouring his left leg, numbed from sleeping on that side. A guard handed him a thick slice of stale black bread—*khleb*—and a cup of thin porridge. The guards hurried the prisoners through their breakfast with continued prompts of "*Est*"—eat—not necessary for Tommy because he wolfed his ration down with a dry mouth. Even before everyone had finished eating, the guards shuffled the group into the open and forced them to strip. Young men with closely shaven heads probed each naked prisoner as they searched for contraband. Rough hands parted Tommy's buttocks and a stubby finger added to his indignity.

After the search, the prisoners passed before a new set of inspectors, these ones female, and Tommy covered his crotch with his hands. As each moment brought new terrors and humiliations, he longed for the numbing days on the train when nothing had happened. The line inched forward. As each man ahead of Tommy approached the row of women, he had his name checked against a long list, and then each was shaved and passed before a group of men who brandished cigars and wore fur coats. Most of them were stout and eschewed the usual communist khaki for a more western style of dress. They moved with the swagger of power, and disdained the weaker prisoners by kicking or spitting at them. The prisoners selected by these camp bosses went into one line, while those not selected were shunted into another. If Tommy was selected, would he go to Siberia? If he wasn't, would he go to a nearby prison or be shot? He trembled as he watched. Some prisoners brashly displayed themselves before the bosses while others shyly shielded themselves. When it was Tommy's turn he hesitated, and then stood apart from the other prisoners feeling exposed and vulnerable. He knew from watching the prisoners ahead of him that he mustn't look the bosses in the eye as they slapped his backside or pushed him along for the next boss to examine, and his heart raced, unsure which line would offer the worst fate.

He surveyed those in the line of rejects he was shoved toward, and judged that his slight build and new skinniness had counted against him. Now he worried that he and the other weak ones would be killed, but for two days they were kept in a cell and fed *khleb*, and on the morning of the third day, guards marshalled the prisoners aboard more boxcars. Tommy heard a guard mention Moscow, and this resurrected his hope that he would finally be sent home. But later, when another prisoner dared to ask, he learned his true destination—a gulag northeast of Moscow.

As before, prisoners filled each boxcar until they pressed up against one another with barely room to breathe. Tommy's car had the same ventilation hole in the middle he'd seen before, but in this car, a barbed-wire barrier divided Tommy's half from the other. Occasionally, prisoners spoke through the barbed wire, but mostly they stared at each other as if the vibrations of the train had left them mute. They travelled so long—a week, Tommy would learn later—that the jostling, claustrophobic conditions began to seem not the result of a journey but like some hellish destination in itself, so that when the slow train finally arrived at the camp, Tommy was again disoriented when he found himself free to move and breathe fresh air.

The terrain surrounding the camp was similar to the rugged conifer forests that he'd wandered as a boy in Kenora, but he had no knowledge of what lay between him and freedom. Another prisoner told Tommy that this was the taiga forest somewhere north of the Volga River, and occasionally he caught the scent of pine needles brought by a light gust of wind, much like Laclu in summer, but the scent never lasted and was quickly replaced by the stink of stagnant water and excrement.

In the late afternoon the commandant, a man who looked barely thirty, stood before the men and welcomed them in German and then in English, saying this was where they would live and work for the rest of their lives. The commandant spoke earnestly and economically, as if he did not want to waste one word. He paced back and forth, speaking firmly and proudly, and then he stood and watched as the prisoners were divided and led to their barracks.

Tommy thought the camp appeared temporary, the buildings hastily constructed of inexpensive materials, and initially he worried that such sloppy construction meant the Soviets had no plans to keep the prisoners alive for long, but he soon learned that this location had been in operation for decades. The spruce-slabbed fence that secured the gulag leaned precariously inward, and what Tommy had attributed to poor construction, he learned was a design meant to prevent escape. Twenty feet outside this first fence, a second barbed-wire one marked the perimeter of the camp.

The spruce slabs of the barracks walls had been nailed together carelessly, leaving large gaps that the wind blew through, and the roof of Tommy's barracks leaked in numerous places, though it was dry over his bed.

Broken windows had been stuffed with scraps of paper and bits of cloth, and at the far end of the large room a single cast-iron stove provided what little heat there was, but guards ordered the prisoners to let it burn out, even on the coldest nights. Timber and slab bunks were arranged in four rows, two rows down each side of a single aisle, so that half the prisoners had to climb over others to reach their beds. Only a few fortunate men got bunks with straw for a mattress, but this was a mixed blessing, as the straw was inevitably infested with fleas. The rest, Tommy included, lay on the abandoned clothing of the dead and used an arm or a bunched rag as a pillow, and everyone kept warm as best they could with tattered cloth blankets and the odd scavenged coat or jacket.

Each day, Tommy woke at dawn, careful to rise before being brutally rousted. After a breakfast of bread, gruel, and water, he was marched to the clearing site, where he discovered that his years of chopping kindling and firewood for his father had provided him with a precious skill that allowed him to work alone with an axe limbing trees, while those with saws felled trees and worked in pairs. In the camps a partner was a liability, and worse than the threat of slowing one down or drawing the attention of guards, a partner could be a spy waiting to report a single disparaging word about Comrade Stalin or the motherland. Working alone, Tommy knew, gave him the best chance of surviving his "life sentence"—the mandatory ten years no one expected him to survive.

He hadn't paid much attention to the forests around him when he was a boy, but now he noticed how a spruce differed from a pine, and pine from fir. He learned to distinguish between their needles, paid attention to the thickness and texture of the bark, and knew how readily each gave up its branches. He learned what lived in the trees as well, and he carried various scents of the forest to bed with him as sap darkened his hands between washings. At night he smelled his fingers to counter the foul odours around him, some of them coming from his own body.

At the end of the workday, Tommy and the others were marched back to camp for another meal of bread and gruel. Those who had been in the camp longest ate slowly, savouring each mouthful, and Tommy learned to eat the same way, even while others watched his plate for anything he might leave behind. He went to bed hungry and woke hungry and all day long his thoughts frequently returned to food, but with the hunger came a determination to survive, even as others around him collapsed. Every man got the same ration, barely enough for a smaller, slighter man like Tommy, and he observed how quickly some of the larger men were reduced to skin and bone. One of his bunkmates had been an accountant in Germany during the war. He was a large man whose fingers bled constantly from the work, and each night for two weeks he coughed so loudly he kept Tommy awake, until one morning Tommy woke fresh, having not been woken during the night. He saw that the German's bunk was empty—the man had vanished like all the others who could no longer labour.

Tommy's supervisor, Igor, sometimes smiled encouragingly at him, but with the other prisoners he wasn't so kind. Igor spoke a broken, harsh English. "Work! Work!" he shouted, and when prisoners couldn't or wouldn't work, he slapped them so hard they fell to the ground. He was particularly hard on Fritz, a German. Tommy heard him boast of a friend who had escaped the previous year and who had got word to him that he'd arrived safely home in Germany. Tommy knew it had to be a lie, but for a few weeks Fritz insisted that he would escape as well, to Germany and the bright young son he had left behind. One day, after Igor had warned him to keep silent and threatened him with a fist, Fritz dropped his axe and refused to work. Igor calmly picked up the axe and chopped into the man's thigh as easily as if he were sinking the axe into the trunk of a tree. He left the prisoner screaming on the ground until a guard mercifully shot him.

Three times a week after their evening meal, the prisoners assembled in the large hall to listen to stern speeches in Russian meant to motivate them. "You are soft. Even children work harder. Tomorrow's quota will be raised and it is your duty to Comrade Stalin and the motherland to work even harder. Quota is all. You are nothing but the quota you meet. Anyone not reaching quota will starve."

At the end of each day, a man named Molotov used a notched stick to measure the number of logs Tommy's group had cut and piled to make sure they had met or exceeded their quota. "Okay," he would say with a nod before walking on to the next group. Meeting quota meant they got to eat that night. In a corner of Tommy's bunk, someone had carved in English, "Today quota. Tomorrow death."

Each week the quota was raised, until Tommy worried that soon it would be impossible for his group to meet the quota, causing Igor to turn on them as well. Often he found the walk to the cut zone more gruelling than the work, and he had to be careful to not stumble or slow his steps, because those who staggered out of line were shot before they got far. Some intentionally stepped out of line, Tommy knew, choosing death over wasting away. One old man had stopped to sit on a stump and a guard shot him from a hundred yards. Guards were rewarded with privileges when they killed the weak, and there were plenty of others to take the dead man's place.

Rise, work, sleep, rise. As long as he worked, Tommy lived. Days and soon months passed. He remained alone, forming no real friendships, because all of this was temporary, it had to be, and to become attached was to make the death and disappearances that much more difficult. Language was another barrier. Few prisoners spoke English, and Tommy made do with gestures and the few Russian words he picked up. Occasionally someone translated. Later, when his Russian improved, he learned that friends were the easiest to betray, and he wasn't about to be betrayed or to betray anyone.

When Tommy had first arrived at the camp, the July heat had made the chopping difficult, and in the afternoons the only relief from the sun was the few minutes between limbing when he was allowed to stand in the shade. Then the countryside had consisted of rolling hills, more like the steppes of Ukraine, easy going, but over the past year they had moved steadily north, first through swamp and then over rocky hillsides that yielded fewer trees, so that the trek to and from the work site now took longer and meant fewer hours of sleep.

Tommy had to work ankle deep in cold swamps limbing harder woods like alder and birch, and on the rugged hillsides spruce and pine clung tenaciously to stingy bits of earth, and he had to be careful that his axe did not catch a rock. A dull axe was as good as a death sentence, and forfeited sleep provided the only chance to sharpen one.

The work changed with the seasons. In summer his axe cut easily through the wood, even through the dense tamaracks they occasionally encountered, and in winter, the cold caused branches to snap off easily, but knee-deep snow made meeting quota more difficult. Every two hours he was allowed to warm himself for five minutes at a fire, but no longer. Guards boiled pine and cedar needles for vitamin C, one cupful for each prisoner every two days.

From May through September the bugs were so bad that Tommy swung his axe gratefully, because it kept them away. Stopping to wipe his brow invited dozens of bites, and mosquitoes were worse than the flies and ticks.

Fortunately, his summers in Kenora had made him more immune to their bites, unlike some unfortunates, who itched and shivered all night.

July and August also brought thunderstorms. The rains were heavier than in Canada, lasting days at a time, but Tommy appreciated them for how they cleaned him as he worked. During winter, the sweat stayed inside his clothes between visits to the bathhouse, and in summer he smelled fresh by comparison.

Tommy's greatest pleasure came with the birds. In spring and fall flocks of geese like those on Laclu flew just above the trees. Men stopped to catch a glimpse of that distinctive V, dreaming of the fine meal one bird would make. One day one of the guards brought down a bird and cooked it for lunch, and the men tore greedily into the meat, even eating some of the bones. Days later the guard disappeared.

"*Davay*"—Move it—the guards commanded each time they marched someone off for interrogation. It was the last word prisoners heard at night and the first word spoken in the morning. *Davay* called them away from warming fires and woke them at night, carrying them from one nightmare into another. It was the word for death, for the end of the world, for the last breath of someone wronged, for the devil, for terror, for despair, for darkness.

On his weaker days, Tommy worried he would be the next to be marched away. If he didn't work hard enough, or if he grew stronger, he could be transferred to Siberia. Sometimes he had nightmares about that. As long as he remained close to Moscow, freedom seemed possible, and he knew only one prisoner in his barracks who had been to Siberia and survived. He was a mathematician named Vladislav, and he survived his sentence because he could do sums quickly in his head, and he was put in charge of tabulating production quotas.

Vladislav spoke fluent English. He told Tommy that he had lost all his family in the camps, including both his sons.

"Not much older than you," he said. "If you want to survive, you have to make yourself useful. That's what I did. Most of the guards are not good with numbers, so they need someone to keep accounts."

He told Tommy that he saw hundreds of POWs in Siberia and that most of them died from starvation or cold. Tommy wondered how many of the men the camp bosses had selected that day near Dnepropetrovsk had survived. Not many, he was certain.

One night Vladislav crawled into Tommy's bunk and lay beside him, his hand cupping Tommy's ear, and whispered, "Comrade Stalin fears the old and their memories, so he kills them. The young think his hand is gentle, so they spy for him. They listen to Comrade Stalin as if the rumours were true that he doesn't shit. If you get out you must tell others what you see here, so that someday the outside world will know. If no one tells, this never happened. Much under Comrade Stalin has *never happened.*

"Don't forget," he said to Tommy, and then he slipped back to his own bed.

"*Davay,*" the man hissed and ordered Tommy to follow him to the cold, dark isolation cell although, as was common,

Tommy had committed no obvious offense. Sometimes the duty guard shouted out at Tommy in Russian. He didn't understand much of what the guard said but he did know he mustn't answer back. The first time the guard opened the thin slot on his door and peered in, Tommy was lying on the metal cot, so the guard entered the cell and forced him to lie on his stomach. He beat Tommy on his back and legs with a baton and then showed him that he must sit on the edge of the bed. When the man looked in on his next round, Tommy was sitting upright, but when he fell asleep and curled on the mattress, he woke screaming to yet more blows.

They left him for several days without food, and each time Tommy heard footsteps in the hall, his insides churned. He had heard that some prisoners had been hung upside down for days until their brains swelled with blood, and others were made to lie naked in the snow until their skin blackened with frostbite.

The days in solitary confinement dragged by in the dreamlike blur between consciousness and sleep, with pain sometimes the only clue as to which was which. He longed to be limbing trees, for at least work made the day pass more quickly. His thoughts returned often to Freda and all she had endured. He thought of her mother and hoped that if she were still alive she had somehow got word and was not still hoping Freda would come home.

As he had come to trust that Freda guided them away from danger and toward the Elbe, he also had enjoyed the brotherly intimacy. Often he replayed the details of those days in an attempt to keep images of her alive as long as possible, but with each passing day the images faded, not only hers, but others as well—small particulars of the good he had known, replaced with horrors he experienced in the camp: beatings, murder, torture, and every day new degradation.

Even the last physical ties to Freda and his father were gone—Freda's bracelet, his father's letters. All that remained of these items was what he remembered of them: the words engraved on the back of the bracelet, *Freda Wenders 1931*, and the way his father always closed his letters, *My thoughts and prayers are with you.*

On the fourth day, the guard brought a bowl of watery soup with two dark lumps of meat in it. When Tommy had eaten, three guards took him down a long corridor to a small room. An officer met him and shook his hand. Like so many others Tommy had seen, he was tall, balding, and stern. Sometimes it seemed the same man followed him from one interrogation to another.

"Sit," he said, and went to his side of the desk. "Why did you work with the Germans during the war?"

"I didn't. I'm Canadian."

"You were found near Berlin. How could a Canadian soldier be near Berlin? Canadians and British armies didn't cross the Elbe."

"I was captured by the Germans."

"But you were not in a POW camp. All here are spies. You are a spy. Did you not sign this?" He slid a paper toward Tommy.

"I signed, but it doesn't make me a spy. I don't read Russian."

"It says here that you are a spy, and you have signed it. This camp is only for spies, therefore you must be a spy. Spies are worthy of nothing, not even labour, but Comrade Stalin is kind enough to allow you that. I wouldn't. You will work, starve, and then you will die. Nothing you have learned matters to us, only your labour. Spies work until they die, that is how things are here in the Soviet Union."

He went to the door and opened it. Tommy's escorts came in without being summoned.

"We will not meet again," the man said.

"*Davay!*" a guard shouted, and Tommy quickly stood at attention. The sergeant tapped Tommy on the back of the head with a thin, knotted stick and marched him back to his barracks.

The next two years were a bleak and featureless waste. Each day was the same nightmare of labour, inescapable hunger, swarming lice, and intolerable cold. He willfully practiced the obliteration of memory, and worked hard to avoid thinking. Whenever possible, he stared into the sun, or at flickering flames, putting whatever he could between himself and the memories he strove to avoid, but some of what he had seen could not be forgotten, and the images he retained were so awful that his body convulsed when they surfaced, and bile rose in his throat before he could stop the recollections—the blackened face and hands of one severely frost-bitten prisoner, skin split and oozing pus; the head of another man severed with a shovel. He trusted no one to watch his back, and so even as he tried to ignore all that went on around him, he had to also watch carefully. Prisoners plotted against and betrayed one another for little more than an extra mouthful of bread, and many of the men in his barracks were so near starvation they were reduced to pale sheets of skin over thin bones. Their screams of agony frequently broke what little sleep he got, and each morning he inspected his hands and feet for sores and bites, horrified by how thin they had become. Like the others, he was wasting away, albeit more slowly. Almost daily he considered stepping out of line on the walk to or from work, like so many others had, and only thoughts of Freda and his father prevented him. He owed it to them to go on as long as his body lasted.

As his second year rolled into his third, Comrade Stalin's purges intensified, and the number of prisoners flowing into camp increased substantially. When the daily death tolls weren't enough to make room for new prisoners, the guards killed with less provocation.

By the late fall of 1947, Tommy had survived all but a few of the prisoners who had arrived with him two years earlier. His experience, coupled with what Vladislav had taught him before he died, provided him an opportunity to switch jobs, so instead of the long and punishing trek out into the cut zone, he worked in the camp office keeping accounts and recording daily quota numbers in ledgers.

If Tommy's working conditions had improved, his existence was no more secure than it had ever been, and in early May 1948, three guards appeared in the middle of the night and woke Tommy and his bunk neighbour, Terry, a young soldier from New York City. Terry had been barely sixteen when he joined the army, and he coped by writing letters to his mother in his mind, which he recited to Tommy, sometimes breaking down when he forgot a part or got something wrong. The two prisoners covered the fifty feet to the doorway as slowly as they could, moving between the narrow rows of beds. Tommy passed within touching distance of nearly thirty beds, and as shadowed figures shifted in their bunks, Tommy knew those who woke said a silent prayer of thanks that it wasn't their turn, just as he had done on many similar occasions. He was grateful to be seen, for as long as one person saw him being led out, he hadn't just disappeared. The guards led them to a black van. Yakir, the commander, sat up front.

Near daylight, Yakir told the driver to stop the van, and the prisoners were ordered out. Yakir spat on the ground in front of Tommy and hit Terry, sending him to his knees in the fetid mud. When Terry slumped, moaning, Yakir laughed and commanded Tommy to lift him to his feet.

"*Davay,*" he said, and his men escorted the prisoners to the edge of a small ravine.

Yakir told them to look down and stay still. Tommy thought, *This is it.* His whole body turned numb and when he closed his eyes and tried to count to ten, he couldn't recall a single number. He opened his eyes and saw how much Terry shook and that tears flowed down both his cheeks. Tommy inched his hand toward Terry until his little finger brushed the other man's. Now Tommy's own legs shook and tears filled his eyes as well.

Behind them Yakir laughed. "Look they're holding hands," he said in Russian, and then ordered, "*Davay, comrades, davay,"* and the guards forced Tommy and Terry to turn around and march back to the van, laughing at the two of them as they stumbled through the mud.

Yakir and his guards repeated this routine for five nights. Tommy was familiar with these tortures. Sometimes Yakir shot the prisoner on the first night; other times he waited two full weeks or more. The drives were usually for the enjoyment and morale of the guards, but in Tommy's case, they were more personal.

"I will dance on your bones," Yakir promised him.

On the sixth morning, Tommy woke with a clear head. Usually, he crawled out of bed in the morning and looked at those around him—many slowly dying, their bodies resisting as long as possible, holding on to the hope that one morning they'd wake and the gates would open—and wondered if this day would be his last, but that morning he woke from his first dreamless night since the war. A thin sliver of sunlight slipped through the muddied windows and landed on the bed near him, and he arched his back and sprang out of bed. He looked down at the heap of soiled blankets where he had just lain, and his impression remained there; he could see thin valleys that marked where his legs had been, and yet they felt strong beneath him. He stood in the doorway, and though the cold morning air riffled through his thin clothes, he felt warm. Somehow he knew his luck had changed.

Yakir and his men came again for Tommy that night, but this time he went alone, for Terry had died during the day. He had fallen on the trek to work and a guard had shot him. The van did not stop at the ravine this time but kept driving. Tommy's heartbeat doubled, and he wondered if his optimism earlier in the day had been unfounded. The longer they drove, the more certain he became that he had reached the end. Tonight they would kill him. His breathing grew shallow and twice he checked the back door to see if he could jimmy it open, for leaping from the moving van had to be better than whatever fate Yakir had planned for him, but he couldn't get the latch to move.

After a few hours of driving, he knew they were taking him to his grave. He stayed awake through sheer raw nerves, and through the metal screen, Tommy watched the back of Yakir's head as he puffed on a cigarette. Whenever he turned to look at Tommy through the wire mesh, he didn't smile, or even sneer as he often did, and Tommy was careful to avert his eyes.

A short while later, Tommy heard Yakir give a sharp yell. He looked up in time to see that the van had veered toward the ditch, and he reached up to balance himself but tumbled inside the van like a pebble in a can. His head banged against the metal screen, and what usually kept him from escaping saved his life.

The van rolled into a ravine, where a swollen river spilled over its banks. Tommy was the only one not thrown from the van. When it came to a stop the back door had buckled open and he crawled out. The two guards were gone, sucked into the river, Tommy guessed, and he found Yakir pinned beneath the overturned van but still alive. The Russian wheezed and sucked at the air, his chest evidently crushed. Tommy stared down into his face, and the man's eyes flicked back and forth in the moonlight several times before they fixed on Tommy. Not once before this moment had Tommy been permitted to look him directly in the eye, and now that blood dripped from the man's mouth, Tommy had to control the urge to wipe it off.

"*Eb tvoiu mat!*" Yakir hissed. I fuck your mother, the worst curse a Russian could utter. His eyes fastened on Tommy, and for a moment they could still command, still frighten him. "*Eb tvoiu mat!*" Once more he cursed and spit toward Tommy blood-red spittle.

Tommy knew that if he simply walked away he wouldn't get far in his tattered clothing. With an NKVD uniform, he at least stood a chance of making it to Moscow. For the longest time, he did nothing but listen to Yakir's disturbed breathing, and then he stepped forward, covered Yakir's mouth with one hand and pinched his nostrils with the other. The man thrashed his head and wiggled his body to try to free his hands, but he was too tightly clamped by the weight of the van. Tommy felt the man shudder, then fade away.

Tommy released his grip, slumped down beside the dead man, and pressed his back into the roof of the van. He took two deep breaths, closed his eyes and counted to ten to clear his head. Then he went to the river and washed his face and hands in the icy water. He returned to Yakir and closed the man's eyes the way his father had shown him.

The river's thunder drowned out even the wind as Tommy rummaged between humps of rock until finally he found a log wedged in a crevice of the embankment. He dragged the log to the van and slid it under the wreckage next to the body, and then he lifted the other end of the log enough to force a boulder under it as close to the van as he could manage. He collected several more stones and placed them next to the larger boulder, imitating a trick his father had used once when he had a flat tire on the narrow, gravelled trail to Burnt Lake, south of Kenora. His father had worked a poplar branch the size of his own massive arm under the front fender of his 1926 Model T, and each time he lifted the car a little, he kicked another rock under it for support.

The light falling in layers through the brush and trees had mottled his father's reddened face, and thick beads of sweat trailed down his father's cheeks as Tommy watched from the safety of a nearby stump. He was barely six.

Even with the aid of the log, the van wouldn't budge at first, but Tommy slowly pried it up enough to get the first stone under. After four more stones, he was able to lift the side of the van enough to slide the dead man out.

Yakir was smaller than Tommy and the uniform fit snugly. He dressed the dead man in his own clothes, dragged him to the river, and eased the body in. The moon came out from behind clouds, and Tommy watched the body bob for a minute before the powerful current sucked it below the surface so quickly Tommy doubted his plan to enter the water himself. He returned to the van and worked until he completely righted it. He put the van in neutral and rolled it over the bank. It floated downriver for a hundred yards before it slowly sank. Tommy then threw the log in the river, covered his footsteps the best he could, and slipped into the cold water too. If he could stay close to the edge, he reasoned, he could float downstream faster than he could walk or run. He had only a few hours until morning when the van would be missed.

The cold water cut to his bones, and within minutes he felt numb from the neck down. The shore moved past with increasing speed, and he fought to stay close to land. The moon weaved between clouds and sometimes disappeared for long stretches, making it difficult for Tommy to mark his progress and to keep the shore in view.

After what he estimated as twenty minutes to half an hour, but as long as he could tolerate the cold water, he crawled onto shore. He had no idea how far he had floated in the brisk current, and despite exhaustion and being near frozen, he managed to keep himself moving. A rocky bluff rose above the bank, and he scrambled up it. Although the moon to the west formed only a pale sliver through thickening clouds, each time its light fell on him he felt exposed and feared that even in this deserted dark people watched.

He walked across a landscape of pine-and-spruce-covered hills, with some larch and birch. The rolling hills occasionally broke at a rocky cliff not unlike the faded edges of the Canadian Shield, and he had to walk carefully, using the moon as a guide. Occasionally he heard a dog bark in the distance or a wolf howl. Other than that, it was eerily quiet, and his breathing seemed unnaturally loud. When he reached a gravel road, he followed along its edges, hiding in the bush when any vehicle passed.

Tommy walked all that day and slept in the evening hidden in the mouth of a small cave fifty feet off the road through dense bush. The next morning the sky through the trees looked no different than the sky back in Canada, yet he knew little of where he was or what the next turn would bring.

A few miles down the road, the bush opened to a rolling, open landscape, shaded only on the south by a thick mesh of birch and spruce. He crossed to that side as quickly as he could run, and then walked on hardened, uneven clay beneath trees so dense and ancient nothing had grown in their shade for centuries. At midday, he neared a farm. A dozen horses grazed in a fenced enclosure separated from him by a small meadow of short, tangled grass. He dashed toward a thicket twenty feet from the horses, crawled into the centre, and lay flat on his stomach. Several horses nickered, sniffed the wind, and tossed their heads in his direction. About a quarter mile to the north, several children played in front of a house, and their busy sounds riffled through the grass toward him. Beyond them, a handful of workers dotted the field.

Tommy worked his way around to the gate and swung it open. He chose a thin brown horse that looked fast, and he combed its mane with his spread fingers while quietly rubbing its snout as he'd done so often as a boy. He held his lips to the horse's ear and whispered to it in Russian. The animal lifted its front legs a little and snorted sharply into the bright morning air, and the other horses paced nervously within the tight enclosure. Tommy leaped onto the horse's back and jabbed both sides with his heels. The horse bolted through the gate and the others followed, scattering in different directions. Behind him, the children started yelling, but he didn't look back. Tommy skirted a stand of trees until it intersected a gravel road, and he followed at a hard gallop for several hours, only slowing the pace when he felt the horse's exhaustion. He had no idea where he was, but he followed the sun, hoping to find Moscow somewhere in that direction. *Straight south of here*, Vladislav had said, *that's where that demon is*. It was also Tommy's only hope, for somewhere in Moscow there had to be a Canadian embassy. Certainly they'd take him in with no questions asked, and he stood a better chance of reaching there than any of the Soviet borders, hundreds if not thousands of miles away. As Vladislav had reminded him often enough, he was in the very heart of the Soviet Union. Too far to walk.

NINE

THROUGHOUT THE SUMMER, Judith had stolen only things she really wanted, but now she stuffed toys, candy, pens, or small pieces of clothing down her pants any chance she could and walked out breezily. Sometimes she gave away the things she stole, other items she kept in a special box under her bed, or threw away after a few days. One day a clerk stopped her at the Shop Easy front doors.

"What's this?" she said as she grabbed the bulge.

Twenty minutes later, two police officers arrived to take Judith home. The older officer helped Judith into the back while his partner got in the driver's side. She had the rear seat all to herself, a seat so new it squeaked when she slid across the vinyl. She sat in the middle touching both doors with her extended fingertips as if for balance. The car smelled of coffee and smoke, and Judith wondered what would happen if she jumped out. The officer who helped her inside stood near the passenger door and lit a cigarette. He puffed once and then got inside.

Judith caught sight of her face in the rear-view mirror and quashed her apprehension by adjusting her hair and toying with her eyelashes as she'd seen her mother do. The officer driving drew his hand back and forth several times along the red lip of the dash in a steady, even sweep. Judith watched his stubby fingers without interest and then went back to grooming herself.

Neither man looked back at her or spoke to her, so she distracted herself further by watching their heads bob to the motion of the car. It wasn't until they turned off the highway toward Burnt Lake that the officer smoking turned to her and smiled as if he had suddenly remembered that she was still with them.

When they reached her house, Adam kicked the rear tire of the police car while Judith sat in the back waiting for the police officers to finish talking to her mother.

They seemed to be taking forever. How much could they have to say to each other? And why did they have to make such a big deal of it? It wasn't as if she'd robbed a bank. All the same, her mother shifted on her feet and looked down at the ground several times as if she was ashamed or at a loss for words. Judith knew that couldn't be a good sign.

"What were you thinking?" Alice asked when the police had finally gone.

She lectured Judith about associating with bad influences at school and grounded her for a week. Judith didn't correct her mother's false impression. Once she saw that her mother would so easily forgive her, she treated the whole affair nonchalantly. Being grounded made little difference to her, stuck out at Burnt Lake, where there was never anything to do anyway but listen to the radio or flip through magazines, but getting caught did force her to be more ingenious. She stayed away from the Shop Easy and began to wear the lined jeans her mother had bought her the previous winter. Judith had tossed them to the back of her closet because she had worn holes in the pockets, but now she remembered that anything she put in the pockets slid down to her ankles and hid nicely inside the pant linings. Wearing those jeans, she became bolder, and once two clerks at Johnson's Pharmacy stopped her with a Parker pen and a tube of lipstick down her pant leg. One clerk frisked her while the other watched. When they let her go, Judith ran for several blocks, a wide grin on her face.

For the next couple of months, she walked downtown from school at lunchtime to shoplift. She moved from store to store so as not to raise suspicion, and occasionally she bought something to allay the suspicions of clerks who followed her.

But in time she became careless again, and was caught twice more and driven home by the police. Only a week later, at Woolworths, she got caught a fourth time when she openly stuffed a blouse down her pant leg and her jeans bulged noticeably. The police didn't take her home then but left her at the station until Alice came from work to retrieve her. Alice cried that time.

"I don't understand you," she said. "Do we need this?" She no longer grounded Judith but spoke to her sadly about values and choices. People often broke the law, she said, they exceeded the speed limit, or drove when they had been drinking. Some people cheated on their taxes or slipped dummy coins into vending machines, but rarely did people think about the consequences of their actions. Judith needed to weigh the consequences the next time she wanted to break the law. Alice said a moment's thrill could never outweigh reform school.

Then, less than a month before Judith's fifteenth birthday, a black Ford pulled into the yard and a man and woman stepped out. They knocked forcefully on the front door, and Alice stood a long time at the door talking to them, and now and then she lifted a hand to her hair to swat away flies.

Judith watched from her bedroom doorway and Adam repeatedly tossed a baseball into a leather glove.

"Take that to your room, Adam," Alice said. Her stomach was all in knots. She would never have believed that Judith would become so much of a handful, and yet when the police had brought her home, she could see in their eyes what they thought. *You're not a good mother. She needs the influence of a man.* At times Alice even believed they were right, that she couldn't or shouldn't raise her children alone, but what choice did she have?

Judith grabbed at Adam's baseball glove as he passed. Adam pushed her, and Judith pushed back.

Alice turned from the visitors and said in a firm voice, "I have company. Why don't you both read in your rooms? Don't make me ask twice."

Adam slammed the door to his room, and Judith closed hers quietly.

Alice offered the visitors chairs at the Formica table. Their eyes held the same disapproving expression she had recognized with the police, but she was not in the mood to be intimidated. She waited until they were seated before she spoke. "I don't want to give her up. I told them that over the phone."

"You're not giving her up. It's only for a while. Trust me, Mrs. Rose. After six months in a foster home, you will see a changed daughter."

Judith had been listening at her door and now burst out of her room. "You can't send me to a foster home."

Alice grabbed her hand and held it. "Don't. You're not helping."

"Let go." Judith pulled her arm away and bolted out the front door.

Alice went to the window and watched Judith race down the path toward the lake. She remembered again how Shirley had run away from home and it seemed now that Judith was becoming just as wild, just as hard to control. Still, what kind of mother would give up her daughter, even for a few months? How could it possibly be in Judith's best interest, whatever they said?

When she returned to the table, the woman glanced at the door still flapping open. She crossed to the door and closed it. Back at the table, she took Alice's hand and squeezed it. "She'll adjust. I want what's right for Judith just as much as you do."

"She's not your flesh and blood. How can you expect me to give her up—?"

"She needs guidance and structure, and with you having to work, it mustn't be easy. She can't keep stealing."

"I've talked to her and she's agreed to stop."

"I've dealt with hundreds of juvenile delinquents. Once they start, they don't stop. It's an addiction."

"She misses her father. Before he died, she was the sweetest thing. She still is some of the time." Wasn't she?

The woman retrieved some papers from her bag and slid them across the table. "We can't take her away without your agreement. What you're signing is a temporary consent. The courts wouldn't be so generous, trust me. You can visit her when you like, although we recommend that you don't for the first few months so that she has time to bond. It's nearly the end of the school year so it could be a good summer break for her, like summer camp. I know this is difficult for you, but think of it as a break for you too, a chance to get some rest."

"I don't want a rest from her. I just want some help." Alice had already been warned that if Judith was caught again, it would mean reform school, and then she would end up like Rudy.

"It's nearly her birthday," Alice said.

"No time is a good time, but I do think you'll be doing your daughter a disservice if you say no. Maybe we should come back tomorrow." The woman picked up the papers and handed them to Alice. "Read them over. You'll see it's for the best."

"How will I know it's a good family?"

"All our families are screened, and we do strict follow-up visits." The woman stood and shook Alice's hand briefly.

Alice did not see them to the door but remained at the table. Later, Judith came and stood behind her in the darkened room, trying to read the papers. She put her arms around her mother's shoulders. They stayed like that for a long time, warming each other, until Judith nuzzled her mother's neck and kissed her.

"They'll be back tomorrow."

"You could fight them."

Alice wiped away a tear. "If you get caught shoplifting again, you'll be sent away for a year or more. I won't have any say then."

"But I won't shoplift any more," Judith said.

"Oh, Judith. That's what you said the first time, and I believed you then, but there's too much at risk now."

"I promise this time."

"How can I know for sure? I don't want you to be sent away to reform school. I couldn't bear that."

"What about me? Don't I get a say?"

The next evening the woman returned.

Judith stuffed some extras into the beat-up suitcase her mother had helped her pack: three pairs of nylon socks and four pink-and-white pieces of underwear recently stolen from Woolworths, a Beatles postcard, two short black cotton skirts, and two matching flowered blouses. Finally, she added *The Diary of Anne Frank*, the only book she cared about.

At the front door, Alice gave her a brown paper bag full of new clothing.

"For your birthday," she said, her eyes filling with tears as she touched Judith once on the cheek.

TEN

TOMMY RODE THE MARE for three days, travelling gravel roads at night and sleeping during the day in the thickest cover he could find. On the second night, he stole eggs from a henhouse, cracking them open with one hand and quickly swallowing their slick contents. They tasted delicious.

As he progressed south, and villages and towns became more developed and common, he knew he was at greater risk of capture. Leaving the road to travel around populated areas slowed his pace, but luck provided him with clear nights so he could follow the stars. And after three years in the Soviet Union, he had at least learned to distinguish the North Star from the others. At dusk and dawn he took readings on the sun to confirm his bearings. He calculated from the speed of the horse and what Vladislav had told him that his current pace would bring him near Moscow after six days of riding. Thoughts of Moscow only increased his anxiety, because once he reached there, he still had the daunting task of locating the Canadian embassy in a completely foreign city. He placed his cheek against the horse's warm neck for comfort.

Near dawn of the fourth day, Tommy had stopped at a narrow creek to allow the horse to drink, when a grouse rising out of the brush spooked it. The horse reared up, threw Tommy, and bolted. He fell hard, and when his head cleared, the horse was gone.

His right knee ached from the fall, so he limped south, and at daybreak left the birch and spruce forest through which he had travelled most of the night and entered a wide plain of spring-greened winter wheat. At the edge of the forest was a small clay hut, and out front a woman stooped over her garden. Tommy watched her until he felt certain she was alone and posed little threat. For the first time since his escape, he approached someone, hoping his uniform would afford him a meal.

"*Zahodete*," the old woman said, and motioned Tommy in the direction of her hut. He had expected caution on her part, but she greeted him with warmth.

She pointed to the bed, and only then did he taste blood and realize that his lip was bleeding. He shook his head and raised a hand to let her know he was okay. He pulled a chair out from the table and sat gratefully. She brought him a basin of warm water from the stove, and Tommy washed his hands and face. He could see no mirror in the hut, so Tommy judged his appearance as best he could by his reflection in the window and saw that his lip was swollen and his whiskers scruffy and unruly.

He returned to his chair, and the old woman sat across from him and stroked his face with her cold hands. She said, "Nickoli, Nickoli," and she kissed his forehead with her leathery lips and held her sallow face near his.

Her warm, jaundiced eyes had a glittering, dark halo at each centre, and she continued to smile and gaze at him for a while and then went outside. She soon returned with a freshly killed chicken and again motioned to the bed.

He felt safe enough to sleep. When he woke, the woman sat in a wooden chair at the side of his bed. She stared straight at him and rocked a little in the chair moaning, "Nickoli." Between the repetitions of this name, she added, "*Spasiba, spasiba.*" Thank you, thank you. The wind creaked through the few trees and tossed more dust against the clouded windows. He shivered, and she stood and rubbed his cheek and cupped her fingers around his chin. Her fingers smelled sweet, as if she had dipped them in sugar.

She brought a plate of roast chicken and potatoes to the bed, as well as a bowl of thick cabbage soup. He took the bowl and held it until the broth heated through to his hands, and then he savoured a mouthful before he swallowed it. He took several more swallows, so that when finally he switched to the chicken and potatoes, he could relish only a few bites before his stomach cramped, unused to such quantity, and prevented him from eating more. He lay down and closed his eyes again, but sleep wouldn't come.

The old woman returned to the kitchen to light her samovar. He watched her fill it with water and then carefully place bits of dry grass in the metal heating pipe that rested beneath the reservoir. When a little flame took hold, she piled dry twigs on top. All the while, she hummed softly or coaxed the samovar, saying in Russian, "Good boy. Yes, bring me fire." Finally, when the coals were hot and the water steamed, she carried the samovar to the table and placed it on a metal tray. After she had carefully positioned it, she danced about clapping her hands. The whole process took nearly half an hour, and Tommy watched from the bed, amazed at the woman's patience. The tea she brought him tasted sweet, and he asked for more when he finished. She smiled and poured another cupful as if nothing pleased her more than to see him drink.

The samovar spiced the air, and he fell back asleep until early afternoon. When he woke, the old woman was pacing in the kitchen, and when the sun caught her face, it accentuated her sunken eyes and wide-open mouth. Her thin body moved stiffly and her fingers were crooked and swollen.

Tommy returned to the table. She put out more soup and tea and he only sipped at the soup this time, afraid he might get ill from eating too much too quickly. She plied him earnestly with her "*Est, est,*" until he downed several more mouthfuls of soup, but had to refuse further to eat more. She looked at him with such concern that he experienced a warm rush of happiness. It had been three years since anyone had cared if he lived.

As the day waned she returned to work in her small garden, and Tommy watched from the dusty window as she moved between the plants, her fingers deftly pulling weeds. She had one knee pressed into the earth, the other raised at an odd angle, and she worked like someone proficient at ignoring pain. He felt a pluck of guilt that brought him to his feet. He went to the samovar and poured another cup of tea, and carried the warm cup to the woman outside. She objected, but he encouraged her and drew her over to the worn step to sit while he continued the weeding she had started. He worked the dry earth with his fingers as the sun warmed his back, and he remembered when he and his father had tended his mother's garden after she died.

At nightfall he readied himself to leave.

"Nickoli stay," she pleaded, although her eyes said different.

When he shook his head, she shuffled to the cupboard and returned to sadly stuff a bit of bread into the pocket of his coat. They were awkward at the door, but a brisk wind made dawdling difficult. His larger hands held hers for a moment and then they parted without a word.

He passed several farms and at daybreak he ate the bread and spent the day hidden in a protected poplar bluff. Clouds of midges swarmed from nearby swamps and filled his ears and nose. He had to cover his head with his coat to sleep.

In the late afternoon, hunger woke him, and he scraped his fingers along the layered underbrush searching for something edible. Finding nothing, he sucked on twigs until he could no longer stand their dank, fibrous texture in his mouth and spat them out. He forced himself to keep walking because he guessed Moscow was still at least a hundred miles to the south.

When he heard a snapping of twigs and saw a blur of grey through the bank of trees, he thought for a moment he was hallucinating. But then he spotted a woman astride a regal, battleship-grey horse, moving confidently over uneven terrain. She encouraged the horse with short, snappy sounds as she skilfully worked the reins and guided the horse between the trees. She wore her black hair pulled up under an officer's hat, and the ends of a red scarf trailed down her back. Her head nodded to the gait of the horse, which changed suddenly when the animal sensed him, and a few steps farther, the horse sunk briefly in soft earth. When it regained firmer ground, the woman bent to wipe mud from her boots, and her scarf caught on a branch and slipped from her neck.

She halted the horse and dismounted in a graceful sweep. She retrieved the scarf, inspected it, and then secured it around her neck before she remounted and galloped the horse toward open country. Tommy watched her cross the next field and turn the horse sharply to the right, vanishing in the trees.

He followed, careful to stay hidden. He crossed much of the field on his hands and knees, poking his head up now and then above the tall grass for a quick view of what lay ahead. Where she had turned east, a road cut through a thickly wooded area, and he felt concealed enough to stand. The careful way the woman had retrieved her scarf allowed him to hope she would show him the same concern, but what he wanted most was her horse. He stopped at a stream to drink, and although the water brought relief to his parched throat, it swelled his painfully empty stomach.

He spotted the smoke long before he rounded the bend and saw the three-story house in a grove of towering spruce. He saw no sign of a dog, so he would wait until dark and then rummage through the garbage for food. A house of this stature must have something he could scavenge. While he waited, he would look for the horse.

The stable was at the rear of the house. A fenced paddock surrounded it, and Tommy could find only the one horse, which disappointed him, as he hated to think he might have to steal the only horse the woman owned, though he saw no stable hand to interfere with him if he did.

After dark, the main floor lit up as if she expected company, or did not care who looked in. He watched her move from room to room, and as far as he could tell, she was alone. From the shadows of a hedgerow, he studied the living room, which spanned nearly half one side of the house. A massive and gaudy crystal chandelier hung in a position that lighted the wooden staircase. The walls were finished in dark wood, mahogany, he guessed, and were lavishly decorated with framed paintings—the specifics of which he was too far away to determine. He peered in other windows, at a dining room and the kitchen next to it. Dark cupboards reached nearly to the ten-foot ceiling. At the far end of the kitchen was an unobtrusive side door, likely meant for servants, as a house this size under the czars would have required servants. Near that door were piles of rubbish, where he hoped he would find some scraps.

He waited until the lights had been out for more than an hour before he ventured close to the house again. The grand sandstone steps were weathered and pocked. He skirted them, and instead crept to the side door to sift through the sacks of garbage. Under some papers, he found several half-eaten potatoes and a heap of partly rotten berries. He gulped it all and then lay against a sack to rest.

"*Davay, Comrade.*" She spoke forcefully.

Her dark hair was down, the scarf gone. She pointed a pistol at his heart.

When he didn't move, she said, "*Davay Comrade,*" more fiercely, and pointed again with the pistol for him to get up.

"I'm sorry," Tommy said, in English without thinking.

"English?"

"Yes, Canadian," he said.

Her eyes lost some of their coldness but she continued to level the pistol at his heart. "What do you want?" she asked in English.

"I was hungry. I didn't mean to scare you."

"Where'd you get that uniform?"

He lowered his eyes. "Off a dead man."

"Where are you going dressed like that?"

"Moscow." He said the name with a foreigner's hope.

She lowered the pistol and motioned to him to stand. "I'm Oksana Yerenko, named after my great-grandmother. Come inside and I'll give you something to eat. You look like a dead man yourself. I thought you were, all shrivelled up next to the trash, but then I saw you breathe. I almost shot you as you slept. That's how much I hate that uniform."

Tommy dried his sweating hands on his jacket, the rough threads catching on his callused palms. "What stopped you?"

She didn't answer, but offered him a chair in the large kitchen and spooned out hot potato soup, which she placed in front of him. He caught the scent of earth and perfume and he couldn't remember how long it had been since he'd smelled perfume.

She crossed to the samovar and poured him tea.

While he ate, she sat across from him, still nursing the pistol. Between sips of tea, she drew on a cigarette. He eyed it longingly. He could count on his fingers the number of cigarettes he'd had over the past three years in the camp, and yet the desire for one was immediate. She offered him one and he slid it from the pack and laid it carefully on the table in front of him. When he had eaten half his soup, he raised the cigarette to his lips. She lit it for him, leaning toward him as she did, and her eyes held his until he looked away, but despite their intensity, they gave up nothing. Her hair was now pulled back in a simple ponytail, and she had a face that needed no makeup or enhancements. Her skin was pale and unblemished, her cheekbones high and well defined, and even set in a stern line, her lips held the promise of a wide, full smile. Her expression was unrelenting, but if it lacked softness, it didn't look capable of hardness either. Tommy gauged her to be in her early twenties, a little aloof, with the distant demeanor of someone older and accustomed to caution.

"Three of my aunts fled Ukraine for Canada," she said, butting out her cigarette. "Winnipeg. Do you know it?"

Tommy nodded. "I grew up near there."

"Is it beautiful? My aunts wrote my mother for years saying how wonderful it was, the land so flat you can see for miles in every direction just like the Steppe. A flat, rich plain for growing wheat, even better than Ukraine. They tried to persuade my mother to leave Ukraine, but she and my father wouldn't leave, and that killed them." She retrieved another cigarette from the pack and lit it without looking at him. "What's a Canadian doing here? Moscow is over a hundred miles away. Are you a spy?"

"No, I was taken prisoner after the war ended, in fact, and I only escaped a few days ago." He hoped he had not told her too much and that she could be trusted not to turn him in, but he was sure she would have done so already if she meant to.

"The Soviet Union is good at collecting people. She's not good at letting them go. You won't get within fifty miles of Moscow, even dressed like that. You don't wear it right. You'll be a dead man. Wearing a dead man's uniform makes you a dead man. Did you kill him?"

"I had to."

"There is no 'had to' in the Soviet Union when it comes to a man in uniform. Only 'yes' or 'no.'" She put the pistol in her skirt pocket and went to the stove.

He noticed that she was nearly as tall as he was.

"I can't take you to Moscow, but you can spend the night, if you stay away from the windows. I can't let anyone see you. Even out here there are spies."

"Do you live alone?"

"Except for the colonel-general, but he's not here most of the time."

His stomach tightened.

"Don't worry, he won't be here tonight."

No good will come of this, Tommy thought. He fought the urge to steal the horse despite her offer of a night's rest, or to run as fast as he could back down the road and off into the bushes, but he needed an ally to help him get to Moscow. The way she had pointed the pistol at his heart convinced him that she feared the same people he did. He would be wiser to stay.

She led him up the broad staircase he'd seen from the window. "The same maple as in Alexander Palace in Leningrad, the colonel-general boasts. With me, he's less the Communist."

On the second floor the wide hallway was flanked by several dark doors. She opened one and led him into a large bedroom.

"This house belonged to a cousin of the czar, and after the revolution ten families lived in it until the colonel-general had them purged. It's his dacha now, his hiding place for me, he says. I'm a caged animal. Even a hundred miles from Moscow I'm under lock and key."

She went to the window and pulled down the heavy shades. "Stay in here and don't open the blinds. I'll call you when it's time to wash."

When she returned, she didn't speak at first but looked at him as if measuring him. "Your bath is ready through there." She pointed at a door he'd thought was a closet. "I have some clothes you can put on in the morning."

Tommy reached out a hand to thank her.

"Never touch me," she said, turning her back, and closing the door behind her.

He slipped into the hot bath and slowly his muscles relaxed as he soaked. When the water began to cool, he checked his body for sores and wounds. Hunger had kept him from noticing that many of his wounds were swollen and infected. More than an hour later, he stood clean and dry before a mirror and shaved. His ribs were visible, and the flesh between each bone looked sunken and grey. When he drained the tub, he was embarrassed at how filthy he'd made it, so he searched for some cloths. Meticulously he scrubbed, coaxing each wave of grey water toward the drain as though he could rinse away three years in the camp.

In the morning Tommy dressed in the clothes Oksana had left on a chair. The shirtsleeves stopped above his wrists and the pants barely covered his ankles but he ventured downstairs. He found Oksana at the stove fixing eggs. "You'll need to let those out," she said, and smiled. "You work inside and I'll work outside. We have chickens and a cow, thanks to the colonel-general."

At breakfast, she blew a puff of smoke out the side of her mouth. "How did you escape?"

Her candidness put him at ease, and he told her about the camp and what had happened with Freda. His relief after the telling was so strong he couldn't speak for a moment, and she filled the awkward pause by offering him a cigarette. He took it and they sat in companionable silence until Oksana eventually stood up. "I've got work to do. I've left you a list of things to clean."

That night, Oksana opened a bottle of wine.

"How did you learn English so well?" Tommy asked.

She looked into the red mouth of her glass for a moment and then set it down. "Before the war, we studied English in my gymnasium—my school—and then, until Hitler invaded, German. One of my teachers said I had a gift for languages. He was a Canadian too, who came over to help the revolution and couldn't leave. He didn't know the door only swung one way. He brought me English books to read, but that was before Stalin ordered all foreign books burned. Then he burned Russian and Ukrainian books too. Before the purges started, it was still possible to believe Stalin would make us great. Before the war, it was possible to be happy at least. Now, who knows? We aren't to expect happiness, only labour. The colonel-general says the state must survive, not those in it. Lives can be plucked from it one at a time, but the state breathes on."

Oksana walked over to the same windows Tommy had watched her through only the night before. He knew now that the wood was not mahogany, as he'd thought, but a lustrous polished walnut. On the floors, Persian carpets protected what must have at one time been high-traffic areas. One painting on the wall was of a girl holding a parasol as she reached out her free hand to test for rain. The paintings didn't strike him as Russian.

"They are French," she said when she saw where his eyes travelled. "As are many of the furnishings. The colonel-general brought them back from the war, from one of the many German mansions he stripped. He has a fetish for things French, as he has reminded me many times, and his mother was French. He threw out all the Russian art because it was full of icons or workers. He said the boss's tastes are not his."

On the far wall, floor-to-ceiling bookcases dominated the room, and on several small tables in between, clay sculptures were artfully displayed. "The sculptures are Russian, but stolen too. He talks like a communist but robs like a capitalist."

She brushed her hand along the recently pulled shade and dust fluttered into the air. "Communist dust, the colonel-general would say. Not Bolshevik dust, but the boss's dust. He calls Stalin the boss. If I repeated some of the things the colonel-general whispers to me about the boss, I would be a dead woman. The colonel-general curses Stalin, but if I said even one word against the boss, he would consider it his duty to kill me. I trust no one, including you, but who are you going to tell? I would be killed for having you here as well."

"Should I leave?"

"Part of me says yes. But I also think we could help each other."

"You would help me?"

"If you helped me, I would. But in the Soviet Union, whom can we trust? It's safest to believe everyone lies, that every word you hear is a lie. But I ask you, is that a way to live?"

"No." He found it difficult to take his eyes off her, and as he listened to her, he imagined her alone in the big house with no one to share or absorb her sorrow as she watched the country around her recede. Who was she before all this started? What had she wanted? She seemed eager to talk, and he didn't interrupt.

"I grew up with Russian lies. Ukraine was greater under Russian rule, they told us, even as they gave us Stalin and his *Holodomor*. Do you know what that is? The terror-famine? They expropriated our land, our grain reserves, and our livestock without compensation. They sold our grain abroad for next to nothing and forced us to starve. Farmers were executed for cooking a handful of their own crop. Mothers killed their children to spare them, while families were reduced to eating their dead. Can you imagine that? *Millions* died. Bodies lay where they fell." Oksana stumbled on the words. She put down her wine glass and gathered her scarf in her hand. "It is too much for me to speak of even after all this time. I shouldn't have survived, and I wouldn't have, except for my father's cousin, who somehow got us permission to move to Kiev."

Oksana sat quietly for a moment unable to go on. Finally she took a long swallow of her wine and began again. "The first place we lived in Kiev was not far from the Dnieper River, and when the war came, it was no longer just a pleasant river where I could wash my feet, but a burial ground for the planes that crashed into it.

"The day the Germans marched into Kiev, I was sixteen. My father laughed. 'We're free from the Soviets at last,' he said. 'Don't be so sure,' my mother said. 'This isn't liberation day, just a change of guard.'

"I didn't know whom to believe. Many people I knew went out into the streets to offer gifts to the German soldiers, and at first our situation improved under them. They distributed food the Soviets had hoarded and spent freely in our cafés and shops.

"But in September 1941, NKVD men left behind by the Russians set off bombs all over the glorious centre of Kiev, and the Germans turned vengeful. First, Jews were told they were being relocated and were loaded onto trucks. Most of them were shot in the ravine outside Kiev called Babi Yar. Imagine. People I had known since moving to Kiev, from my own gymnasium. When the Nazis finished with the Jews, they arrested others. Those not shot in Babi Yar were sent to work in Germany. Most crimes, no matter how minor—and certainly any committed against a German—carried one punishment. A march to Babi Yar, and then a bullet. Thousands upon thousands burned. People I knew. We smelled their burning flesh in the air like the stink from a slaughterhouse, only worse because one never adjusts to murder the way one adjusts to the stink of capitalism.

"My parents hid me in the cellar because girls my age were being rounded up to work for wealthy families in Germany. Many of the shops and cafés posted signs, 'Germans only. Ukrainians not Allowed.' In our own language, we were told we weren't allowed. They stole our city and wrapped their garbage in our manuscripts. Slowly they marched us to Babi Yar, and the longer the war took, the fewer of us remained.

"Germans killed many of the skilled people, even cobblers like my father, but months earlier a German officer had come into my father's shop to have his boots repaired, and he liked my father's work so much that he'd only have my father repair his boots, but he'd never pay him. 'You do it for the fatherland,' he said. Soon other officers brought their boots, and my father spent hours every week on work that paid nothing. One morning I saw him sitting at the kitchen table crying, his hands pressed into his face.

"Every day we lived in fear of Babi Yar. If Father didn't repair the shoes right, if one of us was caught out after curfew, if we walked on the wrong street at the wrong time, we could be taken there, stripped, and shot.

"The harder my father worked, the more boots they brought him. When the Nazis started to lose the war, things grew harder and food scarcer. Still, it wasn't as bad as what came later.

"If my father didn't work for the Germans, he'd be shot. If he didn't work fast enough, he'd be shot. If he kept up with the work, they gave him more. My mother had to clean officers' quarters to help feed us. We grew thin and weak, and my father worked his fingers raw.

"Only when the Red Army approached the city once again did the boots stop coming. Then the streets weren't safe any more, what was left of them, because few buildings remained standing. All day we heard the approaching gunfire of the Red Army. My parents feared the reprisals of the returning Soviets so much they talked about fleeing with the Germans. Everyone knew the army would seek revenge on anyone who had helped the Germans. My father wanted to leave, but my mother couldn't bear the thought of fleeing her beloved country, so they stayed.

"Then word spread that all remaining skilled workers would be forced to leave with the Germans. For the next three days, we hid in the cellar, but no one came to find us. In the chaos of defeat, we thought we had been forgotten.

We remained in the cellar and only my father ventured out at night to scrounge for food. As the Red Army shelling drew near, the Germans made one more search of our street and ferreted us out. We were boarded onto tramcars and driven with the rest out of the city, but at night we escaped and walked back to our small house. We hoped the Germans wouldn't look twice, and they didn't. Along the way every street was cluttered with the rotting corpses of cats and dogs that the Germans shot before leaving.

"For two days, the Red Army bombed us. We huddled in the cellar, never certain if the next shell would land on us or not. One bomb blew a hole in our roof, and in the late afternoon, I snuck out of the cellar and lay on the floor and watched the clouds through the hole. At night, things quieted for a few hours, and then on the second morning, the floor above us caught fire and we stayed below, warmed, finally, by the fire. Father said we were safe in the cellar and the fire would keep the Soviet soldiers away a while longer.

"On the third day, the bombing stopped, but two days later, Red Army gunfire started at first light, and as daylight grew, the gunfire got closer and closer. By then the fire above had burned out, and my parents argued over their decision to remain behind.

"At noon, the gunfire ceased altogether, and the sudden quiet was worse. From the top of the stairs, we saw soldiers moving from building to building. They kicked open doors and dragged women screaming into the street. More than two dozen women lined the side of a building, and then the soldiers pushed them inside and left them under the guard of a handful of men.

"When a Red Army soldier kicked open the door to the cellar, my father raised his hands in surrender, but the soldier fired without hesitation. My father stepped into the bullets to block us from them, and then he slumped to the floor and did not move.

"I screamed as he fell, and they shot Mother as she sprang to my father's side. A young Soviet soldier forced me down on top of my dead mother and raped me. So did two others who came when they heard his gunshots. They beat me unconscious. I awoke on my side in a small room crowded with other women.

"I wore the same ripped, filthy clothes for weeks on end and was forced to lie on my back every night while so many Soviet soldiers followed one after another, pressing their stinking skin against me, and I had to close my eyes and remain quiet or be shot.

"I served Soviet soldiers in a floating whorehouse that followed the Red Army from battle to battle. They housed us in one shelled-out building or another and each day soldiers came to us while battles raged around us. Where before I had tried to hide from the war, I felt as though I now belonged to the war.

"I wished I had died with my parents. And then one night the colonel-general found his way to my quarters. His red eyes glistened in the dark like a rat's. A few days later, he had me taken to his private quarters, in an abandoned factory in Berlin. The walls were stocked with boundless supplies. After the war, he had me transported to Moscow with him, and at first I thought I was free."

Oksana pushed back her hair and took another sip of wine.

"How did you end up here?" Tommy asked.

"Two years ago the colonel-general brought me here. He wanted me as far away as possible from the temptations of Moscow, but still somewhere he could reach in a few hours' drive." She pulled a sweater around her shoulders. Even in June the evenings were still cool. "I could light a fire but I like to sit in the cold."

Tommy sipped his wine and his head swirled. Behind Oksana, a single lamp stretched shadows along the far wall. She gathered her hair behind her and tied it with the red scarf.

As she talked she slowly rolled down the sleeves of her blouse and looked across at him. Her eyes, tempered by the wine, no longer held him with the same suspicion.

"Now I'm at the colonel-general's disposal. He shows up whenever he wishes. Sometimes on a whim, sometimes when things aren't going well at home. He hasn't been here for more than two weeks. If he finds you here, he'll think you are my lover, and he'll kill us both."

"Why does he keep you here if he knows you don't love him?"

"The colonel-general senses my disgust, but he likes to show me that he can have me despite my contempt. One day I asked all the servants to leave. When the colonel-general returned and saw the help gone, he slapped me and said if I wanted to care for the house by myself that was fine with him, but he would never tolerate it becoming run down. I had a duty to him to keep it scrubbed and dusted. If I didn't, there'd be a slow death.

"He knows I could walk out of here tomorrow. He also knows that in a week, or a month, he'd find me."

"Can't you just disappear?"

Oksana shook her head. "Only those with power can disappear. Everyone else is betrayed. The man selling you a ticket. The woman at the market. Someone will give you up for a price or to save themselves. That's the kind of bargaining we've learned to do since the revolution. Stalin has taught us to betray, to seek revenge, to quiet the powerless. And yet many still think he's a saint."

"Surely no one still believes the lies. Don't they see and hear the trains?"

"Of course, but they don't believe Stalin is behind it. They imagine that he's kept in the dark. If I stay here, I will die too. I'm getting out as soon as I can. If I'm lucky and the colonel-general dies, then I'll get out sooner. For the past year I've gone to sleep each night imagining him dead just so I can dream of him picked over by vultures and imagine my freedom.

"On one visit, he brought the gelding to ride. For the first few weeks, I couldn't go near it without it putting up a fuss, but I coaxed him to let his guard down. Eventually, I am going to ride his horse to freedom."

She tilted her head back and drained her wine, and Tommy watched her hold the wine at the back of her throat. Finally, she swallowed and lowered her glass to the table with a tired but graceful sweep of her hand. "I'm no better than him. I eat his food and drink his wine and think of his death. My parents would cry to see me now."

"They would understand."

"What does it matter when they are dead and I am here?"

She rose from the couch and slowly made her way up the stairs, but Tommy sat a while longer, finishing his wine. When he stood, his legs felt weak but warm.

He walked past her room without stopping, and he was gripped with a greater loneliness than ever. These past three years he'd thought about survival and little else. Then reaching Moscow and freedom was just a dream, now it was a possibility.

Tommy sat on his bed and couldn't help but remember how beautifully Oksana's hands moved when she spoke.

He heard Oksana's hard footsteps as she approached his room. He hoped she would stop at his door, but she passed and he heard her stop at the library and muffle a cough before entering. He lay down on the bed and the mattress was soft and luxurious beneath him.

ELEVEN

THE WOMAN FROM THE Children's Aid Society took Judith to the Thompsons, an evangelical family, who farmed on Black Sturgeon Lake, northwest of Kenora. Balsam fir surrounded their farm, and the trees reminded Judith of her father.

"Someday balsams will be the only trees left protecting the rocky hillsides," Peter had once told Judith.

"Then what will happen?" she asked.

"They'll cut down the balsam too, until there's not a tree left, the buggers."

Mr. Thompson stood at the door of the farmhouse as the car pulled up. Judith got out, and the three Thompson girls ran from the house and approached the car. The oldest stood back and inspected Judith as if she were a stray animal she couldn't decide whether to keep or not.

Judith felt the hairs on the back of her neck bristle, and she thought, *I don't belong here.* She wanted to slap this girl, but she knew that would only prove her mother right, prove that she did belong in reform school. Alice had never said that, but Judith knew she thought it.

Mrs. Thompson emerged from the house drying her hands on her apron like some television mom, except she had a small blue square of fabric pinned to her head. The bonnet matched her dress and the dresses of her daughters. She was thin and heavily freckled, with angular cheekbones. A few strands of straw-coloured hair hung in her face, and she raised one damp hand to push them aside and then nodded at the Children's Aid woman. She stopped next to her husband, who stood more than a foot taller than her.

Judith looked at the woman from the Children's Aid Society as if to say, *You aren't really going to leave me with these people?* But the woman shook the Thompsons' hands and patted Judith on the back of her head as she introduced her. Everyone except Judith smiled and they nodded their heads as if that was all it took to make things right.

That night Judith curled into a ball in her bed. The room was the plainest she'd ever been in and beside her bed there were three other beds, one for each of the Thompson daughters. Not a single picture hung on the walls, and every wall was painted white. The beige-checked linoleum didn't add any colour either, and the cotton sheets on her bed were clean but threadbare. She missed her mother and she already wanted to go home, but she had a stubborn streak too—"Just like your *real* father," Cathleen had said once. *How could she? How could she?* Maybe her mother thought she planned to grow up to be a crook, a good-for-nothing like her father. But that just wasn't true. She could have stopped stealing if they had given her a chance.

In the morning, when Heather tried to wake her, Judith refused to move. In the bright morning light, Heather looked all skin and bones except for her round face, which sneered almost every time she saw Judith. She kept her pale blond hair tied in two tight braids.

Heather brought her face just inches from Judith's and said, "We don't want you here." She bumped Judith several times with her knee and then twisted her cheek in a painful pinch, but Judith only blinked her eyes. Heather's breath smelled strongly of garlic and her teeth were in serious need of brushing.

Mr. Thompson came upstairs to check on Judith. When he saw her still beneath the covers with only her head protruding, he went to the window and looked out as if checking on the horses in the back pasture. He stood for a while at the window, with Heather's eyes on him.

"From up here you can see clear to the lake if you look through those tall pines there. When my father built this house, this was my room, and I'd stand here on a hot day, look for that patch of blue, and want to go swimming, but my father never let me. He said swimming was for the idle. I thought then that he was cruel, and at night, the moon sometimes glittered in that spot between the trees, and I wanted to sneak out just once, but I didn't have the nerve. I've never been for a swim in that lake although I've lived here all my life, and some days I still come up here when the chores are finished and look at that bit of blue."

All the time he spoke, Judith didn't move. His voice stopped everything in the room and still he was as far away as Peter, cut off from her by the snug cocoon of covers.

He sat down on the edge of the mattress, its harsh black stripes exposed where Heather had tugged the sheets away. He smiled at Judith. "It's okay," he whispered. "There's nothing to fear. Why don't you get up and get ready for breakfast? I know it's difficult to leave home, but we're here to help you."

She liked how he smiled and she wanted to move, but her body wouldn't obey.

"I'm going downstairs now. You try and get ready for breakfast, Judith. Remember God makes each day for work."

The kindness he'd shown her helped her stifle her laugh.

The minute Mr. Thompson was downstairs, Heather spun back to Judith. "You *stink*. You'll always stink, and if you don't get downstairs I'll pinch you harder."

"Fuck you."

Heather moved to pinch Judith a second time, and Judith lifted a hand to block her. She wanted to punch her, the way she would have punched Adam if he'd been mean.

"You wouldn't dare touch me," Heather sneered. "You touch me and you're dead."

Judith jumped out of bed ready to fight, and Heather ran downstairs. The room was suddenly quiet, and the other sisters smiled at Judith. The youngest, Linda, was eight and she held up Judith's clothes. Judith took them and smiled warily back. She dressed, and then went straight downstairs to the empty table. The dining room was larger than her living room at home. All of the pictures were either of Christ or of the family, and across from where Judith stood waiting for the others she saw a photo of a younger Mr. and Mrs. Thompson. He had a long beard and a straw hat and was very tanned.

Mrs. Thompson came through the swinging door from the kitchen carrying a tray of food. She set down a large bowl of steaming oatmeal and a plate of orange slices, and pointed to the chair near her where Judith should sit. All the children lowered their heads as soon as they sat down. Heather was the last one to the table, and she gave Judith a smug glance before sitting next to her. Mr. Thompson motioned Judith to bow her head.

"Lord, give us strength to cherish what you've provided for us this morning and may our work today be hard enough to be worthy of such a feast as this. May this food nourish us and fill us with your bountiful love. May each of us be tested today and surpass your wondrous expectations."

His words perplexed Judith. God had no mercy. If he did, she wouldn't be here but at home, still in her own bed.

After breakfast, Judith washed the dishes while the rest of the family studied the Bible in the living room. Twice, Mrs. Thompson came back to check on Judith, and when she finished the dishes, Mrs. Thompson had her make the beds and dust everything in the girls' room. Each bed had a similar cotton patchwork quilt, something Judith associated with her grandmother. The one on Judith's bed was purple and white, with "God Sees Everything" embroidered near the top. She snooped in the tall unfinished pine dresser that was the only other piece of furniture in the room. Most of the six drawers held the same skirts and blouses in different sizes. She finished her own bed first and moved on to Linda's, but Heather sauntered in and proceeded to mess up Judith's.

"I just made that. Get off."

"Make me."

Judith stepped toward Heather just as Mrs. Thompson came in. She looked at the unmade bed and frowned, and then she stood in front of Judith and examined more closely the tight red dress Judith had selected from her bag of new clothes.

"A girl's got to look proper," she said as she searched through Judith's suitcase and the paper bag. "I sew all the girls' clothes." She retrieved a set of Heather's clothes and passed them to Judith. "Wear these."

Mrs. Thompson took away Judith's clothing, even the new things. All she missed was Judith's shoes, hidden under the bed.

When Judith had looked into the bag before she dressed, she found a birthday card, a brand-new pink blouse, and the red cotton dress she had put on. When she had held the blouse and dress up to the mirror, they looked so smart next to her skin that she had almost forgiven her mother. Mrs. Thompson allowed her to keep the card at least.

The blouse Mrs. Thompson gave Judith to wear buttoned in the back and had pointed darts in the front to accommodate Heather's breasts, which were smaller than Judith's despite her extra height, so on Judith the darts puckered oddly. The arms were too long and ended in simple gathered cuffs, which bunched over Judith's hands, getting in the way.

Heather's plain, full skirt was long enough to cover her already shapely calves, but on Judith, the hem dangled below her ankles and she had to hoist the skirt to keep from treading on it. They all looked like pioneers she had seen in photographs at school, and she could hardly believe Mrs. Thompson was serious.

"Face and hands are all that should be visible," Mrs. Thompson said. "There are some extra rubbers at the front door. Once you're finished in here, go out to the barn. Mr. Thompson's waiting for you there."

Judith followed him inside and choked on a pungent blend of manure and piss. She put her hand over her nose and mouth and stumbled forward into the dark stink, not daring to look at her feet to see what she stepped in. Judith lost sight of Mr. Thompson in the dark and walked right past him.

"It's not so bad," he said.

She spun around to face him. His eyes caught the glow of the outside light.

"You'll get used to the smell. We stockpile the dung behind the barn and let it cure. Dressing, we call it, dressing for the earth. It makes things grow. We all excrete, and you have to admit there is something worthy in the smell. It lets us know we're alive. Here. Take the shovel."

As she held the shovel, uncertain about how to use it, Mr. Thompson pointed to the stall behind her.

"Start in there. Once you're finished, come and see me. It's your job to clean the barn every day. Take the dung out to the pile behind the barn," he said, and then left.

Judith stepped into the stall and let the shovel drop too quickly, so the dung splattered her. Small piles had collected around the stall, and she sunk the shovel into one pile until it oozed full.

How could anyone call this dressing? She gripped both hands at the very end of the handle, as far from the dung as possible, which prevented her from lifting, so she dragged the shovel behind her to the back door. As she walked her skirt hampered her and pieces slipped off, so by the time she was outside, the shovel was scarcely half full and the hem of her skirt was filthy. She tossed the remaining bit on the manure pile and dragged the shovel behind her as she walked back in no particular hurry. A half-hour later, Mr. Thompson checked on her. When he saw the trail she'd left along the way to the back door, he took the shovel himself.

"Here, let me show you how I do it. Hard work helps you become strong in both body and mind, but honest labour means working with, not against, yourself. For years I've waited for my daughters to grow up and help around the farm, but now that Heather's old enough she says she doesn't like to get her hands dirty, so I let her help in the house instead. I wanted a son, but the Lord blessed me with daughters." He smiled when he said that, as if to indicate that daughters were all right as well.

"For years my father helped on the farm, but there's only me now. The Children's Aid said you'd be a big help, and I'm looking forward to that." He filled the shovel a little over half full and placed one hand near the bottom of the handle and his other hand at the top. "Don't be afraid to get dirty. Dirt washes off, so don't worry about that." His hands were already caked in dung, but he didn't seem to mind. He showed her the tap near the front of the barn. "If the smell gets to you, wash off here as many times as you want." He smiled and waited, as if he expected her to say something.

"Thank you," she said. She could think of nothing more.

"Hard work is the best cure there is. Once you're finished in the barn there's plenty of other work to do."

When he left, Judith leaned on the shovel handle for support and surveyed all the piles still to be cleared. She wanted to drop the shovel and run away before he gave her even more work, but what would that prove? That she was a delinquent, just as they all thought. Judith decided, right then and there, that she would withstand whatever challenge this man gave her. She cleaned up the trail and went back to work in the stalls.

That night in bed, she couldn't escape the smell. The other girls giggled in the dark and she knew they were talking about her because all three of them huddled in Heather's bed. She pushed her face as hard as she could into the pillow and remembered how her mother used to sit on the edge of her bed and push her hair back before she said goodnight. She hadn't done that as much lately, but Judith supposed that was her fault. She hadn't thought she wanted the attention, but now she did.

She missed the sounds her mother made outside Judith's room each evening, too, and the little peck her mother gave her each morning before Judith left for school. Her mother's kisses had begun to make her feel embarrassed and resentful, as if her mother wanted to keep her from growing up, but she saw now that she hadn't meant any harm. It was nice to know someone cared. What surprised Judith most was that she even missed Adam.

She fell asleep, as she would most nights after, believing that the next day her mother would understand she'd made a mistake and would come for her.

TWELVE

OKSANA SHOWED TOMMY HOW to dust the pysanky eggs that she kept on the shelf in the living room. "They are illegal under Stalin. My mother painted eggs every year during the last week of Lent, not to ward off evil as some believed, but because she loved their beauty. She tried to show me how to blow out the contents of each egg with delicate, short breaths, but I didn't pay attention. I was a good little Party sister by then, enthusiastic for the great modern age ahead. I wanted to forget the old ways. Now I display my pysanky and wish I could make them. The colonel-general was content to give them to me, but he would kill me if he saw me making new ones. Capitalist relics, he calls them."

One large blue egg had the drawing of a Cossack brandishing a sword. "An ostrich egg," she said and handed it to Tommy. "Be careful, it's empty inside."

The egg was light, and Tommy ran his fingers gently along its sensuous, near-perfect surface.

Oksana told him the meaning of the drawings on the eggs. "My favourite is this one. The Spider." She handed him a black duck egg with variegated markings surrounding an orange circle with spiralled tentacles that Tommy had mistaken as the sun.

"The spider means patience. The colonel-general doesn't know what any of the symbols on the eggs mean. He thinks they are just brightly coloured with curious patterns. He doesn't believe in religious symbolism. I dust this one with extra care, for I am like that spider."

She burst into the house. "The colonel-general's gelding reared up, so he can't be far off. Come, I will show you where to hide."

She led Tommy to a place in the woods near enough to the house that he could watch the colonel-general come and go yet far enough away that he wouldn't be seen.

Tommy saw the black limousine ease up to the house. The car idled for several minutes before anyone got out, and then an older man dressed in full uniform emerged. He was too far away for Tommy to make out his features, but he watched as the colonel-general walked slowly up the steps. The door shut behind him and the car returned the way it had come.

Seeing the colonel-general's uniform, even from a distance, brought back all Tommy's fears of the camp. He'd once seen a colonel-general select men at random, men who were never seen again. Tommy realized at that moment how much trust he was putting in Oksana. All she had to do was breathe a single hint and Tommy was as good as dead. And what if it wasn't Oksana who betrayed him but Tommy himself, taking Oksana with him? What if he'd forgotten something, left even a cup or knife out of place, left a sock out? What if the colonel-general could smell Tommy on the furniture, in the bedroom upstairs? He would kill Oksana, and Tommy wouldn't hear anything until it was too late.

Five hours later, the car returned.

The following day, Oksana called Tommy from his work. "Come see what I've done." She led him down into the cellar past cobwebbed rooms to a corner in the far end of the house. She pointed at a solid concrete room.

"This was the old root cellar. It's been empty as long as I've lived here. Nothing but cobwebs and spiders."

When both of them were inside, she bolted the door. "See? I made it so it locks only from the inside, and the door seals. You can stay here whenever the colonel-general visits. You can even bring a candle and a book. If you read Russian."

"A little, but what if something happens to you? How will I know?"

"I'll knock twice on this door when it is safe. If I don't knock, it's too late. The colonel-general is my worry, not yours."

Tommy's strength increased, and now each afternoon, after their main meal of the day, he got down on his hands and knees and scrubbed the wooden floors and stairs. He cooked meals and cleaned the bathrooms, always mindful that anything out of place could raise the colonel-general's suspicions.

"He has spies everywhere, but he hasn't used them since I moved from Moscow. Before that, I couldn't venture into the street without a shadow. Sometimes when I went out I'd return to a ransacked apartment. Not once did they find anything, and I plan to keep it that way. Each visit, I see him inspecting every room. Once, he poked his head in the fireplace and peered up the chimney. He trusts no one, least of all me, and he's wise to do that. If he finds the slightest trace of you, he'll tear the place apart until he unearths you."

In an effort to repay Oksana for the risk she took in helping him, Tommy did little tasks for her. He sharpened her axe, watered the plants, and ironed her blouses. Sometimes she thanked him, other times she didn't seem to notice.

And as they settled into the last weeks of spring and the early days of summer, they alternated between evenings alone in their respective rooms, and evenings filled with conversation and wine after dinner. Mindful that the colonel-general could surprise her at any time, she often sat facing the windows and rarely looked completely at ease. On those evenings with Tommy, Oksana always went to bed first. She seldom said good night, but made a sudden exit upstairs. Sometimes he thought she had merely gone to the washroom. After fifteen or twenty minutes he would realize she wasn't coming back.

Alone, he thought about Oksana almost obsessively. Clearly he owed her his life, but his attraction felt stronger than a response to that debt. Each day he discovered something new about her that pleased him. Even the cold, steady attention of her eyes appealed to him, as did the way she held her fork, or squeezed an armload of wood and walked on her tiptoes across the kitchen floor. He noticed how she smelled: flowery scents in the morning that drifted across the table, and then later in the day a hint of musk, ending each evening with a damp, organic scent that turned his head as she approached.

Although her strength and wild eyes reminded him of his mother, she was so exotic she disarmed him. Yet her presence also soothed him, and when he looked across at her at the dinner table, he thought it was her proximity more than anything else that was mending him. For five weeks, each night his last thoughts were of her. When he woke, sometimes it was from a dream of her. They were lying together, or somewhere safe, but always there was the idea of her and him, and then the sharp realization that what existed between them was formed out of necessity, nothing more. To want more, to expect more, was to flirt with a painful death. But he felt something more that he was afraid to put a word to yet. It couldn't be love. It was too early for such a delicate, certain word.

Because of the war, and his time in the camp, merely existing felt complicated, razor edged, and everything, from shaving to smiling, seemed to require so much more effort than it used to.

When they drank wine in the evening and talked, he hungered for more of her, was fascinated by her. She noticed him too, not with the same, fired interest but with the patience and calculation of someone careful, and although she had told him the brutal facts of her life, she remained guarded about her feelings.

Oksana killed a chicken and roasted it using a traditional Ukrainian recipe. She cut the chicken into pieces and baked them with slices of carrots, onions, and garlic. She basted often with bouillon, and with Tommy's help she prepared potato perogies, and *babka*, a sweet bread. Oksana told Tommy this had been her favourite meal as a girl. Many families served *babka* only at Easter, but her mother liked to cook the bread every Sunday, like Oksana's grandmother.

After the dirty dishes had been cleaned and put away, she brought out a fresh bottle of wine and poured them each a glass. She took a long sip, and Tommy recognized the focused look she had whenever she wanted to address something serious. Finally she put down her glass and looked directly at him.

"I've enjoyed your kindness these past weeks. It's been years since anyone has been kind to me. But please don't expect anything in return."

"I don't."

"Are you certain? You mustn't fall in love with me. For your sake and mine. I don't need love. I need to escape this hell and find a new life. Then I'll have time for love. You're a good man, Tommy, but cemeteries are full of good men. My father had a saying. 'The dead grow cold without a fire.' What's your fire?"

"Getting home alive, and taking you with me," he said, finally saying aloud what he had been planning in his head for days.

"Don't ...," she started and then caught herself. "If you make it home, you should forget me."

"I couldn't do that." Tommy downed the rest of his wine, hoping to dull the sting of Oksana's words.

Several evenings later, warm winds from the Barents Sea brought the first summer storm, gathering along its way the scent of pine and beech. The densely forested hills to the west and north of the dacha broke the brunt of the storm, but thunder and rain still rattled the windows.

"My grandmother believed storms were demons we let out by some mistake we'd made that day or the day before. She would go from room to room with her broom trying to sweep the demons out of the house. I thought she was old and foolish, but now I wish she were right and we could just sweep all the evil away." Oksana shivered even though the evening temperature was still pleasant, and several times she pulled a blanket around her. "I must be coming down with something."

"Do you want another blanket?"

"No. Come sit beside me. Don't get any ideas."

Tommy sank into the plush stuffing of the couch and she slipped her arm around his shoulder and drew him to her. It was the first time Oksana had approached him and for the longest time he didn't move, barely breathed. He had not been this close to a woman in more than three years, and they laughed about how much he shook.

Then Oksana turned serious again. "Why should I help you get to Moscow? People are arrested for merely talking to foreigners."

"You shouldn't put yourself at more risk for me, but I could take you with me to Canada."

"How would you manage that?"

"The Canadian embassy in Moscow will help us."

"You think you can walk into the embassy and everything will be okay?"

"Why not?"

"You've been in the Soviet Union for three years and you still haven't learned a thing. What makes you think there are no spies there? If I went with you, the colonel-general would find me before we had even entered the building."

"I've noticed he seldom visits more than once a week."

"That's how long he dares to be away from Moscow, those few hours. Any longer and he would be the next shipped to Siberia."

"Well, if we left right after his visit, we could be safely out of the country before he found out you were gone."

"I'll think about it." Oksana stood and looked down at Tommy. "Good night," she said. "Good night, Tommy."

Tommy remained on the couch. It was more than an hour before he stopped trembling, and then he went up to bed.

Tommy felt something else too. Jealousy. Not so much because the colonel-general had touched her, was with her now, but because he had a place in her life that Tommy didn't have. Tommy was the promising stranger, nothing more.

Tommy had conjured faces for the colonel-general. Sometimes he was handsome, rugged, with the weathered face of a career soldier. Other times he was an ugly man, with unbalanced features and deep wrinkles from the weight of lies and deceptions.

The colonel-general's next visit marked Tommy's second month there, and he could not contain his curiosity about the man any longer, so despite Oksana's warnings, he tiptoed to the bottom of the stairs to listen. At first, the colonel-general's Russian was difficult to follow—he spoke differently than others Tommy had heard, with a few Ukrainian words here and there—but eventually he understood much of what the older man said. Between the words, glasses clinked.

"They are all fools. They think the boss will save them. He would cut their throat just as quickly as I could cut yours, Oksana. I loathe them all, including him. I spit in his eye and yet each week more disappear. I can't turn my back for a minute or I'll be a dead man. Even this dacha could do me in one day. Or you. Oksana, your beauty could do me in."

"Have you heard rumours?"

"Now I have your interest. Each time you are different. First you don't resist, and then you won't let me touch you. Now we barely talk. Why should I keep you here?"

"So I can listen."

"What good is listening? I could have a choice of a dozen whores if I wanted. All of them would listen, and pretend to love me at least."

"Suit yourself, then."

"Why can't you at least pretend to love me?"

There was a long silence, and all Tommy could hear was the tap of the colonel-general's boot.

"You hate me and yet you stay. Do you think I'm a fool like the boss, who doesn't know what you really think behind my back?"

There was a pause, and then the colonel-general said, "Stay. What is your rush?"

"This talk makes me tired."

"You could rub my neck like you used to. Then you listened and even laughed when I said something you liked. Now you barely say a word. Do you think I don't notice?"

Tommy was still awake when she knocked on the root-cellar door the next morning. When he opened it, she raised her hand as if to slap him but stopped herself.

"Don't ever leave this room again. You may not value your life, but I value mine. Thank God he's gone back to Moscow early. An important meeting, he said, but I think he's suspicious."

Tommy flinched. "I'm sorry." He didn't know how she knew he had been eavesdropping.

Her tone was cold. "Don't be sorry. Be smart."

She turned toward the light, and he saw that the right side of her face was blotchy.

When she saw him looking, she ran upstairs. "Don't look at me," she said.

He found her at the sink with her back to him.

"Stay away," she warned.

"Are you okay?" He reached out a hand but moved no closer.

"I'm fine. Besides, it's not what you think."

"What, then?"

"He is very dangerous."

Later, when Tommy went into the living room, he saw that the shelf that held the pysanky was empty. On the floor beneath it, the smashed shells had been swept into a neat pile. He turned to get the broom and Oksana was behind him, her eyes narrowed with rage.

"Leave them," she said.

At breakfast, Oksana spoke quietly. "You saw the ones who made it to the camps. They are the lucky ones. Many don't make it. Some are cemented in walls. Others hung upside down until they die. That will be our fate. A slow death. The colonel-general's specialty is slow deaths. He talks to his victims first, to find a way into them. Pries until he knows what they fear most. Then he gives it to them. He'd kill you before my eyes and put me out in the cold until my skin turns black. Once, he stopped a train on the way to Kolyma and summoned every second woman and her children out of the cars and into minus-forty cold. At gunpoint, he forced them to undress and left them there. He laughed as the train pulled away and they stood in the falling snow. He laughed all the way to town, and boasted about it for weeks after.

"Today is my mother's birthday," she said, bringing him tea from the samovar. "I wanted to be a Ukrainian dancer, like my mother and her three sisters. They travelled from town to town with their father. That was how she met my father. He repaired her shoes when she came to town. She stayed behind with him while her sisters travelled on, and it's they who are still alive in Canada. Sometimes love is what kills us." She paused, and then she said, "Do you think I could be a dancer in Canada?"

"I don't see why not. My mother was a dancer too. Every Saturday she used to push aside all the furniture in the living room and dance ballet for my father and me. My father would put on one of her favourite 78s. At first, I got bored easily and sometimes yawned and my father would give me a warning look not to disappoint my mother. Then she taught me to dance, and the year before she died, I finally saw how lightly she moved her feet and hands, how gracefully she spun and twirled in the air. Later I realized that one day a week she got to hold on to her dream a little longer."

"My fondest memory of my mother comes from before we moved to Kiev. She danced at my cousin's wedding, and my father smiled and clapped his hands so enthusiastically, I could see on his face the delight and love that had driven them together and that had made my mother leave dancing behind. I wouldn't willingly leave my dreams behind just for love. I have postponed my dreams, but I haven't abandoned them. Besides dancing, I would like a daughter someday. I will teach her Ukrainian and all the old songs. I want a two-story brick house, much smaller than this, but one a family would have room to move around in. Do they have such houses in Winnipeg?"

"Streets of them. Many as big as this. Even bigger."

"For those with money."

"There are many we could afford."

"Many we couldn't too."

"Yes. But there would be no NKVD to come in the middle of the night and take it all away."

"Not yet."

"There are shops off Main Street in Winnipeg where I can buy used furniture from Kiev, London, Paris, New

York. Dark wood, light wood, you can have your pick, cherry, oak, maple, ebony."

"I'd want a piano, and a fireplace. Sculptures by the front door. Oak floors. I want a brick house like this one, but with a modest number of rooms. Perhaps a maple staircase, and three bedrooms, no more. Running water and a proper kitchen."

"You can have electric appliances," Tommy said.

"Even if we make it past all the spies on every corner, what makes you think Canada will be so generous?"

"In Canada we don't need papers to move from province to province. We can travel freely where and when we want." Tommy wanted to boost his own hopes as much as Oksana's.

"Under the czar we had freedom too," Oksana said. "But only for the rich. Now Stalin protects our freedom. During the war he passed a new decree. If you were late five minutes for work you were docked a month's pay. If you were late twenty minutes, you were sentenced to seven years in a work camp. Once my mother slipped on the ice and had to run to work. She was four minutes late and was docked a month's pay. She thought her co-worker had advanced the clock, but she didn't complain because she thought she might be sent to a camp instead. That's how well Stalin protects our freedom."

Tommy had nothing to reply. "Maybe we could live near your aunts," he said.

"Wouldn't they be surprised?" She put her head on his shoulder and they sat in the quiet.

Tommy wondered if she believed a word of it. He wanted to believe, but even he found it difficult. He wanted to move ahead without the heft of the past, but he was no longer sure that such a future remained possible.

The next day Oksana, sober-faced, turned to Tommy and spoke words he could tell she had held back until now. "Before the war, there was a young man, Joseph. I met him not long after we moved to Kiev. He'd been studying music when the war broke out and was four years older than me. When all the schools were closed, he sold utensils in the streets. He moved from street to street to avoid the German police, and he visited me at night when Father worked in his shop. Mother was sweet on him, and she encouraged him to visit. Before the war, both his parents had been schoolteachers, but when the Germans closed the schools, there was nothing for them to do. One night Joseph came home to find his parents gone, driven to Babi Yar, the neighbours said.

"When he asked me to marry him, I agreed. He gave me this red scarf, and when I told Mother, we talked late into the night until Father begged us to go to sleep. The next morning I rushed to visit him, but he was gone, sent west by the Germans.

"After the war, Joseph traced me to Moscow, and surprised me. But one of the colonel-general's spies saw him leaving my place and within a day the NKVD arrested him because of his time in the West. He needed to be re-educated to our ways. He'd been too exposed to the filth and depravation of the West, the colonel-general told me. I could see in his eyes he was beside himself with glee. He claimed he sent Joseph into hiding for his own good. The colonel-general would keep him safe until the purges stopped. Then we could be married, he would not stand in our way. Very generous of him, I thought. Later he moved me to these woods, miles from Moscow, far from his wife and family, far from the temptations of other younger men. I thought I could love no one, but if Joseph came back, I wanted to try. I believed for a year that he was hiding, waiting for me, that someday the colonel-general would come and say it was safe and I could go to him. When I looked at that scarf, I saw him, and when its rough wool rubbed against my face, I imagined it was his hand reaching me from his hiding place.

"But after a few months, I knew. The colonel-general had sent him to his death. If he was hiding it was in his grave, and each night the colonel-general visited, I betrayed him again. He'd left me his red scarf to remind me of his love, but now it reminds me of his blood.

"I didn't need to ask the colonel-general about Joseph. I knew. I felt it each time his hands touched me. He thought I belonged to him.

"I live in this big house and all I have that's mine is Joseph's scarf. When you sat at my table that first time, I saw Joseph, not because you resembled him but because you looked hungry and hunted, the way he must have looked not long before he died."

Tommy shivered to think he had been someone else's ghost, and yet he felt grateful that for one moment her Joseph had lived through him.

"Do I still remind you of Joseph?"

"No. Your face has filled out. Besides, you cleaned the bathroom after your first bath here, and you pulled your hand away when I told you not to touch me. I'm not sure Joseph would have done either."

A few nights later, Oksana came to his room and stood by his bed without saying a word, but even in the dim light, he saw that something in her expression had changed.

"Slide over and lie still." She crawled in next to him, took his hand, and rubbed each of his fingers. "I couldn't sleep. Soon, the days will turn colder and then the snow, and you know how long our winters are. I couldn't last another winter here. You're thoughtful. I like that. Patient too. You're not in such a hurry like most men. They think big muscles make them strong, but sometimes you make me smile, and that is better. I haven't smiled much in a long time, and I don't know what can come of this, but maybe we can go to Canada, as impossible as that seems."

"That can't stop us from attempting it," he said, trying to remember when he had seen Oksana smile. He couldn't say he had, although he had often tried to elicit one.

She grasped his hand so tightly it hurt, but he didn't move. "I've been in this house too long. It's time to walk away."

Through the remaining two weeks of August and into September, Oksana went to Tommy's room each night and lay next to him. She wore either her red or her navy full-length cotton nightgown, each with its embroidered hem. The long sleeves and cuffs bunched nicely at her wrists, and sometimes she waited for him there when he came to bed. Other times he woke in the night to find her lying next to him. Occasionally she took his hand, but most of the time, they lay side by side and talked. He knew that if her touch had anything to do with desire, it was only the desire not to be alone.

One night a powerful wind snapped off branches and shook the house. A tree crashed down yards from the dacha. In the dark she came to him, and he could make out the watery halos of her eyes and nothing else. She lay next to him and whispered, "I couldn't sleep."

"When I was a boy and there was a storm, my mother would sing to me louder and louder until she drowned out the wind."

"My mother would sing to my father after work. She would sit with him near the fire and sing while he tugged on his pipe. For years, I wanted that life. They say in Ukraine that the wind is your future, not your past."

"My mother told me if you shout your wishes into the wind, they will come true. On windy days, we would stand outside and shout. After she died, I wished into the wind for her to come home. A part of me still believed the wind could bring her back. For a while, I even believed that she'd told me that secret so I could call her back to life. My father caught me once and told me not to expect the impossible. I was a kid and at first I hated him for that. Now I see that he didn't want me to be disappointed."

"We could go out in the wind now and try it." Oksana got up on her elbows so she could see Tommy better.

"Someone will hear us."

"Tonight I don't care. Tonight I want to believe your mother's story."

"What would we tell it?" Tommy asked.

"To take us away from here, of course." She got out of bed and ran to the front door and threw it open to the full force of the wind. The door banged against the house, but Oksana didn't try to catch it. She stood on the massive stone steps and cupped her hands to her mouth and shouted into the wind, "Get us out of here!"

Tommy joined her and cupped his hands and shouted the same at the top of his lungs.

They continued to shout until the wind brought a heavy, driving rain. They stood and let the rain flatten their hair against their faces. Only when they both shivered from the cold did they go inside and close the door.

Oksana towelled the rain from Tommy's face and hair, and he did the same for her, and then they returned to his bed.

In sleep she turned away from him, and he remained on his back making out strips of ceiling in the dark. He shut his eyes. He didn't want this moment to pass, but he also wanted to leap forward in time, to know if the wind had made their wish come true.

THIRTEEN

THE SECOND MORNING, she woke to the odour of manure even before the sun rose, and as she lay surrounded by farm noises she thought ahead to her birthday, two weeks away. Each year on her birthday her mother counted out the candles and pressed them one at a time firmly into the thickly iced cake she had made. Peter would stand back with the camera pointed at Judith as she blew into her wish. At her last birthday, less than two months after Peter's death, she blew out her candles and wished Peter could come back. Later she wished he had been there to take the pictures because her mother seemed awkward with the camera and she held it too close to Judith's face, so that when they got the prints developed, Judith looked like a smiling bug, her face distorted, someone else's.

When Peter's birthday came in August, Judith found her mother crying in her room. She remembered then what her mother told her as a child: "Birthdays are the one day we get to be special."

Even if her mother couldn't rescue her before then, Judith knew she would come for her by her birthday. She could last until then, and she'd do everything right so Mr. Thompson would say so, and her mom would know she could trust her again.

Breakfast consisted of the same oatmeal and orange slices as the day before. Judith kept her eyes a little open as Mr. Thompson prayed, so she could watch everyone. Mr. Thompson held his eyes tightly closed like a child pretending to sleep, and as she had yesterday, Heather jiggled her leg next to Judith's. Judith stole glances at her face to see if she opened her eyes too, but she didn't, and when Judith nudged against her, the leg stiffened.

After breakfast, Judith cleaned the stalls more quickly, and the shovel didn't feel as heavy as it had the day before, although much of her body ached. If she didn't exactly enjoy the work, at least the smell bothered her less, and not once did she let the shovel slip from her hands into the brown slop at her feet. She also devised a way to knot her skirt so it hung just below the top of her boots. Her legs were still completely hidden so she felt safe from Mrs. Thompson's disapproval.

Near lunchtime, Mr. Thompson checked in on her. He scanned the clean barn and said, "My father always worked hard. He came to this country after the First World War, from England, where his father had a farm. Once farming gets under your skin, it's hard to get rid of it, and he worked until the day he died. He got up early that day and sat at the table drinking his coffee. 'Michael,' he said, 'we need to clear that north block this summer. I don't want to die until it's cleared. I'll go take a peek after I finish in the barn.' Then got up and walked bow-legged to the barn. It was the last time I saw him alive. Funny what you remember about someone after they're dead. All those years I never noticed how bow-legged he walked until that morning, and then an hour later, he died in this very barn, shovelling dressing. I found him lying in it." He paused and then said, "I'd like to die like that, in the middle of work, partway through the day, far enough along from morning that my muscles ache, but not enough to want to stop."

Judith smiled, already understanding a little of why he might feel that way.

"Strange how we spend so much time around these animals, care for them day and night, and yet we know little about them. All we see are stalls filling up with excrement every day. Now and then a horse or cow might show some affection or recognition, but beyond that, there isn't much. I saw plenty of animals die by the time I was your age. Some I even buried, but it didn't affect me. Death didn't bother me one bit until that day my father died.

"When I found him, I bent down in all that dung, feeling for any sign of life, and I couldn't take my hands off him. I kept hoping that he wasn't completely dead, that somewhere inside, he was still there and could feel my hand and hear me. A week after I buried him, I started clearing the land he set out for the day he died."

"My father died too," Judith said. "I kicked him when he was dead, but that didn't bring him back to life."

"I'm sorry. I didn't know."

Mr. Thompson walked to the tap and ran some water over his handkerchief and wiped his brow with it. "Let's forget all this talk about death. Some things need time to heal." He looked into the sky with one hand shading his eyes. Then he looked back at Judith, and his eyes were sad. "Not even July yet and the heat's started. It's going to be a long, hot summer."

Judith nodded and ran water over her hands to wash away the dung. "When I saw my father lying on the ground I thought that death must be heavy to keep him pinned down like that. I don't ever want to die."

Mr. Thompson stripped his rumpled hat from his head and soaked it under the tap. "You must miss him."

Mr. Thompson saying that suddenly made her want to cry harder than she had since Peter's death, and she dunked her head under the cold water so he wouldn't see.

That afternoon, he took her out to mend fences, and as Judith left the smell of the barn behind, she realized that she liked working with him because he spoke to her like an adult and there was none of the tension that existed between her and her mother.

"I love mending fences. I could do it all day, every day. Especially on a hot day like today when your pores open up and you can feel the air ripple on your arms. Sweating is healthy. It's how our bodies clean themselves. My father used to eat garlic until he sweated. When I was a boy, I hated to go near him because he smelled so strongly of garlic, but when I got older, I didn't mind. The odour of garlic still reminds me of him every time I step into the kitchen and catch a whiff of it."

Judith held the barbed wire while he nailed. He never complained if she performed a task incorrectly, and the longer she worked the more she found herself wanting to please him. Several times in the thick of work, she caught herself smiling. She tried to imagine his father lying on the floor of the barn and Mr. Thompson reaching down to lift him up and carry him. If Peter had been covered in manure, would she have gone near him?

Later that afternoon, after a long, silent patch of work, he dropped his hammer between his feet and looked west toward the lake. "See that mare out beyond the pond? I'll teach you how to ride her if you keep up the good work."

Judith squinted at the mare. "I don't think so. I don't want to." Even from this distance, the size of the horse frightened her.

"Suit yourself, but if you change your mind, she's out there."

They went back to work, but Judith stole a glance in the mare's direction whenever a lull in the work permitted. Several times that afternoon she dropped the wire, or took too long getting more nails, but Mr. Thompson just moved quietly inside the work.

At supper, Mr. Thompson led prayer with a very short one that concluded, "Lord, thank you for bringing Judith to our home so that we might be able to point her your way, to show her through her labours that you will find a place for her in your heart." He didn't end his prayer with "Amen" as he usually did, but said only, "Let's eat."

"You'll need a little extra after a difficult day like today," he said and filled her plate with a heaping portion of mashed potatoes and roast beef. Judith caught the disapproving glance that passed between Heather and Mrs. Thompson, and held her plate firmly in her hand. Heather barely touched her food, but Judith ate hers quickly, not looking up until she finished. She had never been this hungry. She bit her tongue but didn't stop eating.

"May I be excused?" Heather asked, looking pained, as if Judith's appetite actually disgusted her. Mrs. Thompson nodded, and Mr. Thompson smiled and looked across at his wife. No one spoke at supper except to ask for a dish or to be excused. At the end, only Mr. Thompson and Judith remained.

Judith washed the dishes while everyone else collected in the living room to read the Bible, just as they did after breakfast. Mrs. Thompson played "The Old Rugged Cross" on the piano, the same hymn Judith's mother sometimes sang as she cleaned the house, and Judith heard the children's reluctant voices while Mr. Thompson bellowed at the top of his lungs. The thought of her own mother drew Judith to the living room, and when they finished the hymn, Mr. Thompson motioned her to join the rest of them. At first she felt too shy to move, but his kind smile allowed her to slip in beside Heather on the couch. Heather acted as if Judith wasn't there, but Judith smiled at her all the same.

The next week, Judith asked Mr. Thompson to show her how to ride. The mare was white with two large brown circles on each side of her face. Mr. Thompson offered the horse an apple, which she snapped from his hand so quickly Judith flinched.

"This here is Abigail. That was my mother's name. Abigail, meet Judith. Don't be afraid. Horses feel and think the same as us, and once a horse trusts you and loves you, they do for life. Remember, a horse will test you at every turn, but you have to be sensitive and know when to be tolerant and when to pull on the bit. With a horse, everything must be negotiated, like a family. Never force a horse to do something it doesn't want to do.

"Of all the horses, Abigail is my favourite. I delivered her myself. Her mother was a wild one, but Abigail is so gentle I'd trust her with a baby. I'll help you up, and then I'll lead her by this rope until you feel comfortable."

Up close, the horse was even bigger than Judith expected and she couldn't imagine getting on her back, but Mr. Thompson locked his fingers together and told Judith to put her foot in the cradle of his hands.

"This is the only proper way to mount a horse. It's called giving a hand up. My father showed this to me, and now I'm showing you."

Judith hesitated for a moment and then raised her foot cautiously to Mr. Thompson's hands. She felt his hands gather the strength to lift her onto the horse, and he guided her as she swung up and into place. Her long skirt was a nuisance and rode up to her thighs, but Mr. Thompson averted his eyes and said nothing.

They walked several times around the corral, until Judith felt comfortable enough that she could have taken the reins, but when Mr. Thompson asked her if she wanted to try it on her own, she shook her head. Her legs hurt so much when she dismounted that they trembled.

"Next time, then," he said as he stroked Abigail's back. Judith nodded and walked stiffly back toward the house.

All the next day, she worked hard, and by evening she couldn't wait to go out with Mr. Thompson to the horse. He taught her how to mount by herself, and she eagerly got on Abigail's back, not caring how much her legs hurt. She even took the reins and guided Abigail once around the corral.

For the rest of the week, they went out every evening, and finally Judith rode out into the back forty on her own. Abigail found a creek nestled under the cover of a few remaining spruce, so Judith dismounted and let her wade halfway into the creek to drink. As she bent over and splashed some water on her face, she longed for the smell of her mother as she knelt down to give her a kiss, or to see Adam sitting at the kitchen table playing with his food. Mr. Thompson was kind and the way he looked at her told her that he was capable of loving her, but the possibility of that was not enough. Every night she read the birthday card her mother had given her signed *Love Mom and Adam*, but with each reading it felt less true.

On her birthday, Judith frequently stopped work and looked toward the road for her mother's car. As the day progressed, she switched from biting her lip to kicking at the ground until she saw Mr. Thompson glancing at her and stopped before he felt the need to question her. In the evening she rode Abigail out to the creek and lay by the running water. She sucked on a stone and watched the sun's pink finish to the day, and when the sky began to fill with evening stars, and with the hardened, sun-parched ground under her back, she closed her eyes and sang "Happy Birthday" to herself.

It was dark by the time she rode Abigail back to the house, and Mr. Thompson was sitting on the front steps.

"Better get some sleep. We've got another early morning tomorrow."

"It's my birthday," Judith said, joining him on the step.

"Well, happy birthday."

Judith saw in his smile that he meant the words.

"Wait here," he said.

The screen door squeaked as it closed behind him, and while she waited, she watched the night sky and wondered if her mother was asleep already and if she had even remembered her birthday or had forgotten all about her.

Mr. Thompson stepped from the house clutching a small package in his large hand. "Here, it's not much. You should have given us a warning."

Judith unwrapped the yellowish foil and six barrettes fell into her hand.

"Do you like them?"

"Yes," she said, and then she hugged him quickly and ran inside before he could see her tears.

Lying on her bed, she held the barrettes and knew her mother wasn't coming. For the past week or more she had convinced herself that her mother would wait until her very birthday to surprise her. Now she knew that was just another fantasy, like all the rest. Even her mother couldn't be depended upon. She pulled the covers over her head and almost tossed the barrettes to the floor, but then she remembered Mr. Thompson's face when he handed her the gift. He really wanted her to have something, but what she wanted most was to hear her mother's car stop out front of the house and for Adam to come running in to say happy birthday, her mother not far behind, saying, "Sorry we're late, but happy birthday, sweetheart. Now pack your things, we're going." She imagined her mother thanking Mr. Thompson, shaking his hand. "No problem," he would say. "We liked having Judith around, but she belongs at home."

She fell asleep still grasping the barrettes.

Except for Heather, the Thompson girls were too young to do much work around the farm, so Heather minded the others during the day, taking them to Black Sturgeon Lake every afternoon. Two days after Judith's birthday, when there was a lull in farm chores, Judith joined them.

The water was icy, as it was still only mid-June, but Judith didn't mind the cold and happily treaded water as she watched families collect on the beach. She watched a mother walking with her daughter along the sand. The child's laugh skipped across the water to Judith, and the glare off the water stung her eyes. *Were we ever as easy together as that?* she wondered.

She splashed her face and then swam out toward the middle of the lake. Heather called for her to come back, but Judith paid no attention. She swam until her lungs hurt, and then she swam back to join the Thompson children. On shore, she dressed slowly while Heather glared at her.

"You think he likes you, don't you? He takes you out on the horse, but he laughs at you and says you're stupid behind your back."

"That's a lie."

"I hear him talking to Mom. They don't want you here except they need the money. And because of that I've got to a share a room with someone like you who stinks and steals." Heather walked up to her. "You're a thief. You stole my barrettes."

"Go to hell!" Judith said, picking up her pace to leave Heather behind.

When they got back to the farm, Heather whined that Judith had kept them late by refusing to get out of the water. One of the sisters started to say that it was Heather who had dawdled, but Mrs. Thompson grabbed Judith by the ear and pushed her toward the stairs. "Never again. That's the last time you're going to the lake. Now get to bed and stay there until morning." Judith stumbled, and Mrs. Thompson was about to pull her hair again when Mr. Thompson gripped her arm.

"That's enough." Mr. Thompson took Judith's hand and helped her up. "Are you all right?"

"I'm okay. Leave me alone." She pushed his hand aside and ran up the stairs.

When the girls came to bed, Heather put her face close to Judith's. "Open your eyes," she said. When Judith ignored her, she stood a little back from her and spit in her face. Judith waited until Heather slipped into her own bed before she wiped her face on the sheet, and then she heard the other two sisters giggle.

For the next several nights, Judith practised getting past the sleeping sisters, and when she felt brave enough, she even tiptoed to the door of Mr. and Mrs. Thompson's bedroom and watched them sleep. Part of her knew Heather had lied about Mr. Thompson, but she could never stay with them until Christmas. She had to go home, even if she risked her mother's anger. If Judith could only talk to her, she knew she could convince her that she'd never steal again. She wouldn't be any trouble at all.

Several times, she ventured out into the front yard and sat with the dog so that he became comfortable with her midnight prowls. She took him out to the barn to visit Abigail, and she talked quietly to the horse and stroked her, careful to rub under her chin. Once, the barn door swung open and banged against the side so loudly she felt certain she had been caught, but only moonlight swept in.

She practised unhitching one of the cows and guided her to the exit. She wouldn't have time to lead them all out, but she hoped that once a few were free, the rest would follow. The cows would serve as a distraction, so even if the dog gave her up, or the horse, she would have time to reach the highway.

Heavy cumulus clouds filled the sky the night she left, but undaunted, she walked toward the barn. The dog followed her as he always did. She left a bone for him to chew on in the barn and lit one of the coal-oil lamps so she could see as she guided some of the cows toward the back doors. One of the cows was reluctant to leave her stall, and even when Judith tugged at her halter, she wouldn't budge. Finally Judith slapped the cow's side, and the cow bolted, knocking over the lamp, which smashed in flames. Judith kicked at the shoots of fire, but her efforts only spread them into a pile of hay, so she ran for Abigail, freed her and the other three horses, and guided them to the exit. Smoke already filled the barn and she barely got out before flames engulfed it. The dog was barking wildly and Judith saw a light go on in the house just as she rode Abigail through the front gate. Beyond the main gate, she felt suddenly free and urged the horse into a gallop.

She looked over her shoulder and saw a red glow in the gaping barn door. She smelled flesh burning, and heard several cows bawling. Thunder sounded overhead and a few drops of rain splattered her hot face. She imagined the sad look on Mr. Thompson's face as he watched the barn burn. He had been kind and she respected him, but he'd hate her now. It would no longer matter that Heather had lied, because Judith had done something much worse. In her haste to escape, she had hurt the one person she liked. She couldn't avoid blame for bringing the lamp into the barn, but if only she could have saved all the cows, he might have recognized that she hadn't meant to start the fire.

More lightning filled the sky, and then thunder so loud Abigail reared and Judith nearly slipped off even as she clung to the reins. When Abigail settled back down, Judith gave her a quick jab to her side.

The fire would distract them for a while, but eventually they would search for her. She only hoped it would be much later before they called the police.

After riding nearly fifteen minutes, Judith couldn't smell smoke any more, and instead the smell of fish told her she was beside Black Sturgeon Lake. On the far shore, she saw porch lights shimmer on the lake's surface in long strips of light, and she heard a wolf howl. Spooked, Abigail turned and bolted back toward the Thompsons'. Judith tugged hard on the bit to stop her, but just when she managed to turn the horse around and guide her back toward the highway, rain poured down on her, and Judith had to trust Abigail's instincts. Within a mile of the highway, the horse stopped on her own. Judith dug her feet into Abigail's side, but the mare held fast. Judith tried to wait her out and then gave her two final kicks before she dismounted in frustration.

Her clothes were soaked, and she shivered and pressed herself against Abigail's steaming flank. In the east night already relented. She walked around the horse several times, but Abigail just snorted into the cool air. "Come on, girl," Judith said. She stroked the horse's snout, but Abigail would go no farther. Judith slapped the horse's hindquarters and sent her back toward the farm before she ran for the highway.

The rain stopped and the storm passed on to the east. Few cars appeared at this hour, but whenever one passed she hid in the bushes, afraid it might be Mr. Thompson.

His car came out of the dark just as she could see the highway ahead. She knew it was him as soon as she saw the lights. She ducked into the bush and watched his car pass within thirty feet of her. He would turn her over to the police and she would be sent to reform school for sure. A boy at school had been there, and he said they beat him daily.

Mr. Thompson drove alone, searching slowly, and he stopped up the road and called her name, and then drove on. Soon he came back the other way, nearly at a crawl. When his car had vanished around the curve, Judith ran.

The fire had ruined her chances of going home. She couldn't face the shame she would see in her mother's eyes, and even if her mother agreed by some miracle to let her stay, the police would send her away anyway. Or the Children's Aid woman. At the highway, she ran toward Winnipeg, stopping only to stick a thumb out at any vehicle that passed. At first none stopped, but as the daylight grew and she became more visible from a distance, a few began to slow down, and one eventually stopped. Two men sat in front and one in the back seat. The man in the passenger seat rolled down his window.

"Look what we have here!"

Judith stepped back a little, and the man jumped out of the car. He was nearly as tall as Mr. Thompson. Judith bent down and picked up a big rock.

When the man advanced toward her, she threw the rock. It caught him just below his left eye.

"Come on, Frank. Get back in the car. She's just a kid, for Christsake."

The car edged ahead a little, and at first Frank took no notice—he kept his eyes fixed on Judith. Then the car moved a little faster, and Frank chased after it until it slowed and he slammed the side with his fist. He jumped back inside.

"Stupid bitch!"

Judith stood trembling while the car sped off up the highway, and then her legs buckled and she rolled into the bush. She lay shaking as a few more cars passed. She thought how it would mean nothing to anyone if she stood in the middle of the highway and waited for a transport to run her over.

FOURTEEN

OKSANA JUMPED FROM THE BED and went briefly to the window to consider what she had just done. September had passed, and Tommy had been with her nearly four months. In recent mornings, the sun had taken until eleven to completely clear the taller beeches and oaks to the east. This morning, it managed to poke only a few pale fingers of light between the leaf-laden branches, to illuminate the squirrels hunting through the woodpile. She paused only long enough to see one sprint across the top of the firewood, its claws invisible. Oksana dropped the knife as she fled the room.

For weeks now they had worked out a plan of escape. She couldn't say for sure when it became their plan and not just his. It wasn't as though she woke one morning and knew that she wanted to go with him, or even that she loved him. At first they were together during the day, then more in the evenings, and finally their conversations changed to include what they saw or liked in the other.

One day, as soon as the colonel-general left for Moscow, they would ride his horse to a village to the southwest, cutting a diagonal course between Jaroslavl and Ivanovo instead of south toward Gorky and the main road west to Moscow. Oksana knew where a car could be stolen in the village, and for more than a year she had been waiting for her chance. From there they would drive to Moscow, where she had contacts who could direct her to the Canadian embassy. Once inside, Oksana would seek asylum with Tommy's sponsorship. They could even be married there to please the authorities. Marriage was not something she took lightly, and she would prefer to wait, but if marriage was necessary to reach Winnipeg she would marry Tommy with confidence that their union would last.

In speaking of Winnipeg, Tommy had constructed a city for her not unlike her beloved Kiev, one carved through by two winding, restless rivers, a city of extremes, summer and winter, one that was the gateway to commerce and a great surrounding rich and prosperous plain. It was an infant city by Kiev's standards, but like Kiev it was committed to the arts, to the best in its citizens. What appealed to her most was Tommy's description of the concert halls, ballet stages, and theatres. He described a place that was on the verge of outliving its powerful past and now fought to hold on to its glory. The streets were broad, he said, wide enough that even the tallest buildings would not shade everyone walking below.

They had planned to flee by the end of October, before the cold weather hit, but the colonel-general's visit last night had changed everything.

Earlier in the evening, his eyes, lit by excessive wine, had darkened to hard, cold orbs. "I can smell him. Don't think

I don't know. He'll suffer worse than Joseph. With him, I was kind. This one waits until I'm gone and then he slips in here. You are his whore, not mine. I could slit your throat and drive across Moscow with your head on my lap and no one would care. I could tie your body to the trunk of my car and no one would care. The dead don't matter. They have never mattered. I could put a hose in your mouth and fill you with water until your insides exploded and no one would care. I stole you away from death and now your death is mine. I will do it slowly, better than I've ever done it before. Just for you."

He slapped her and then drank another glass of wine. "Stay away from me. You stink," he said, and then he lay down in bed, certain of her powerlessness. Often when he drank he tried to make her lie one more time, tell him how much she loved him, worshipped him. This time she said nothing, so he slapped her.

She knew he was bluffing again. If he really knew Tommy was in the house he would already have had them killed.

The knife had been there for months, long before Tommy arrived. She'd held it and sharpened it, lain it next to the revolver. The revolver was for strangers, the knife for him. It could cut through flesh like butter. Just one slice and it would be over.

She opened the drawer and retrieved the knife, cold against her palm. She knew she had to make the cut deep enough because she would only have one chance. As she waited for the right moment, his breathing stopped altogether. It wasn't the first time it had happened. He suffered from sleep apnea, and once, before Tommy had arrived, the colonel-general had stopped breathing for more than two minutes before he started again. Now she prayed his heart would stop and he would save her the trouble of killing him, but before she had counted to sixty, he took a greedy gasp and her unrealistic hope was quashed.

She waited until his breathing became regular again, then she put the blade to his flesh and sliced across his neck in one quick firm, motion. She jumped back when he sat up and reached out in front of him, and she heard the hiss of air escaping the wound. He spoke only the sputter of a word, and then his head dropped back to the pillow.

As often as she had imagined killing him, she took no pleasure in it now. It was necessary, that was all, and she couldn't allow herself to think or feel.

At nine o'clock the car would be back. The driver would find the colonel-general and then what? She dressed and went to the kitchen, stuffed food into a sack, and hurried downstairs to Tommy.

"Wake up," she said and pounded on the door. Tommy opened it immediately, his eyes still sleepy.

"We must go. Now. Hurry. The colonel-general is dead."

"Did you kill him?"

"I don't want to talk about it. Just dress quickly."

The horse smelled the colonel-general on Oksana and kicked wildly at the stall. Death brings notice of itself, travels from body to body. Twice she ventured toward the horse and twice it attacked her.

Tommy eased open the stall and walked up behind the mare. The animal reared once and then settled as he mounted. He coaxed it out of the stall, and then Oksana climbed on in front of him, her hands grasping the horse's mane. She nudged the mare to life. It protested once more and then bolted out the barn door. She dug her heels into the horse's side and it galloped past the house and down the gravel road. Neither looked back but bowed their heads to allow the horse better speed. With her head down, Oksana pressed her knees hard into the gelding's warm sides. Tommy held on behind, pressing his face against her.

Horse and riders cast small shadows in the rising sun as they sped across the wakening countryside. The gelding's charcoal flanks blended with shadows as they followed a line of trees, camouflaged except when caught briefly by the sun. The car coming for the colonel-general would already have left Moscow and would be winding along the familiar roads. Oksana dropped her head lower so she could breathe freely and Tommy did the same. He held her tighter than she held the horse.

They rode southwest without stopping. The village Oksana sought was only an hour away, but they couldn't approach it until dark. All the same, Oksana wanted to get as far from the dacha as possible before the driver discovered the colonel-general.

Oksana stayed to side roads and avoided even the smallest of villages until they neared the one where, on two previous occasions, she had seen a brand-new Moskvich sedan parked with keys in the ignition. The car belonged to a local party official who believed no one would dare steal it.

She stopped in a grove of trees outside the village. As soon as they dismounted, Oksana clapped her hands together and gave a sharp yip to scare the horse off. They hid throughout the entire day, sleeping when they could, talking anxiously occasionally, but mostly lying side by side staring at the sky through the trees. In late afternoon they ate half the bread, cheese, and apples Oksana had put in the sack, and as soon as it was dark they walked to the car.

Tommy stepped up on the running board of the passenger side as Oksana got in behind the wheel. The car started after the third turn, and Oksana sped out toward the road. A few barking dogs trailed behind them. Lights in several houses went on, but otherwise the night remained undisturbed.

They drove for half an hour, and then Oksana backed the car between two dense hedgerows in the far corner of a large cemetery. "Parked by the dead, we're safer. No one will disturb a car here, even at this hour."

They planned to approach Moscow in the morning to avoid suspicion. Driving at night in the Soviet Union meant trouble.

Oksana fell asleep with her head crooked into Tommy's shoulder. He stayed awake listening. These past months had stretched to the point where he barely remembered another life. He finally closed his eyes and slipped into a calm, hopeful sleep.

At dawn, they woke to rain. They sat quietly together, listening to the rain pebble the car's roof, and then ate bread and cheese without speaking. Oksana started the car and let it warm up. She looked out at the clearing sky.

"No more rain today," she said. She shielded her eyes from the rising sun and then looked south toward Moscow. "By tonight, we'll either be safe or dead."

They waited until the road had some traffic, light as it was, before setting out, and the trip took less than an hour. Outside Moscow, Oksana stopped the car on a side road, and Tommy got into the trunk as planned. They had entered the city of suspicion, and Oksana could be arrested for even being seen with a foreigner.

Tommy could feel the car slow and speed up, and he imagined Oksana's slim, determined fingers curled around the steering wheel. Even when the car stopped, no sound of her travelled to him. He longed to hear her voice one more time, afraid that her soft instructions to get in the trunk were the last words she would say to him.

The car stopped abruptly. Tommy heard voices, none of them Oksana's, and then the door opened and shut. The car sped off, this time with some urgency. He feared that a soldier had pulled her out and jumped inside and was now driving furiously toward prison. He braced himself as best he could, but he jostled wildly as the car twisted and turned through the streets. He banged his head and groaned. The car stopped a second time, and this time he heard Oksana call his name as she worked the lock. When the trunk sprang open, he stepped out and straight into her arms.

He heard her crying as they embraced and he felt her back give a little. Oksana kissed him for the first time on the lips, and she held the kiss before she pushed him away.

"We must go quickly," she said. They were alone in a narrow alley. She took his hand and pulled him toward the street up ahead. They emerged from the alley hand in hand, lovers out for a stroll, except that Oksana's fingers were stiff and slippery in his. Two militiamen in long blue coats with red-and-white tabs were stationed in front of the Canadian embassy on Starokonyushenny Pereulok, a safe but busy part of the city. The embassy was a grand two-story sandstone building with two pillars in the front and a marble entrance, and like its neighbours on the street seemed more French or Italian, even Roman with its harsh corners and bold facade.

They strolled casually back to the alley.

Oksana was undeterred. "Most buildings in Moscow are guarded. I expected as much. This is what we will do."

They each approached the building from opposite sides so the militiamen wouldn't suspect they were together. Oksana walked toward the building holding a folder of papers she'd found in the glove compartment of the car. She tripped and fell in front of the militiamen, spilling the contents of the folder. One of the men helped her to her feet while the other collected the papers. They didn't see Tommy slip inside the building.

Oksana quickly joined him. "I told them I had a job interview. For once the colonel-general's name was useful. I said he recommended me for the job."

The security guard in the foyer stood at attention when they approached. Tommy noted that he was unarmed. He told the guard he wanted to see the ambassador. "There is no ambassador at the moment. There is a chargé d'affaires, but he is away in Leningrad."

As he spoke, the man looked more at Oksana than at Tommy. He asked her in Russian if she was with Tommy. She nodded and took Tommy's hand.

Tommy asked to see whoever was in charge. The guard returned a few minutes later with a severe-looking young man with a moustache. He shook both their hands and introduced himself as First Secretary Boyd. He ushered them into his office. Before sitting at his desk, Boyd turned on the radio and Russian voices blared from the speaker. Tommy thought the radio inordinately loud, but Boyd waved his hand to take in the room and then pointed to his ear.

Tommy recounted his story, and asked that they be sent to Winnipeg.

Boyd listened intently, giving Oksana two inquisitive glances when Tommy told him her story. Tommy did not mention the dacha or the colonel-general, only that Oksana had helped him come to Moscow and that he wished to marry her.

When Tommy had finished his story, Boyd leaned back in his chair and stroked his moustache. Then he excused himself.

"Your people are not very welcoming," Oksana said.

"Everything will be okay," Tommy said. He wished he felt as certain as he sounded. The radio now blared drab Soviet music. The musicians approved for broadcast were no match for the great Russian composers, who were no longer heard.

Tommy slid his chair closer to Oksana's and they held hands and waited. On the wall behind Boyd's desk was a large clock flanked by pictures of the King George VI and Prime Minister Mackenzie King. He had taken such pictures for granted in his youth when he saw them in classrooms and offices, but now they brought a rush of emotion. He squeezed Oksana's hand and she squeezed back, but she remained unusually quiet. His own heart raced as the realization sunk in that he had finally made it safely to the Canadian embassy. For three years he had dreamed of this very moment.

Boyd returned and sat down again behind his desk. "Do you have any papers?" he asked Tommy.

"I have nothing. Even my identity disks were taken by the Soviets."

"I see."

"And you, do you have an exit visa?" he asked Oksana.

"No."

He fished in his pile of papers for a moment and then excused himself a second time.

"I don't like this. I need to get out of here." Oksana moved toward the door.

Tommy rose. "Oksana. Wait." He saw the look of panic on her face.

Boyd opened the door, surprised to see them standing. He waved them to their seats.

"May I be candid? This room is the only one that is not bugged in the building and I can't be one hundred percent certain of that. The guard in the foyer could be a spy. Certainly the militiamen are spies. Everything we do is tracked. We are under siege." He placed his hands flat on the desk and looked from one to the other. "So suppose your story is true. Even you will have to admit it sounds incredible. We can protect you here until we contact Ottawa by encoded telegraph later today, when their offices open. But within no time the Soviets will know you are here." He turned to Oksana. "Your case presents a different problem. We have a small staff here. When Gouzenko defected in Ottawa in 1945, he revealed Canadian spies providing information to the Soviets. Relations between Canada and the Soviet Union have been chilly ever since. We have not had an ambassador here since 1947. Although in Canada we could grant you asylum, it is a much different situation here. We face the risk of being accused of smuggling spies out of the Soviet Union."

"Is there any chance you can get us out?" Tommy had his first feelings of real foreboding.

Boyd look at them and smiled patiently. "Even embassy staff who marry Russians have trouble getting their spouses exit visas when they are transferred. We are very isolated here. We have little contact with Soviet citizens. We meet with Soviet diplomats, send dispatches by mail or encoded telegraph if they are too sensitive. That is about all. Even amongst our local staff, I am never certain who are spies. The NKVD could already know you are here."

"We should go," Oksana said.

"No, you are safer here. They aren't as likely to come inside these doors. You won't last out there. Not with your friend. Frankly, I'm surprised you made it this far. I will see what I can do, but it may take some time. For now, you can stay here, but for your own good, you should not leave the building."

Tommy and Oksana spent the rest of the morning and most of the afternoon in Boyd's office. They spoke little, conscious of the microphones, and although they lay on the office floor at one point, they could not nap.

Boyd returned in the late afternoon. "We have a wire from Ottawa. There are certain questions about your war experience that Ottawa wishes clarified."

"Such as?"

Tommy felt Oksana stiffen at his side.

"You have never been officially discharged from the army. Until yesterday you were considered killed in action.

"Obviously I'm alive."

"And if your presence here is detected, there may be nothing I can do. If you're believed dead already, the Soviets may decide they have nothing to gain by resurrecting you. The good news is that you've gone unnoticed so far. Getting you out presents other problems. There are few civilian flights from Moscow abroad at the moment and we could not risk the train to Leningrad. Fortunately, I've learned there is a cargo flight leaving for Stockholm tomorrow. I will see about some papers for you both."

Tommy and Oksana slept little that night. Soon the stolen car would be discovered, and then what? Tommy wished they had left it farther away. He had expected his countrymen at the embassy to greet him with open arms. The missing war vet and his fiancée. He could have written the headlines himself, had already imagined them in the *Winnipeg Free Press*, but he and Oksana had been out of touch with world events for too long. He realized now he had been naive to think that once he reached Moscow the last three years would be magically resolved. Moscow was as much under siege as it had been during the war, only this time from within.

They watched the sun come up from the direction of the Moskva River, the sky heavy with yellow cloud. They held hands, and without saying so, each knew that today would determine the rest of their lives.

When the sun rose higher, Boyd appeared with a bag of fruit and bread for them. He had the cheerful manner of someone with good news and he seemed genuinely happy for them when he produced some doctored papers. "Good enough to get you both out on the cargo plane. You're Canadian diplomats returning with our mail."

At ten that morning, they left in Boyd's car. Traffic was light, because few people had cars, but the streets were filled with people. Tommy watched as the city rushed by. Three years he had dreamed of Moscow, and now it was vanishing before him in a blur.

Next to him Oksana faced the window, her hands limp in her lap. "You know," she said, not looking at him, "I will never be free of Moscow. Its twisted, weathered streets will be inside me forever."

They travelled southwest toward Vnukovo airport. Boyd had explained that no one, not even the crew, suspected that they were anyone other than what their papers said. Tommy feared a checkpoint at every street. Oksana seemed remarkably calm beside him.

The driver took care of the first stop, and all went well. At the airport, he braked at the cargo area, where a single guard watched their plane approach. The guard took both their papers and went into his office. He returned with them stamped for exit. Tommy and Oksana walked up the metal boarding stairs and into the nearly empty hull of the plane. Cargo planes arrived in the Soviet Union full and departed empty.

Four rows of passenger seats had been fitted near the front of the plane. Two older men already occupied two of the seats. Tommy and Oksana sat next to each other and buckled themselves in. Tommy could feel Oksana tremble beside him, and he shook too. He willed the crew to close the doors and get the plane off the ground.

Oksana leaned close to him and whispered, "I love you."

I love you too. He only mouthed the words, but she watched his lips as he did, and then looked in his eyes and stretched her mouth in a half smile. He extended his feet and tried to appear relaxed. Then he looked out the window and saw a guard boarding the stairs. Tommy's face remained expressionless, but his hands sweated and he clasped them to control their shaking. Now what? Why didn't they close the doors and leave before something went wrong?

The guard entered the plane, looked at the other passengers, and then focused on Oksana and Tommy. He approached them and asked to see their papers again. Oksana and Tommy sat rigidly next to each other as he peered at their passports. His examination was brief.

"One moment," he said in Russian.

Oksana asked if anything was wrong, but he turned and left the plane without responding. "He's being a good, officious Russian," she said to Tommy.

But he saw in her expression the same wariness she had worn the day he arrived at the colonel-general's dacha, when she had stood with a gun pointed at his chest.

The guard re-appeared at the cargo door. He called to her and waved her to come with him. She rose. Tommy got up, but she pushed him back into his seat. "No," she said. He rose again to follow her to the door. "No," she said again. He recognized the hard tone from before.

Their papers were already stamped. Surely they couldn't detain her now. The guard pushed Oksana ahead of him, and Tommy reached out to grab him, but the man pushed him back. When Tommy stepped forward again, Oksana had already reached the bottom of the stairs, and two men in NKVD uniforms flanked her. Tommy stepped out onto the stairs, but two more NKVD men appeared and started up toward him.

"Davay," one said as he pushed Tommy back into his seat. Through the window, he could see Oksana being forced into the back of an NKVD van. Then the door to the plane was shut and one of the soldiers pointed his gun at Tommy. If he left his place, there would be no trial, no gulag, only a bullet.

He gripped the arm rests of his seat and his heart felt as though it would beat right out of his mouth. How could this be happening? Then. *The bastards. The fucking bastards.*

The plane waited a long time before takeoff, and Tommy hoped that by some miracle Oksana would be released. But then the plane taxied out, and in no time they were in the air. Tommy felt Moscow sink away from him, and for the longest time he kept his eyes painfully closed. What had he done? Or more to the point, what could he have done? And what must Oksana be thinking? That he had betrayed her to gain his freedom? She looked so vulnerable, so uncertain, when she glanced back from the door of the plane and disappeared into the monstous machine from which he had just escaped.

The man next to Tommy obviously wanted to say something, but Tommy turned away from him and clenched his teeth against him and against his own great stupidity. For three years he had nurtured the fragile dream of freedom, even as every moment taught him despair. Only a moment ago it had felt entirely possible as he had dreamed it, and now here he was in the air, his release a few hours away, but for what? He might have felt gratitude, indeed he knew that intermingled with everything else, he likely did feel immense relief that he had at last left the murderousness, the inconceivable madness of the last few years behind, but for what good, without Oksana? She was the only woman he had ever loved, and what did it say about his ability to love that he could feel any happiness at all? For all he knew, she might soon be consigned to the very horrors he had escaped, worse by far than the loathsome life she had lived with the Colonel General, and it was Tommy who had convinced her that escape was possible.

Good god, what must she be thinking? Would she believe that he had ever intended all that he said, or would she think he had sacrificed her to save himself? After all that had happened to him, couldn't he have seen this coming? He should have planned for it, worked around it. He should have gone after her. But if he had tried to get off the plane, they would have shot him. If they hadn't, he would never have had a second opportunity to leave. And no matter what he had done, he knew with desperate certainty, he would never see Oksana again.

He held his eyes tightly closed, unable to look at the cargo door she had been forced out. They might as well have reached in and torn out his heart. At least then his pain would have a single, identifiable source. The plane banked, and he pushed his knees into the seat ahead of him for support. He crooked his head sideways and opened his eyes, searching for the sun. When he was in the camps, he had sometimes stared into the sun in an attempt to block everything else out, but all he could see out the window was a bank of clouds.

III

*Now when these things
begin to take place,
stand up and raise
your heads, because your
redemption is drawing near.*

LUKE 21:28

FIFTEEN

KATERINA WENT TO THE KITCHEN to slice some *babka*. Out the window Tommy saw the bare maples and oaks that lined the road to Katerina's farmhouse, and beneath them a recent dusting of snow.

"My sisters will be here shortly," she said. "Russell was up late with a sick cow so he's resting, but he might pop his head out later. We don't get many visitors from the city, not once the snow hits, at least."

Katerina's kitchen was small, with flat white cupboards and a painted table pushed up to the window. Tommy saw they lived modestly, with few hints of Ukraine, except in the living room, where he had seen pysanky eggs on a shelf next to a cabinet radio.

She brought a tray from the kitchen and placed a cup of tea in front of him. "Aneta and Ionna are looking forward to meeting you. It's been a long time since we've had much news from home. Too long."

Katerina had told him they had not heard from Oksana's mother or father since the beginning of the war.

Aneta and Ionna both looked away when Tommy told them about Oksana and her family, but Katerina held his gaze until her eyes filled with tears. She told him that Oksana's mother and she had been very close, hardly separated until Nadya married.

"We feared all three had died during the war. So at least Oksana survived. That's something. They would have been happy here. Petro could have set up a shoe repair shop in Winnipeg, Nadya could have taught dancing classes. But to have gone that way . . . Here." She thrust a plate at Tommy. "Have more cake. There's plenty." Katerina pressed a date square and another slice of sweet *babka* on Tommy before she passed the plate to Ionna.

"Oksana's parents lived for her. You would have liked them. Petro was the best cobbler within a hundred miles, and Nadya—how my sister danced. They tried a long time to have a child, and finally the angels brought them Oksana. I remember the day Nadya laboured and how Petro paced in their small kitchen. That girl was the happiest baby that ever lived, and as she grew, she talked all the time. In school she won all the debates." Katerina stopped to dry her eyes, and she smiled widely through her tears. "She laughed at everything, and made others laugh with her, but she was smart. Everyone predicted a great future for her in the Party."

Tommy could easily imagine Oksana leading others in the Party, but the war had changed her. Oksana had rarely smiled. When she did, sometimes it was tenderly, but most often her lips twisted as a result of wry observation. He couldn't remember a single time when she laughed freely.

Katerina brought out the few family photographs she had collected. Cameras had been scarce in the Soviet Union, so she had only one picture of the four sisters together, dressed for a performance. Oksana bore a stronger resemblance to her aunt Katerina than to her mother, although Nadya pinched her forehead the same way Oksana pinched hers when she concentrated.

The most recent photograph of Oksana was taken when she was ten. She had braids in her hair and stood beside a pony. Tommy saw hints of the woman he knew— the same wide mouth and full lips, the same roundness of her eyes. Petro stood behind her in a snow bank, his hand waving tentatively. Oksana grasped the pony's mane with one hand and looked defiantly at the camera. Tommy could tell by the puffiness beneath her eyes that she had been crying, and Katerina told him that her father had sold Oksana's pony for food, and that only minutes after the picture was taken the new owner led the pony away.

"I want to go back for her," Tommy said.

"Oh no," Ionna said, glancing at her sisters. "They'd never let in you in, and even if they did, any attempt to find her or contact her would only cause more suspicion and get her arrested."

"That's true," Katerina agreed. "There's nothing we can do. If anyone can get out, Oksana can. She was as strong as her mother, perhaps stronger, but there's nothing you can do now. Nothing any of us can."

"I can't just wait. I need to do something." He told them that his first impulse after receiving a dishonourable discharge from the army was to board a plane back to the

Soviet Union. Instead, he flew to Ottawa to visit the Soviet embassy, but that got him nowhere. The embassy didn't track relatives or lovers, it promoted trade and good will between the two countries. He called the Canadian embassy in Moscow and was curtly informed that they had no knowledge of an Oksana Yerenko. When he asked for Boyd, the first secretary was always out or busy and never returned his calls.

"In the Soviet Union," Katerina said, "people vanish every day, but Oksana will get word to us if she can, you'll see. As with all things in the Soviet Union, you must wait."

Tommy knew that with each passing day the news could only be worse. Yet the sisters convinced him, and by the time he left Selkirk he had agreed not to make matters worse by returning to the Soviet Union. Hardly an hour passed when Tommy did not think of Oksana. To say his life was diminished without her could not begin to express how he felt. The lack of any news from the Soviet Union made everything he imagined possible: She was dead, or worse, tortured. He prayed it was not true.

To relieve his anxiety, he smoked marijuana, something he had avoided when it was available to him during the war, but a fellow veteran smoked to ease the pain of his shattered legs, and he had suggested that Tommy try it. So long as he was stoned, he didn't feel. As soon as he stopped, his body ached with not knowing.

More than anything, he wished there was something he could *do*. He might as well be living in another time period, for all the good he was to Oksana. He missed her the most at mealtimes, though he couldn't explain why, and so he learned to cook elaborate dishes he imagined presenting to her, but eating them alone made them flavourless.

When he remembered her most clearly, he was reminded that she had always spoken frankly and practically, even when she had struggled for the correct word in English, and in his heart he knew she would have sided with her aunts. He could almost hear her admonishing him not to be stupid, or pathetic, to use logic, not emotion. There was nothing he could do, except exactly what Katerina had said. He could wait, as they and others had waited for many years before him.

But still when he closed his eyes at night, he saw Oksana being pushed into the NKVD van. He wanted to remember that she had looked up at him, but he could never be sure the memory was anything more than his own necessary construction. They had been duped, all of them—Oksana, Tommy, even Boyd. The papers had come too easily. The Soviets may have wanted Tommy out to prevent a scandal, but they would never have let one of their own go.

In the coming months and then years, word from Oksana never did arrive. Tommy called the family or visited at least once a month, usually with Katerina. Aneta died in 1952, and Ionna not long after, and when Russell died, Katerina moved to a house in Winnipeg's East Kildonen and spent the summers at Victoria Beach with her daughter.

Katerina was still lucid, and each time Tommy visited he learned more about Oksana and her family.

In 1957, after nearly a decade with no word, Katerina phoned Tommy to say that Oksana's cousin, Dimitri, who had recently fled to France, had written to her with news of Oksana. A friend of his had been imprisoned in one of the Siberian camps shortly before Stalin's death, and there he met an Oksana Yerenko. Over several months he and Oksana had struck up a friendship, until she became ill and died only three months before Stalin's death, in March 1953.

Katerina's voice broke, and the receiver felt heavy in Tommy's hand. His legs trembled so much he had to sit on the floor. He had known this moment would come, had expected it, had even believed that he was prepared for it, and still he had hoped. Even as the months of silence became years, even knowing that if Oksana were alive she would have found a way to get word to them, he had managed to hope she was well and in Moscow, living as best she could there. He thought he had come to accept that he wouldn't see her again, but to hear it confirmed this way was like having his chest sliced wide open.

Dimitri's friend had not said how long Oksana had been in Siberia, and Tommy hoped it had not been since 1948. After the long train journey to Vladivostok, she would have faced another journey by cramped ship north to the port of Magadan. There she would have been led from the ship when the sky was not yet light, and Tommy could almost hear the growl of the engine and the sound of tires chewing into heavy, fresh snowfall on the Kolyma highway. No one would have spoken, and metal would have creaked against metal as the van turned north. Regardless of the details, she was gone.

He hung up the phone and went to his study. He closed his blinds, lit a dozen candles, and sat in the amber light. He took out a bottle of vodka and drank, but even that didn't ease the ache that he felt would consume him. His shoulders shook, and silent tears streamed down his face.

In the years following the news of Oksana's death, Tommy wrestled daily with the knowledge that his freedom had cost her life. Any moment spent alone seduced him with his morbid fantasies of all he might have done to wrest Oksana from the NKVD, instead of watching helplessly as she was dragged to her doom. So he turned to the only business that made sense to him. He bought a two-story house on Flora, and he began the long job of completing the necessary renovations for its operation. To further occupy his mind, he collected books and works of art and expanded the large study he currently stood in to house his collections, but nothing eased his nightmares except the marijuana he smoked when sleep proved impossible.

Sensing the weight of the book in his hand, he remembered why he'd come upstairs and returned his copy of Crime and Punishment to its place in the bookshelves. He'd finished the book the night before and wasn't in the mood for another, although that didn't stop him from running his fingers along the rows of books, mostly novels and poetry, or perusing one here and there before returning each of them. He really *wasn't* in the mood, he decided, and instead he examined the largest of the pysanky eggs that lined the oak window ledge behind his desk. Most of the eggs he had found in shops along Main or Selkirk, but this particular one was special. A blue-green fish swam over an underlayer of solid black, and white flowing leaves circled the fish. The craftsmanship was exceptionally skilled, so the egg stood out amongst the others for its beauty as well as its size. But more than that, Katerina had given it to him, and it was forever a link to Oksana. He rubbed a few bits of dust off the egg's polished finish and returned it to the shelf. Across his desk he saw his father's certificate of undertaking that he'd found buried in a box after his father's death. He had framed it in rosewood and it hung next to a photograph of his father in a suit.

Usually Tommy found his study the most comfortable room in the house, and he would sit in his stuffed leather office chair and read or do work surrounded by books and a few things collected from his past, but today, he felt more restless than usual, as if reading Dostoevsky had stirred up his own painful memories of the Soviet Union.

He thought a drive might do him good, and soon he was aimlessly cruising the streets of Winnipeg. He drove east for nearly three hours to Kenora and stopped at the cemetery, a couple of blocks from the paper mill. Regardless how many times he walked the final twenty paces to his parents' graves he always felt his heart speed up.

Today he stayed longer than usual, and even straightened up some twigs and branches the wind had collected over their graves, not brushing them aside but absently lining them up neatly around the edge of the plot. When the afternoon heat caused him to perspire he walked slowly back to his car. On the drive back to the city he didn't pay much attention to the scenery, and hardly noticed the change from dramatic rock cuts to flat prairie.

When Tommy first spotted the girl, he wasn't certain that she was hitchhiking, she stood so far off the road. She was practically in the ditch, and rather than look at Tommy's approaching car she peered down into the grass as if she was about to scramble into it. Most hitchhikers this far from the city would have had their thumb out long before Tommy's car reached them. Part of him wanted to drive on, but he couldn't pass her by when he was the only car in sight. He slowed a bit, and the girl thrust out her thumb at the last second. Tommy pulled over on the shoulder. In the rear-view mirror he watched her approach, struck by her odd pioneer costume. She could have been going to the corner store, or to a costume party.

SIXTEEN

JUDITH APPROACHED THE black Chrysler New Yorker. The driver lowered the electric side window and waited for her to come alongside.

"I can take you as far as Winnipeg," he said. He looked away and patiently let the car idle as if he had all the time in the world. She preferred that to the slow once-over of most men. Nor did he say, "Get in," like the last guy.

Judith peered in at the driver. He had a high forehead and faded brown hair. He was well dressed, fashionable like the men in the pages of the magazines Judith read every chance she had at Johnson's pharmacy. When she was satisfied that he looked harmless enough, she let herself admire the claret-coloured leather of the interior. The car had bucket seats, and the wide gap between the driver and passenger seat appealed to her. The seats shone, as did everything in the neat interior.

Judith took no chances and climbed into the back seat. She was surprised how easily the door shut, and how new and fresh the car smelled. The air conditioning blasted even into the back seat and Judith felt a pleasing chill as she ran her hand along the cold leather seat. She raised her skirt enough to allow her to cool the back of her legs against the leather.

For the first few miles, they rode in silence, except for wind noise, and there was little of that. Judith had never ridden in such a new, quiet car. She could see through the gap between the front seats that the man did not have his foot on the gas and yet the car maintained a steady speed.

"Don't you have to use the gas pedal?" Judith asked.

"Autopilot, Chrysler calls it. Others call it cruise control. It keeps the car at a set speed. This is the first car I've had with that feature." He caught her eyes in the rear-view mirror. "I'm Tommy Armstrong."

"Judith," she said, and leaned forward to give the hand he offered a quick shake.

Someone her age on the road alone was asking for trouble, Tommy knew, but he kept this to himself. He also wasn't used to the scrutiny she gave him before getting in the car, not that he had minded. Sometimes a little suspicion was wise. Tommy turned on the radio, keeping the volume low.

Now she was on her way, Judith reconsidered her plan for when she reached Winnipeg. The thought of finding her way through the confusion of streets now terrified her. Shirley was her only contact in the city, but Judith had little desire to face her aunt alone.

Judith hadn't been to Winnipeg since early the previous summer, when her mother took her and Adam to visit Shirley and Cathleen. As they neared the city, her mother had annoyed her by saying, "You were born in Winnipeg," as if she didn't already know that. Her mother had annoyed her often last summer.

She especially irked Judith when she tried to sound understanding. "All girls get a bit cranky at your age," she would say, and that made Judith want to scream that she wasn't like all girls. *Why do adults always think they've lived everything I've lived?* she had thought then. It had been her first summer without Peter, and she wished—still wished—that adults would leave her alone. Yet here she was, alone, and so far she didn't feel any better.

Shirley and Cathleen lived in a large house that smelled of cats, although Shirley didn't keep one. "The bastard who lived here before us had twenty cats. I wouldn't have stayed here a day, except the landlord lowered the rent so much I couldn't afford to say no. I was between jobs, after all. Once cat pee gets into carpet you can't get it out."

"Shame to ruin such lovely carpet," Alice had replied, and that annoyed Judith too.

Shirley had a good job downtown, so Judith wondered why she and Cathleen still lived with the cat pee smell, especially since, unlike Alice, Shirley was never afraid of moving on.

It annoyed Judith that her mother said nothing to Shirley about the smell, nor did she want to talk about it on the way home, even though Judith kept coming back to it any chance she could. After a while, her mother kept her eyes on the road and acted as if she didn't hear what Judith said.

Judith didn't know whether Shirley still lived at the same address. For all she knew her aunt had fled south, as she had threatened to do so often. The closer Judith got to the city, the less she wanted to knock on Shirley's door. Shirley would insist on calling Alice, and Judith worried that neither her mother nor Shirley could prevent her from being sent to reform school. What she had hoped when she set out for Winnipeg was that Shirley would hide her until the whole matter blew over, but she realized now that going to her aunt's had never been an option. Shirley was too loyal to Alice.

"I was just visiting my parents in Kenora," Tommy said. "In the cemetery. I do that whenever I get a chance."

Before she could catch herself, she said, "My father's dead too. Not my real father. He's a bastard."

She hadn't planned to tell this guy anything. He was as old as Peter and what could she have in common with him? But her mouth worked faster than her brain sometimes. She'd need to be careful. He could try anything now that he knew she didn't have a father, but she'd be ready this time. She'd jump out of the car if she had to.

"My mother died when I was only eight," Tommy said, and he watched her fidget in the rear-view mirror.

They rode in silence the rest of the way into the city. He had no close friends, and he had not allowed himself to get close to a woman. Now here was another wounded child needing care and some explanation while he confronted a fist knotted inside him that he didn't know how to unclench.

Judith watched the outskirts give way to the newer treeless neighbourhoods, and then finally the clutter and noise of the downtown itself. Now she'd have to fend for herself on these busy, alien streets.

"Where would you like me to drop you?" Tommy asked when they neared Portage and Main, the heart of the city.

"Anywhere's good," Judith said. Except now that she had got here, she didn't want to get out.

"Are you on your own?"

"Yes, I'm fine." She opened the door before he could get too nosy.

"I've got a place in my back yard. It used to be a carriage house, but I had it converted and I let people use it once in a while. You can stay the night there if you want—it'd give you a chance to get your bearings. It might leak, but otherwise it's cozy."

"No funny stuff?" Judith said. *Watch the older guys—they like them young,* Shirley had warned her.

"God, no. You can lock the door. I won't even come around. Except to leave some food if you'd like some. I could put it outside on a tray."

It would be easier, even sensible, to simply let her go on her way, but he also knew where she'd end up.

"Do you have a family?" she asked.

"None living. I've got an idea. I'll give you the key and you can check it out. If you like it and want to stay, just lock the door and you have the place to yourself. You won't even see me until morning. And only if you want to. When you go you can leave the key on the table, like a hotel. No questions asked."

Judith didn't tell him she'd never been to a hotel.

"I'll stay in the car until you're safe inside. There's a phone in there, so feel free to call someone if you need to."

"And you'll stay in the car?"

"I'll do whatever makes you feel comfortable."

SEVENTEEN

Dear Judith,
Adam is asleep, and I am sitting at your desk, the one
Peter made for your twelfth birthday. He worked for a
month to get it just right and he hid it under a blanket for
you to find. His reward was the way your eyes grew wide
when you finally uncovered it. I don't know why I'm writ-
ing about your desk.

These past months, with no news of you, have been
worse than the ones right after Peter died. The uncer-
tainty of where you are leaves me feeling drained of
energy, and my imagination torments me. I try not to lose
hope, but it's so hard, it's like my mind won't let me think
anything positive. If the news were good, wouldn't you
have called? I searched for weeks and then months, many
of them in Winnipeg with Shirley, but now all I can do is
wait for you to return on your own. The police told me
that only one certainty exists with runaways: those that
survive eventually come home. As long as your dead body
does not show up, there is hope. I can't believe I even
wrote that down.

You don't know how much I miss you. Every morning I wait for you to emerge from your room and make these past months all a bad dream. I'm truly sorry for any hurt that I've caused you. Every chance I get I dust in your room or line up the books on your desk, little things to make your welcome as warm as possible. I want you back more than anything in the world and I will do anything to make that happen. Adam misses you too and has worked as hard as anyone at trying to find you.

Lately I've been finishing Peter's old projects to keep myself from going crazy. I hired some men to haul away his old junk, and I finally got a proper bathroom put in, complete with plumbing and white tiles around the tub and shower. And I repaired where the kitchen floor heaved, laid linoleum, and covered the old studs with drywall. I painted the walls cream, you wouldn't believe how good it looks. I sold the piano to pay for some of the renovations.

I had the sawmill hauled away, except the wooden frame. I burnt that one evening near sundown. I just stood there and watched it turn into ashes until that's all that was left. When they cooled, I shovelled fresh snow over them. Peter would understand what that means, even if I can't really say it in words. "You go on ahead without me," he often said when I asked him to go for a swim or for a walk down to the lake. If he didn't want to join me, he never wanted to hold me back.

I visited Mr. Thompson. He seemed really nice (his wife wasn't there). He made coffee, and he pulled out my chair like a gentleman. I said sorry to him about the barn, but he refused my apologies. He said you didn't mean any harm. I was afraid he'd be angry, and I figured he'd be really strict. But he was nice. I didn't think you would run away from someone like that. Then I thought, maybe you were running from me? Judith, that would break my heart.

I know I've made mistakes with you, and I've kept secrets from you, but I plan to change that starting now. We need to be open with each other and I realize I have not done a good job of that myself.

I should have told you a long time ago that Rudy was your biological father, but Peter loved you even before you were born, and we both wished and hoped you into being his daughter too. He suggested the name Judith, after Judy Garland, because of her red hair in *The Wizard of Oz*, and when I first set eyes on you, I knew the name was perfect. You should have seen him beaming. I realize now that we were wrong to keep all that from you, even if Rudy was long gone. It was never meant as a lie, but we should have been straight with you right from the beginning, as soon as you were old enough to understand.

What I want more than anything now is news that you are all right. When you come back—God, please come back—and finish high school and go on to university, Adam and I will move with you to Toronto or Winnipeg, anywhere you want to go. Maybe I wouldn't work as a waitress any more if we were in a big city. I would try something new. I could work in a department store maybe, maybe I could become a teacher or a nurse. I want you to be proud of me.

*And I'm not angry! I only want you home. Please
come home and give me another chance. From now on
everything will be better, I promise.*
    Love Mom

Judith woke thinking she was back at Burnt Lake, but as
her eyes scanned the room, the now familiar painting on
the wall opposite her bed reassured her that she was still in
the carriage house. Until she came here, she hadn't realized
that people put paintings in bedrooms. Her walls at Burnt
Lake were decorated with posters she had received in the
mail and with pictures she clipped from magazines.

The furnishings too were unlike anything she was
accustomed to. They were made of wood and looked old,
in a pleasing way, not at all like the few things her parents
had purchased at Campbell's Furniture in Kenora. Those
items had been made of wood veneer, though she only
learned the difference when Adam broke a corner off the
coffee table and exposed the pressed wood inside. She was
particularly proud of the low teak bookcase Tommy had
recently bought her to organize the books she had collected since her arrival. The top shelf contained those volumes she had already read but wanted to keep, and the
second held a generous number she had yet to read. The
third shelf was reserved for library books and the one closest to the floor contained a stack of magazines she still
flipped through occasionally.

When she was dressed, she went to the main house.
Tommy had prepared bacon and eggs, which he served
with thick slices of toasted rye bread. He smiled at her, and

for a moment, with the sun reflecting off his war-ruined teeth in such a way that it disguised the blackened fillings that otherwise marred his smile, she saw that someone her mother's age might consider him handsome. Certainly he was better looking than Peter had been, though the fillings, along with scars on his cheek and forehead, gave him a slightly malevolent look that had made her uneasy at first. She had grown accustomed to his smile, and was fond of the many wrinkles around his eyes. She smiled back.

"The flowerbeds along the fence need to be cleaned up before the snow."

"I'll do them this afternoon."

He nodded, and Judith liked it that she could please him so easily. He had been looking happier lately, and she knew the change had to do with her. When he finished eating he cleared his dishes and left them in the sink for Judith. When he cooked, she cleaned.

Tommy went out back to the shelter of the Manitoba maple, and through the kitchen window Judith watched him puff as she ate her eggs. He had cut back on the number of joints he smoked, but he hadn't given them up altogether, and they made him different. A bit silly and absent minded.

"I only smoke them when it gets too bad in here," he told her once, pointing to his head.

He was much better off financially than her mother could ever hope to be, yet he had few real friends, though there were often others about. She wasn't his only charity case, and Judith couldn't count the number of times he had taken stragglers in and let them stay for a while.

He helped them find work and sometimes he even provided them with money, telling them there was no need to repay it.

"I've had my share of hardship, and relied on others myself" he said, by way of explanation. "It feels good to help."

Tommy had the biggest brick house on Flora, with numerous windows that gave it a bright, airy feel, and he had explained when she first arrived that he ran a booze can, one of several that flourished along Stella and Flora, alongside a healthy share of churches.

At first Judith hadn't known what to make of the idea. She'd heard her aunt Shirley talk about booze cans, but somehow they had always seemed dangerous and seedy, not better than her own house or any house she could ever have imagined.

But Tommy assured her that bootleggers in the city were nothing like the ones in small towns. "The police turn a blind eye. In fact some of my best customers are off-duty police officers. You're as safe here as anywhere in the city."

True to his word, he ran a perfectly respectable business, and in three months she had never been disturbed in the carriage house by the nightly comings and goings at the main house.

But although he had been direct with her about most things, he was as vague about his past as she was, and only recently had she dragged out of him that he had been in the war and had been wounded there. Since then, he had told her a few of his experiences, like what it felt like to jump out of a plane or have a rat nibble on his ear, but nothing that would explain a sadness so deep even a fifteen-year-old could recognize it. To encourage him, lately she had begun to tell him a few things about herself.

One topic that remained off limits was her mother, although in recent weeks Judith had wondered often what her mother must be thinking and feeling. The police or Mr. Thompson would have contacted her about the fire a long time ago. Was she angry? Did she hate her? Probably she wished Judith had never been born, but even if she did, Judith couldn't stand the idea of her mother worrying about her. She wished she could let her know she was safe, but how? If she telephoned, couldn't the police trace the call somehow? She'd heard they could do that, and if they found her, she'd go to reform school for sure. And if she sent a letter, they would know from the postmark that she was in Winnipeg, and if the police knew that, wouldn't they double their efforts to find her? She had considered telephoning her mother and asking her outright to promise not to tell the police, but if Alice had allowed the Children's Aid Society woman to take Judith, wouldn't she turn her over to the police as well?

Besides, she was probably as happy as she could be, right here. Tommy gave her responsibilities and allowed her to make her own choices, and he paid her well for doing the jobs he didn't like doing himself, like gardening and cleaning. And he allowed her to keep her own schedule. Her mother had always insisted Judith do her chores on certain days. Tuesday nights for laundry, ironing on Saturdays.

——

When Judith finished clearing up after breakfast, she returned to the carriage house and read until early afternoon, when she went to work in the flowerbeds. Last week she had raked leaves for hours, and by the look of the flowerbeds it would take even longer to pull out all the dead stems and pile them in the corner of the yard where Tommy had shown her how to alternate plants and leaves to make compost. The air was cool now, and she could use the money.

In July and August the heat and humidity had made the afternoons stifling, and the evenings had been worse yet, but she had enjoyed watching the flowers bloom and fade, and now there wasn't a single one left—no peonies, poppies, nasturtiums, or bellflowers—only the stalks that had once held them. She hadn't been keen to get her hands dirty at first, she'd had enough of that at the Thompsons', but by the middle of July, when the heavy heads of the peonies needed staking, she propped them up proudly.

When she finished with the first flowerbed, she washed up in the carriage house and got ready for dinner. She and Tommy always started dinner preparations at five sharp. Today, as Judith measured out ingredients for the biscuit recipe he had placed on the counter, she watched him chopping garlic. He did it so much more methodically than her mother, fanning his broad knife in a half-circle, chopping quickly first one way through the small mound of garlic and then the other until it was thoroughly minced. Her mother had been happy with large chunks of garlic, which she quickly tossed into the frying pan, but Tommy carefully slid the minced garlic off the chopping block and into the pan with three calculated passes of his knife.

She stopped her mixing to stare at the quickness of his hands.

"You can't stop mixing once you start. The biscuits won't rise properly," Tommy reminded her. He finished chopping green onions and deposited them into the pan with the garlic.

Judith folded the dough over and over, pressing each fold under with the heels of her hands as he had shown her. She loved the soft give of the dough.

"How did you learn to cook so well? Were you ever married? Or did your mother teach you?"

Tommy stopped what he was doing and looked for a moment like someone caught in a lie. She expected him to evade her questions as he'd done several times in the past, but he returned to his preparations and surprised her by telling her more of his war experiences, and then about Oksana, about cooking with her and dreaming. She had wanted children and he had wanted to have them with her. Oksana dreamed of dancing and of teaching her daughters to dance. Tommy and Oksana had even talked of teaching others to dance as both their mothers had wanted to do. Most of all they would have grown old together.

They fell silent.

Finally Judith spoke. "Were you a hero?"

"Definitely not. There aren't many heroes in a war, and I certainly wasn't one. I was an ordinary kid," he told

Judith. "I hadn't even thought about Europe other than the little bit of history and geography I took in school. I wasn't prepared for war. I thought I was, but once I was over there, I knew I was lost. But I couldn't just walk away."

"Why not?"

"Guys who tried to walk away usually ended up dead. Others vanished and no trace of them was ever found. In a way I was one of those. We had to kill, and hide, and walk past the dead until we had fewer and fewer words for any of it. Before the war I thought I might want a family some-day, but after the war it seemed impossible." Tommy took the dough from her and began to roll it out.

"Because of Oksana?"

"Yes."

She hadn't really expected him to say yes. She didn't know what she had expected, but his simple yes, with no further elaboration, left her feeling careful, and she didn't know how to respond. The war was distant and easier to talk about than the death of someone he loved. She had been hearing about the war all her life, but she'd never met anyone who had fought in it.

"What was that like? Did you have to kill people?"

Tommy stopped rolling out the dough. "Look. I under-stand that you're curious, but the war isn't like anything. It is the worst possible experience any person can have. I did and saw things during the war that I'm ashamed of, that I can't ever take back. I killed a girl your age. I didn't mean for her to die, but I killed her all the same." Tommy stopped. "God, it's been nearly twenty years, and in all that time, I've never told anyone that."

Judith stood motionless and silent. Tommy didn't seem like a killer.

"Her name was Freda."

Tommy began cutting the dough, and now Judith watched his hands in a new light. Had he killed her with his bare hands?

"I never knew much about Freda, except her age and where she was from. She had a mother who loved her, much as I imagine you do."

He sounded crosser than she was used to, and he must have seen the hurt look on her face, because he turned away. Judith found her mouth taking on a stubborn set whenever he mentioned her mother, but she felt something new too, the desire to confess secrets of her own, so she told him about being sent to the Thompson's, even about the fire, something she had been certain she would never tell anyone.

Tommy listened, and reassured her that he believed the fire had been accidental, then he repeated the few words Freda had spoken to him, and he told Judith what he had surmised about her life. Some of the details he must have only imagined because he said that he thought she had been happy before the war, that if not for the war she would have grown into a fine person, with many friends and admirers. He stopped then, as if he understood there was no way he could know what might have been.

Judith interrupted only a couple of times to ask for more details. She understood his silences now. His stories weren't any easier to tell than hers.

"Why did you say you killed her?" Judith said at last. "The Americans did that." She wished she could say something more helpful, but she didn't know what.

"I'm still responsible."

They stood through a long and awkward silence. Judith stole occasional glances at him and chewed her bottom lip, and Tommy looked from her to the biscuits he shaped.

That night, Judith tried to concentrate on her book, but she kept losing track of the story as she replayed Tommy's revelation. She slept but woke later feeling restless. She went for a drink of water and saw that it was nearly three in the morning. When she looked out the window, she saw Tommy's house still brightly lit, and in the windows, men stood talking to other men until they disappeared from one window and appeared in another. A woman came into sight and then out again. The window closest to the carriage house was large and four-paned, with stained glass in the top two panes. She could see the back of the burgundy couch and the oak bookshelves.

Her eyes darted from pane to pane as she searched for Tommy's thin frame. When she couldn't spot him, she went back inside, sat by the window, and watched until only the kitchen light was left on. Then she crossed the yard to the back door. Tommy was cleaning up. He looked tired, but his eyes flared a little when he saw her.

"Did we wake you?"

"I couldn't sleep."

"Can I fix you some warm milk?"

"Sure," Judith said, unsure what she really wanted to say. "I was thinking about Oksana and Freda," she finally managed.

"I shouldn't have told you so much."

"No, I want to know. It made me sad for you, that's all."

"It was a long time ago." He said it lightly, as if there was nothing more to say, but the awkwardness was still there between them. The milk came to a boil and he removed it from the burner and added a drop or two of vanilla to each cup.

"This will help you sleep," he said. He took a sip himself. "And me, too."

They both drank in silence, and in the east window Judith watched the first pink hints of sunrise.

After Judith left, Tommy went to the study and closed the door. He sat at his desk and contemplated lighting a joint before going to bed, but tonight there was no appeal in it. Before Judith, he had avoided telling anyone about Freda, or the war, or all that happened after, including Oskana, partly out of shame, partly because he didn't want to be seen as one of those men who cried into his beer, and mostly because there really hadn't been anyone he wanted to tell before. He hadn't meant to say anything tonight, either, but it was out before he could check himself, and he couldn't think why.

He had spared Judith many of the unsavoury details, like how Freda had looked in the tent and in her grave, and he didn't describe the cruelty and even eagerness on the faces of the soldiers. He described her physically in great detail, because Judith had asked, but had he traumatized her? Was she afraid of him, is that why she couldn't sleep?

She had seemed to understand, but how much could she, at her age?

He still woke some nights drenched, the nightmares vivid even after twenty years, and all the dreams brought back images of Freda lying in the tent, of the family at the farm, and of all the others that died nameless to him, their faces half gone. All the same, since Judith's arrival, the dreams were less frequent. His intention had been to help her, but something in her presence was helping him as well.

As September turned into October, Tommy knew Judith should be in school, but she was still skittish whenever they left the house, and he assuaged his conscience by convincing himself that, for the moment, she could learn as much reading in the safety of the carriage house. Yet if she stayed much longer, he would have to insist she enrol in a school come January. He still pressed her occasionally to call her mother and let the woman know she was okay, but Judith balked whenever he mentioned it, and he didn't want to push too hard. Besides, Judith talked more about her aunt than her mother, so something must have happened to strain their relationship. Until she told him otherwise, he could only imagine what sort of backward abuse she ran from, and the way he saw it, she was better with him than anywhere else he could imagine.

Tommy temporarily closed his booze can, telling his customers and Judith that he needed a holiday. He didn't need the money, and if the customers left for another house, some of them would return when he reopened, if he reopened. Most mornings he woke refreshed, and when he had showered and dressed, he walked to Dunn's Bakery for a sweet bun for Judith. It made his day the way her face lit up each time he handed her one after breakfast.

He brought a copper samovar up from the basement and set it up in the kitchen on a small metal stand. He had packed it away when he learned of Oksana's death, a too poignant reminder of the time spent with her, but now he kept a flame lit all day under a dark brew.

When the first snows arrived, Judith took long hot baths in the carriage house, where she filled the tub to brimming with hot water and luxuriated in the jasmine-scented bubble bath Tommy had bought for her. She felt a tiny bit guilty because she didn't reciprocate Tommy's many special gestures as often as she might, but when she mentioned this to him, he taught her graciousness by saying that her company was pleasure enough. So occasionally she bought flowers for his desk or forbid him to enter the kitchen while she tested her skill at baking cookies. Once she carved *Thank you* in a fresh bar of soap and left it in the downstairs washroom. He came out waving it.

"Your family really *must* miss you," he said. "You've got to at least call them, or allow me to."

"She'll send me to reform school," Judith said, with far less conviction than she might have a month earlier. For the longest time, she had believed that her mother would turn her in, and that the consequences would be dire, but lately she wondered which she dreaded more, her mother's betrayal, answers to her own questions, or the possibility of life with a shared bath. To avoid the answer, she promised herself that by winter, the police would have forgotten about her and it would be safe enough to contact her mother.

One day in early November, Judith saw her aunt Shirley on East Main. Judith had been on her way to the corner store on Selkirk to buy magazines when she spotted Shirley half a block ahead, right in the middle of the sidewalk, plain as day. She knew it was Shirley because of her unique walk. Her aunt kept her head straight and hardly moved her arms.

"You've got to walk with grace," she had told Judith once. "Most people flap their arms around as if they were birds about to take off. Look at your mother and do the opposite."

Now Shirley was walking toward her with her eyes fixed straight ahead while she listened to the man next to her. Judith's heart leaped and for a moment she wanted to run straight up and give her aunt a hug, but at the last minute she ducked into a shoe store instead, and watched her aunt approach. Despite the cold, Shirley's coat gaped open to her brightly coloured dress, hemmed an inch above the knees. She had her hair bobbed the way Judith had seen on models in *Seventeen*, but didn't dare do herself. Most women Shirley's age would look silly in such a get-up, but Shirley pulled it off. In fact, Judith had never seen her aunt look so good.

Shirley was smiling as she went by the storefront, and Judith couldn't remember Shirley ever smiling much. She had always seemed edgy and on the verge of anger, so that for years Judith had been both in awe of her and half-afraid.

Judith hid in the store for ten minutes, and then she went back to Tommy's without buying a magazine.

She tried to convince herself that she was mistaken. She hadn't seen her aunt in nearly a year, and the woman had been smiling, after all. But she knew. Shirley had passed her on the street and she had hidden from her. Unbidden, the lyrics from the "House of the Rising Sun," came to her. She knew exactly what it meant to turn your life bad and want to turn it good again. So much of her present life felt good and complete, but she couldn't deny that her mother deserved more than these months of unforgiving silence.

"I want to see my mom," Judith told Tommy the next morning. "And I'd like you to meet her. But I don't want to stay there," she hastened to add. Her matter-of-fact delivery belied the churning she felt inside.

"I'd like to meet her too," Tommy said. "Should you take your things with you, in case you change your mind?"

"I won't change my mind. I like it here better."

"I'm glad to hear that, but won't your mother have a pretty big say in all this?"

As they neared Kenora, the trees pushed close to the highway and Judith's palms began to sweat. She pushed her hair back for the hundredth time and tried not to feel all stopped up, as if she were about to step into a trap and knew better. Over and over she argued with herself. Tommy had accepted responsibility for the events of his life, and she needed to do the same.

She looked across at him, his eyes alert as his hands made small, timely adjustments to the road. He hadn't smoked a joint in weeks, and he had an appointment with a dental specialist next week. It's a shame he hadn't been already, but her mom would see past his teeth. If not for Tommy, she might not be making this trip, and if he could survive all he'd been through, she could set this one thing right.

The snow was thicker here, and it swirled up around the car whenever they passed another. At the end of this highway, some new version of her old life waited. The light outside the front door of her mother's house might already be on.

ACKNOWLEDGEMENTS

I WISH TO THANK the Canada Council for the Arts and the Alberta Foundation for the Arts for their generous financial support during the completion of this novel. I also wish to thank the DeVry Institute of Technology for a sabbatical to work on earlier drafts. My thanks, too, to the following people, who shared information and experiences along the way and provided invaluable insights: Greg Gerrard, Cathy MacKay, Peter Slezak, Henry Mycan, Ron Johansson, Brian Hilles, Pam Hilles, Cathi Whyte-Tetrault, Robert Tetrault, Jack Tempman, John Hilliker, Wendall Holmes, Julia Iscariot, Yuri Gerasimov, and Falk Huettmann. Much thanks to my editors, Suzanne Brandreth and Maya Mavjee, for seeing the possibilities. Their careful detailed readings and editorial suggestions were always valuable, insightful, and sensitive. To my agent, Dean Cooke, for offering editorial guidance in the beginning when it was needed most, as well as helpful suggestions along the way. Also thanks to Nick Massey-Garrison for various timely suggestions, to Shaun Oakey for his keen eye, and to Martha Kanya-Forstner for editorial input; and all the people at Doubleday Canada and Random House Canada including Valerie Gow, Stephanie Gowan, and Carla Kean. And to Austin, Breanne, Amanda, Woody, my mother Hazel Hilles, the memory of my father Austin Edwin Hilles, and my paternal grandmother, Estelle Hill, whoever you were. And to my cousins: Grace, Bonnie, Raymond, Ronald, Dennis, and Bruce, and my uncle Paul.

Besides the Internet, libraries, and archives, numerous books were helpful during the course of writing this novel, including: *Babi Yar*, A. Anatoli Kuznetsov; *The Gulag Archipelago*, volumes I to IV, Aleksander I. Solzhenitsyn; *One Day in the Life of Ivan Denisovich*, Aleksander I. Solzhenitsyn; *Man Is Wolf to Man*, Janusz Bardach and Kathleen Gleeson; *Soldiers of Misfortune: Washington's Secret Betrayal of American POWs in the Soviet Union*, Jim Sanders, Mark Sauter, and R. Cort Kirkwood; *POW/MIA: America's Missing Men*, Chimp Robertson; *Moscow Journal*, Harrison E. Salisbury; *Our Man in Moscow*, Robert A. D. Ford; *Moscow Despatches*, John Watkins, edited by Dean Beeby and William Kaplan; *Canada's Department of External Affairs*, volume I and II, John Hilliker and Donald Barry; *The House of the Dead*, Fyodor Dostoyevsky; *Journey into the Whirlwind*, Eugenia Semyonovna Ginzburg; *Kolyma Tales*, Varlam Shalamov; *Torn Out by the Roots*, Hilda Vitzthum; *True Stories*, Lev Razgon; *Transit Point Moscow*, Gerald Amster and Bernard Asbell; *An American in the Gulag*, Alexander Dolgun and Patrick Watson; *From Poland to Russia and Back, 1939–1946: Surviving the Holocaust in the Soviet Union*, Samuel Honig; *Gulag: A History*, Anne

Applebaum; *Hope Against Hope*, Nadezhda Mandelstam; *Inside Russia Today*, John Gunther; *The Fall of Berlin 1945*, Antony Beevor; *The Fall of Berlin*, Anthony Read and David Fisher; *Six Years of War*, Volume I, Col. C. P. Stacey; *Citizen Soldiers*, Stephen E. Ambrose; *D-Day: June 6, 1944: The Climactic Battle of World War II*, Stephen E. Ambrose; *Parachute Infantry*, David Kenyon Webster; *London at War*, Philip Ziegler; *Reporting World War II: American Journalism 1938–1944* (Library of America, 77); *Reporting World War II: American Journalism 1944–1946* (Library of America, 78), Paul Fussell; *Unauthorized Action: Mountbatten and the Dieppe Raid*, Brian Loring Villa; *The Oxford Companion to World War II*, I.C.B Dear, General Editor; *Six War Years 1939–1945*, Barry Broadfoot; *And No Birds Sang*, Farley Mowat; *On Killing: The Psychological Cost of Learning to Kill in War and Society*, Lt.-Col. Dave Grossman; *The Industry of Souls*, Martin Booth; *An Intimate History of Killing: Face-to-Face Killing in Twentieth-Century Warfare*, Joanna Bourke; *No Safe Place*, Warner Troyer; and the film *My Mother's Village*, directed by John Paskievich.

Most of all I wish to thank my partner and best friend, Pearl Luke, without whom this book would not exist. Pearl read the manuscript in countless forms and offered many crucial editorial suggestions. As well, I am forever thankful for her continued moral support, wisdom, and love.

ABOUT THE AUTHOR

ROBERT HILLES' first novel, *Raising of Voices*, won the Writer's Guild of Alberta's award for best novel. In that same year, he also won the Governor General's Literary Award for Poetry for *Cantos from A Small Room*. He and his partner, Pearl Luke, split their time between Calgary, Alberta, and Salt Spring Island, British Columbia.

BOOKS BY ROBERT HILLES

POETRY

Look The Lovely Animal Speaks
The Surprise Element
An Angel In The Works
Outlasting The Landscape
Finding The Lights On
A Breath At A Time
Cantos From A Small Room
Nothing Vanishes
Breathing Distance
Somewhere Between Obstacles and Pleasure
Higher Ground
Wrapped Within Again: New and Selected

FICTION

Raising Of Voices
Near Morning
A Gradual Ruin

NON FICTION

Kissing the Smoke